# FLAMINGO ROAD

## ALSO BY SASSCER HILL

### The Fia McKee Mysteries

*Flamingo Road*

### The Nikki Latrelle Racing Mysteries

*Full Mortality*

*Racing from Death*

*The Sea Horse Trade*

*Racing from Evil*

# FLAMINGO ROAD

## A FIA McKEE MYSTERY

*Sasscer Hill*

Minotaur Books
New York

FLAMINGO ROAD. Copyright © 2017 by Sasscer Hill. All rights reserved. Printed in the United States of America. For information, address St. Martin's Press, 175 Fifth Avenue, New York, N.Y. 10010.

www.minotaurbooks.com

Designed by Omar Chapa

Library of Congress Cataloging-in-Publication Data

Names: Hill, Sasscer, author.
Title: Flamingo Road / Sasscer Hill.
Description: First edition. | New York : Minotaur Books, 2017. |
Identifiers: LCCN 2016055982| ISBN 9781250096913 (hardcover) |
    ISBN 9781250096920 (e-book)
Subjects: LCSH: Thoroughbred Racing Protective Bureau—Fiction. |
    Government investigators—Fiction. | Undercover operations—Fiction. |
    Women detectives—Fiction. | Horse racing—Fiction. | BISAC: FICTION /
    Mystery & Detective / Traditional British. | FICTION / Mystery &
    Detective / Women Sleuths. | GSAFD: Mystery fiction.
Classification: LCC PS3608.I43773 F58 2017 | DDC 813/.6—dc23
LC record available at https://lccn.loc.gov/2016055982

Our books may be purchased in bulk for promotional, educational, or business use. Please contact your local bookseller or the Macmillan Corporate and Premium Sales Department at 1-800-221-7945, extension 5442, or by e-mail at Macmillan SpecialMarkets@macmillan.com.

First Edition: April 2017

10  9  8  7  6  5  4  3  2  1

*For my husband, Daniel C. Filippelli, and my sister,*
*Lillian Hill Clagett*

# *ACKNOWLEDGMENTS*

For law enforcement support, my thanks to Frank Fabian, former president of the Thoroughbred Racing Protective Bureau (TRPB) and twenty-year veteran of the Federal Bureau of Investigation. He and James Gowan, former TRPB vice president, kindly met with me at the TRPB home office to give me the lowdown on TRPB operations. Jim Gowan took an extra step and read the final manuscript of *Flamingo Road* to check for TRPB procedural errors.

Mark Pryor, the excellent mystery novelist and assistant district attorney in Austin, Texas, who was kind enough to read the manuscript and catch a police procedural error in time to fix it.

Scott Silveri, former chief of police, Thibodaux Police Department, Thibodaux, Louisiana, who patiently and quickly answered my "what-if" questions on police procedures.

A special thanks to Richard Couto of Florida's Animal Recovery Mission, who allowed me to interview him and whose actions to save horses from slaughter inspired me to write this novel.

From the medical world, I thank Craig W. Stevens, Ph.D., professor of pharmacology, Oklahoma State University. His knowledge of Dermorphin use was invaluable.

From the racehorse world I thank John Kenney, DMVD, and racehorse trainer and consultant David Earl Williams, M.S., Ph.D.

A big thanks to my critique group members, Mary Beth Gibson, Steve Gordy, and Bettie Williams.

As always, thanks to the wonderful members of Sisters in Crime who have helped me along the way.

And finally, to the two people who allowed Fia McKee to live and breathe, my agent, Ann Collette, and Minotaur editor, Hannah Braaten.

# FLAMINGO ROAD

# 1

My name is Fia McKee, and I was a Baltimore City cop until
that November night when I drove through West Baltimore
alone. Alone, because the department requires their cops to patrol
in single-man units. It's their way of stretching the law farther into
the crime-ridden city.

I eased my blue and white cruiser along the streets surround-
ing Lafayette Park Square, passing by St. James Episcopal Church
and a stark ten-story apartment building, where a faint scent of
mold soiled the night air. An odd mixture of nineteenth-century
brick row houses lined the square. Disintegrating buildings with
decayed walls and boarded-up windows crowded against happier
homes that had been carefully restored to their former beauty.

Rolling to the corner, I hooked a right onto West Lanvale,
the square's southern perimeter. Scanning the deserted park on
my right and buildings on my left, I let the Ford's big police engine
purr me toward the Methodist church at the end of the block.

Someone had shot out the sodium-vapor lamp over the alley

that ran between the stone parish house and the church on the corner. I let the cruiser idle a moment. Above the slate roofs, brick chimneys, and church spires, a small slice of November moon did little to illuminate the dim alley.

A flash of white movement caught my eye.

Two people—dark faces, dark clothes—struggled in the alley against the church wall. A white scarf wrapped around the neck of . . . a woman? I hit my searchlight and pinned them. Yes, a woman, her fingers tearing at the fabric stretched around her throat by the hands of a large man.

The guy seemed oblivious to the sharp beam of my lamp. He must have been high on something. I radioed in my location and the assault to dispatch, then I was out of the car, running through the cold and into the alley.

I pulled my service Glock. "Police! Let her go. *Now.*"

The man seemed unable to see or hear anything beyond his need to destroy the woman he'd slammed against the stone wall. His lips curled in an ugly grimace. He twisted the scarf with such force the woman's shoes lifted away from the pavement.

I shouted another warning and ran toward them. He didn't see me, didn't stop. The fight drained from the woman. She was going to die.

I closed in. The man saw me. His head snapped back. Just enough. I aimed for his ear and squeezed off the shot. He went down. The woman, choking, fell to her knees, then gulped air off the pavement like it was an oxygen mask.

The man lay motionless near my feet, blood pouring from the entrance hole. The woman darted a glance at me, her almond-shaped eyes devoid of emotion. Her gasping filled my ears. Then I heard a rapid, shallow panting. I recognized it as my own.

I checked the man for a pulse, not really expecting one. I felt no beat, and though he wouldn't officially be declared deceased until he arrived at the hospital, there was no question in my mind he was already a corpse.

A shuffling movement caught my attention. The woman was trying to crawl away.

"Oh no, you don't," I said, grabbing her arm near her shoulder, moving around to see her face. "You have to wait for a medic. You may need to go to the hospital."

Her hands began to shake. The fear I hadn't seen before widened her eyes. "No! I have to leave. I can't be involved in this."

"Ma'am, can I see some ID please?" What was it with vics? Half the time they clung to me and the other half they tried to rabbit. If the woman had carried a purse, it was long gone, but her peacoat looked bulky enough. "Do you have a wallet? Maybe in your coat? I need to see some ID."

She rubbed at her throat, sucked in some air, and slid a hand into her coat pocket. I leaned forward, clasped her wrist, and said, "Take it out easy, okay?"

She withdrew a wallet and when she handed it to me, her eyes had gone dead again. "I got *nothing* to say to you, lady cop. Nothing at all."

With a mental sigh, I took her wallet and flipped it open. A Maryland driver's license said she was Shyra Darnell. I was more interested in another piece of ID behind the plastic window next to the license. A permit from the Maryland Racing Commission. A hot walker's license from Pimlico racetrack, a world from my past. A world I knew well.

Shrill sirens sounded in the distance. I stood up, looking away from the coffee-skinned woman and the dead man on the pavement. Above me, the moon floated over the church spire, as if wanting to drift to the rural land north of Baltimore, where I'd grown up. A place where the vastness of the sky and light of the stars weren't hidden by brick, mortar, and stone. Or by the anxious, closed-in feel of this city.

The sirens drew close. The twirling flash of blue and red lights exploded into the square. I heard another squad car and saw lights where the ground swept down behind the church to the next street.

Glancing back, I stared at the man I'd shot. This probably wouldn't go well for me.

# 2

My supervisor, Ladner, sat behind his scarred desk staring over his drugstore cheaters at Detective Gravelin of Internal Affairs. Ladner, as usual, chewed on an unlit cigar.

My foot started jiggling, something I do when I'm nervous. I pushed my five-foot-six frame more firmly into the metal chair, suppressing the motion.

Gravelin occupied the room's guest chair, his posture stiff, his eyes cold as he said, "You have the right to remain silent."

I'd never imagined being on the wrong end of a Miranda warning. I felt a rushing in my ears and focused on the mole just to the side of Gravelin's nose. A single black hair sprouted from its little dome.

As he droned on, his words left me cold and isolated. Sitting in the wobbly, side chair backed against the dirty beige wall of Ladner's office, I worked on my best poker face, keeping my legs uncrossed, feet square on the floor's ratty green carpet.

"Do you understand these rights as I have read them to you?" Gravelin asked me.

"Yes, sir."

Fortunately, Gravelin had agreed to meet us in Ladner's office, instead of making me come to his lair over at the IAD building. Ladner and I had decided against calling in a legal representative from the Fraternal Order of Police, agreeing on a wait-and-see posture. At least for now.

"Maybe," Gravelin was saying, "if your witness, Ms. Darnell, would talk, I could confirm your story. But so far, Officer McKee, you're the only one saying this guy was trying to strangle her."

"It's possible, sir, that Darnell won't talk because she's afraid of something," I said patiently. "Something that relates to the man who tried to kill her. You saw the marks on her neck."

Gravelin shrugged. "If he's the one that put them there."

This IAD guy was unbelievable. Did he think I had strangled the woman? It wasn't helping that the department had been unable to identify the man I'd shot. And no one they'd canvassed in the neighborhood had seen or heard anything.

"My problem, McKee, is you have this history of striking first and following procedure later. It's called 'excessive use of force.' Are you sure you didn't have a prior relationship with the man you shot?"

"Sure. He's an old enemy of mine. And I grabbed a woman off the street and strangled her to make my story."

"Don't fuck with me, McKee."

Ladner rolled his chair back a couple of inches and a strong scent of cigar wafted in my direction. "Take it easy, Gravelin. Fia only has one prior incident on her record."

"That we know about," Gravelin said.

"The man in that case," Ladner continued, "was beating a child."

Gravelin punctuated his next words by jabbing his finger at the folder he'd spread open on the edge of Ladner's desk. "She didn't have to knock the man senseless with her baton."

I stared at the folder. That report was like a bloodhound. Damn thing followed me everywhere I went.

"And last night's incidence makes two, Sergeant Ladner, not one." Gravelin glared at the report, and gave me a hard stare. "You sent this first guy to the hospital with a severe concussion."

*I should have smacked him harder.*

"I felt it was necessary, sir. He was about to kick his son in the head." *Again.*

Gravelin sighed as if the weight of the world was on his shoulders. "Baltimore PD doesn't need officers like you, McKee, and—"

"Hold on," Ladner said. "She does damn good police work. Lowered the crime rate in her patrol area. She—"

Gravelin stood abruptly. "Yes, I understand she's like an avenging angel. As I said, we don't need officers like that. Suppose this guy's family comes forward and sues the city?"

What could Ladner say? I didn't want to put him or anyone else in a bad situation with the brass. But damn these people that crawled the streets like poisonous spiders. *Somebody* had to stop them.

Gravelin curled his lip at me. It made his mole wiggle. He turned back to Ladner. "I recommend you put Officer McKee on administrative leave at least until we finish the investigation." He didn't wait for an answer, just stalked out of Ladner's office, closing the door hard behind him.

Ladner sank a bit in his chair. "Fia, you know I have to follow his recommendation."

"Sure. Of course you do."

Ladner smiled. "Thank you for not giving me a fake smile and saying you could 'use the time.'"

"We both know better than that." I'd had no life since my dad had been murdered five years earlier. They'd never found the killer and the case had gone cold. Turning to law enforcement had filled in a void. And provided an outlet for the anger that flickered like a pilot flame inside me.

Ladner put his palms on his desk. "You finish your paperwork on this yet?"

"I'll have it on your desk before I leave."

He nodded, and as I walked from the room, he came through
the door of his office and followed me out. He headed to the
street so he could light up that cigar and leave me to deal with
the questioning looks and curiosity of my fellow officers. I was
saved by the chime of my cell phone. I tucked my head down,
hunched my shoulders, and answered.

"Fia," the caller said. "It's Patrick."

The brother I rarely spoke to. "Is something wrong?" I asked,
walking toward my metal desk.

"I can't call to say hello?" he asked.

"Did you?"

He paused a beat. "I could always count on you to cut to the
chase, Fia."

"Patrick, what's wrong? I can hear it in your voice and we
both know you never call me to say hello."

"Whose fault is that?"

*Oh, boy. Here we go.* I pulled out my desk chair, sank into it,
took a breath, and leveled my voice. "It doesn't matter whose fault
it is. Are you okay? Is your family all right?"

He was silent a moment. I pictured his pretty, but distant
wife Rebecca, and his little girl Jilly. Wait, she wasn't a little girl
anymore, she was . . . fifteen. Was that possible? Yeah, if I was
thirty-two.

"If you must know," he said, "Rebecca and I are . . . having
problems right now. She's got this—she's staying in Sarasota."

I suspected another man. "I'm sorry, Patrick. Did she take
Jilly with her?"

"No."

I waited for more but he was quiet. Rebecca hadn't taken Jilly
with her? But then the woman had always been about clothes,
cocktails, and let's-have-a-good-time. I felt bad for my niece. I

hadn't seen her since she was ten and she'd come up to Maryland with Patrick and Rebecca for our dad's memorial service.

The heater vent near my desk clicked on, blasting hot air laden with tiny carpet and paper particles, filling the air with the smell of dust. I could almost taste it. What did Patrick want?

He took a breath. "Jilly's got school. All her friends are here and, oh, Christ, Fia, she's wild! I have no control over her."

I didn't like the way this was going. "How long has her mother been gone?"

"About a month. Rebecca's just a bitch. She has no interest in Jilly and the school's been calling me. Jilly's skipping classes and if it wasn't for the horse I got her, I think she would have run away."

"You got her a horse? You *hate* horses."

"She's just like you were, Fia, wild and horse crazy."

So he'd bribed his daughter. I almost expected him to say this was my fault. What a mess.

"Fia, Jilly could really use some support. And . . . she's your *niece*."

Now I knew what he wanted. I leaned forward and pulled my case file from the shooting closer. "Isn't there someone else down there that can help you?"

"Fia, she's *your* family. She needs you. Don't you have any leave coming to you?"

Out of the corner of my eye I saw the door to the squad room open. Ladner came in with the stump of his cigar crammed in the corner of his mouth. He headed toward me, rolling a wave of cigar smell my way.

"Hold on a minute," I said to Patrick.

Ladner looked down at me, his mouth tight. I knew that expression. He was angry. I followed his irritated glance to the glass pane set in the door to the squad room. Gravelin stood on the other side in the hall staring at me, one hand gripping my "incident" folder.

The two cops that sat opposite each other at the desks closest to mine flicked nervous glances between Gravelin and me, then they both got busy with their phones and paperwork.

"Fia," Ladner said. "I need you to finish up that report and clear out." As he spoke, he stabbed a finger at me. I was pretty sure the angry gesture was for Gravelin's benefit. At least I hoped it was.

"Fia? Are you still there?" Patrick, on my cell, waiting for an answer.

I nodded hurriedly at Ladner. He pivoted and walked back into his office.

"Hold on another sec, Patrick." I'd never gotten along with him, but he was right. Jilly was my niece, and I remembered how hard it had been when my mother ran out on Patrick, my dad, and me. "Okay, I guess I could take some leave."

"Really? Fia, that's great."

I hadn't heard his voice sound like that since he was a little boy—all small, grateful, and relieved.

"Jilly will be so glad to hear you're coming."

"She will?" I asked. The kid didn't even know me.

"Well, this is part of the reason I called you. She's really scared. We've had some trouble down here. There's some lunatic running around killing horses in the area. In our neighborhood."

"What do you mean, 'killing' horses?" I asked.

"They're being butchered. It's awful, and Jilly's afraid for her gelding. She said she wished you were here. Since you're a cop."

I didn't tell him I might not be a cop much longer. "Okay, okay. I'll get a flight. Or maybe drive," I said. "I've got some things to clear up before I leave." My fingers traced the smooth manila of the Shyra Darnell and John Doe folder as I ended the call with Patrick.

I knew nothing about teenagers. The prospect of facing my niece seemed more frightening than facing a man with a gun.

Especially if she was like me. What was that old saying, "payback is hell"?

There was something else I had to do first—speak to Shyra Darnell. I knew the trouble it could get me into, but I wanted to know what she was afraid of.

And I wanted to know whom I had killed.

# 3

According to the statement she'd made, Shyra Darnell lived in the on-site housing that Pimlico provided for its backstretch workers, the people who cleaned stalls, fed, and groomed the horses.

To reach the racetrack, I drove north through Baltimore on 83. A sharp, cold wind scuttled trash on the edges of the freeway beneath a gray lid of dense clouds that covered the city. After exiting onto Northern Parkway, I passed by some of the priciest real estate in Baltimore, until the neighborhood disintegrated abruptly as I neared the track.

I hadn't wanted to ruffle anyone's feathers by arriving in a police car. Of course my Mini Cooper wasn't exactly stealthy.

I'd seen it at a used car dealership, and immediately had fallen in love. Starlight blue with a black roof, checkered flag mirror caps and black bonnet stripes. I told myself it got great mileage and had aftermarket built-in OnStar, but who was I kidding— I'd thought the car was totally cool. Tricked out with after-factory dark-tinted windows and silver rims, the car was a wicked match for my radically short, electric blond hair and double sets of gold-and-silver earrings.

But my present circumstances killed the happy-new-car buzz as dead as a swatted fly. Now I just wanted to keep my job. Yet here I was planning to question a hostile witness from an investigation I'd been ruled out of.

When I turned onto Pimlico Road to reach the backstretch, I passed a huge parking lot on my left still there from the days when crowds had flocked to the Maryland races. The curve of the dirt track's far turn rolled past me on my right and catty-corner across the track I could see the decrepit old grandstand so sadly in need of renovation.

I ran my window down and the smell of horses drifted in, the memories galloping in hard behind. The last time I'd been here my dad was alive. We'd brought his best horse down from the farm, and I'd ridden her, busting that filly out of the gate for a speed work that had taken my breath away. I remember the grin on my dad's face as he held up his stopwatch and gave me a thumbs-up. God, I missed him.

I inhaled sharply and closed the past away. Pulling the Mini up to the stable gate, I parked to one side, and climbed out. A cocoa-skinned security guard ambled out of the gatehouse. Nodding at him, I stepped in close and showed him my badge.

"How are you this morning?" I asked. I'd purposely not called ahead and timed my arrival for eleven. The track closed for morning exercise at ten, and most of the grooms and hot walkers were done by now. I hoped to catch Shyra in her room.

The guard gave me a suspicious look. "What brings the city police to Pimlico today?"

"Just some routine follow-up. I need to talk to Shyra Darnell."

The guard's closed expression opened with interest. "Heard about that. She's the one almost got herself killed."

"Interesting you'd put it that way."

"What way?"

"Do you think she made someone want to kill her?"

He took a half step back. "I don't know anything about that. Let me get her room number." He stepped into the guard-house and leafed through a ring binder. "She's in barn fourteen, room ten."

I thanked him, climbed into the Mini, and drove through the gate, past the receiving barn where my dad and I used to bring our horses in when they raced.

As I drove by, a woman pulled an equine pulmonary scope from a Chambers and Warner vet truck. She was tall, with broad hips and light brown hair. Had to be Wendy Warner. She had been my dad's vet. They'd worked hand in hand, were good friends, and after my mother walked out, I'd wondered if they might have been more than that. She must be almost sixty by now.

I'd always liked Wendy, but I didn't want her to see me. The Mini's dark tinted windows solved the problem, and I rolled on by, leaving her in my rearview mirror. Ahead, the gravel road dipped sharply downhill and suddenly the long Pimlico barns lay below me like rows of dominoes.

I arrived at barn fourteen and cut the engine. The grooms' quarters crowded above the stables, looking like the second floor of a cheap motel. Clothing hung to dry on the railing, and after I climbed a set of steep metal stairs, I had to step around dirt-encrusted shoes set outside many of the rooms.

There was no plumbing in the groom's quarters, and the bathrooms on the backside turned pretty nasty when lug-soled boots tracked in sand and manure. Especially when it mixed with water spilled from sinks and showers. But the rent and utilities were free, and, for some of the inhabitants, Pimlico's security and razor-wire-topped fence made it the safest place they'd ever know.

I found number ten and knocked. Shyra swung the door inward and heat from her HVAC unit blasted across my face.

She was tall and large boned with high cheekbones, a wide nose, and the almond-shaped eyes I remembered. Her skin was the color of coffee with cream. The wool hat she'd had in the church alley must have covered the tightly braided cornrows she wore today. Her turtleneck failed to hide the top edge of a reddish ligature mark.

Her eyes narrowed in recognition. "What do you want, lady cop?"

"Thought I'd check on you. See how you are." I knew she was forty, but she looked fifty-five or more.

The door to the room on the right opened and a Latino man stuck his head out. "You all right, Shyra?"

"I'm fine." The lines around her mouth compressed in irritation. Glancing at me, she said, "You'd better come in before anyone else sticks their nose where it's got no business."

I stepped inside and she pushed the door closed behind me. The tiny room had a cot against one wall with an orange bedspread. The scent of pizza leaked from a microwave that whirred on a plywood shelf set above a small refrigerator.

A chest of drawers, hooks on the opposite wall, and a desk with a metal chair completed the room's decor.

Except for the altar on top of the dresser. A bronze figure of Christ was mounted to a tall dagger that thrust so deep into the wooden chest it had splintered the surface. Wilted flowers surrounded the image of Christ and someone had draped strings of beads around the porcelain necks of what appeared to be Catholic saints. *Weird.*

Not a room to sit down and have a cozy chat. I remained standing.

"Ms. Darnell, you were pretty shook up the night you were attacked. Have you remembered anything about the man or that night that might help us identify this guy?"

Shyra thrust her lips out slightly and raised her head defiantly.

"Everything I know is in that statement I gave. Why do you care so much, anyway?"

The room was hot, and the smell of manure, molasses, and hay that rose from the stables below grew thicker and heavier.

"I never shot anyone before," I said.

For a moment she stared at me, startled, as if it had never occurred to her cops didn't go around shooting people all the time.

"What's the name of the man I killed to save your life, Shyra?"

Her eyes got that dead look I'd seen in the alley. "I don't know."

"I think you do," I said, pulling the fifty-dollar bill I'd brought with me from my Windbreaker's pocket.

Her gaze flicked to the bill, the momentary interest I saw in her eyes rapidly displaced by fear.

"Nuh-uh. I don't know nothing."

"What are you afraid of, Shyra? I can help you."

"No. You can't. Nobody can. You don't *know* him."

"Who?"

She backed away from me. "Get out." Her voice rose. "Get out!"

I raised my palms face out. "Okay, okay, I'm leaving. In fact, I was never here." I placed the fifty on her desk with my card. "If you need help, if you change your mind, call me. Use the cell. I may not be in the office."

"Get out," she whispered.

I pulled her door open and stepped onto the balcony. An icy wind hit the side of my face. I hunched my shoulders and headed for the stairs. I hoped the fifty would keep her from mentioning my visit to anyone, especially someone from IAD like Gravelin.

I'd taken a huge risk and learned nothing. Except somewhere out there was a man that terrified her.

# 4

Three days and more than a thousand miles later, I exited off Florida I-75 South onto Griffin Road, and after steering my Mini around a stubborn armadillo stationed in the middle of the pavement, I entered the township of Southwest Ranches, a community that lay fifteen miles southwest of Fort Lauderdale and thirty miles northwest of Miami.

Patrick lived here with Jilly.

Lowering the car's window, I breathed in air warmed by the afternoon sun. After the leafless trees and frozen concrete of Baltimore, I found the scent of growing plants and damp earth intoxicating.

Staring with interest as the Mini rolled slowly along Griffin Road, I passed one expensive-looking ranchette after another. Brick or stucco walls guarded many of the long, single-story homes. Some yards had hedges, bamboo, and palm plants so thick I had no idea what they hid on the other side. In spots where the vegetation grew sparsely, I saw white plastic or chain-link fences on the sides and backs of the properties—cheaper extensions of the expensive frontage walls.

A few buildings looked like stables. As if in confirmation, a horse's whinny echoed from behind a house on my left.

Patrick lived in a horsey neighborhood? As a child, he'd been so jealous of the horses and had hated the endless hours Dad devoted to them. Me? I'd just gone to the track every chance I got and loved every second of it.

My OnStar navigation voice broke through my thoughts, instructing me to turn right onto Thoroughbred Lane, left onto Lead Pony Lane, and stop at number seven.

A prefab, sand-colored stone wall rose between me and my brother's house, but the double wrought-iron gates guarding the drive stood open. A pair of cabbage palms flanked the entrance. A brass wall plaque read, NUMBER 7, MCKEE.

As I motored between the gateposts, the house remained hidden. I drove along the drive as it curved around a splashing fountain before disappearing behind a jungle of greenery. Looked like brother Patrick's real estate business was doing okay.

After rolling past a perfectly mowed lawn, through the carefully manicured jungle of palms and waxy, thick-leaved bushes, I cut the engine before a smooth stucco house painted the color of butter.

When I climbed out, the scent emanating from the purple flowers bordering the house was so sweet and heady, I knew how Dorothy felt when she arrived in Oz and passed out among the poppies.

The front door opened, and Patrick stepped out beneath a portico. He walked across a stone terrace toward me. At thirty-eight, he was still lean, his hair glossy and dark, but his blue eyes had lines around them that hadn't been there five years earlier. His lips that had been so full and smooth were thinner, and creases I hadn't seen before bracketed his mouth.

"Thanks for coming," he said, continuing to move closer

until he stepped right into my no-comfort zone. He'd always treated me this way—as if being the older brother gave him the right to disregard my privacy. And he'd liked to tell me how to behave and what to think. Always a bad idea.

A thin, leggy, teenage girl appeared in the doorway. Big blue eyes, dark hair. Had to be Jilly.

"Hey," she said, her expression guarded.

I moved a half step back from Patrick and smiled at her. Glancing at my brother, I said, "She's beautiful, Patrick. You did good."

Jilly's body seemed to relax. She moved across the terrace and stood closer, on the edge of the drive. Three sapphire earring studs gleamed from the outside edges of her ears. A diamond stud pierced one nostril, and on her left breast, the ears and head of a small black-and-blue horse tattoo peeked above the edge of her skimpy tank top.

Patrick frowned. "She'd look better if she'd get rid of some of that junk she wears. It's not legal for her to have a tattoo at her age, but she got it done." He shook his head at the hardship of having such a difficult daughter. He probably didn't think much of my double set of gold earrings, either.

Jilly acted like she hadn't heard her father's comment, looking at me instead. "Cool car."

"Thanks. We'll have to go for a ride."

"But not now," Patrick said quickly. "You probably need to decompress after that drive." He stared at me, frowning. "Fia, what's with your hair? Why would you cut it that short? You look like a man."

"Dad." Jilly rolled her eyes. "It's looks totally cool."

No wonder I'd avoided him for five years. I didn't want to get in the middle of this argument and was almost relieved when I saw a police cruiser roll around the edge of the garden jungle. Almost.

The white car with the words BROWARD COUNTY SHERIFF emblazoned on the side pulled up behind mine and stopped. The deputy in the passenger seat stayed in place, but the driver got out and walked around the hood of the cruiser. He appeared to be studying my car.

Staring at him, I realized I didn't miss the weight of the gear he had strapped around his waist or the nuisance of the wired radio clipped on his shoulder. I did miss the service Glock I'd had to turn over to Ladner, but I had brought another gun with me. And though I held a permit to carry for most every state, cops get a little edgy when they find a Walther PPK handgun stashed in your glove box. I hoped he didn't have a reason to look inside the car. I'd just as soon avoid questions.

"Good afternoon, Officer," Patrick said, then waited for the other man to speak. The deputy nodded at Patrick. I couldn't make out the name on the green and white badge pinned to his chest as he glanced at the Mini.

"This car belong to you?" he asked Patrick.

"It's mine," I said. "I just drove down from Maryland."

"She's my sister," Patrick said quickly. "Fia McKee. She's visiting." He introduced himself and Jilly.

I noticed the passenger cop was typing on a laptop. Probably running my tag. "Is there a problem, Officer?" I asked.

"We had a call," he said. "People get anxious when they see an out-of-state car cruising the neighborhood."

I *had* stared at every house and yard I passed. Had someone thought I was casing the place?

The deputy continued, "This horse killing has people unnerved."

Jilly's face paled. "I hope you catch this guy before he comes here."

He smiled. "We're working on it."

He glanced at the three of us and handed a card to Patrick. "All right, then. Keep your eyes open for anything unusual and call if you see something. You folks have a nice evening."

The passenger cop gave a brief wave from the cruiser's

window as it navigated the circular drive before disappearing into Patrick's greenery.

An hour later, I sat on the guest bed gazing outside the sliding-glass door of the bedroom. A patio, pool, and a fenced-in pad-dock that was maybe an acre, lay behind the house. The drive ran alongside the enclosure and led to a prefab stable crowned with a brass cupola. More fencing and paddocks appeared behind it.

Jilly leaned on the paddock railing watching a well-fed black and white paint as if nothing in the world existed but the horse.

My cell phone rang and looking at the ID, I saw it was Lad-ner. When I answered, I heard him suck in some air. He must be outside with a cigar.

"You enjoying the weather down there?" he asked.

He wasn't calling to talk about the weather. "You got any-thing for me on this IAD investigation?"

"Gravelin's fairly closemouthed," he said. "But I did hear something about your witness, Darnell."

I gripped the cell harder, hoping IAD hadn't heard about my visit to Pimlico.

"She's disappeared," he said. "Her room at the track is empty, like she cleared out."

Had I driven her away? Or had her fear of the man she'd mentioned?

"Any idea where she went?"

"No." He paused and I heard him take another puff on his cigar. "But the guy that lives in the room next door said a woman came to visit her. A woman with short blond hair. You wouldn't know anything about that would you, Fia?"

"No, sir," I lied.

"Sure you wouldn't," he said. But he let it go. "It's good you're down there. Stay put and keep out of trouble."

I released a breath I didn't know I'd been holding. "Yes, sir."

He disconnected, and I looked out the window. Jilly had

climbed through the fence railing and had her arms around the neck of her horse, her face planted in the fur on his shoulder. I had always loved doing that, breathing in the rich horse smell. The horse curved his neck, and nuzzled the small of Jilly's back.

Deciding to shower and change, I padded across thick white carpeting through the room Rebecca had decorated in turquoise and white. I shook my head at the gaudy lamps and wall fixtures and could almost hear her decorator saying, "with gold accents."

I sighed, thought about my conversation with Ladner and wondered what had happened to Shyra. I wished she had let me help her. Maybe I had already helped her too much.

# 5

Around seven that evening the three of us went to a local Italian restaurant for dinner. We sat in a booth dipping crusty bread into olive oil, breathing in the scents of tomato and garlic that drifted from the kitchen to our table.

To avoid land mines on our road into sibling territory, Patrick and I had a glass of the house Merlot, and I encouraged Jilly to tell me about her horse Cody. I hoped to keep the conversation in a demilitarized zone.

But more than that, I loved talking about horses, especially after a couple glasses of wine. I listened to every detail about Cody, his new tack, what he liked to eat, his favorite naughty tricks.

"You should have seen him the first time I asked him to cross this wooden bridge over the canal," she said. "He put one hoof on the first plank and just sort of pawed like he was testing it. So, I clucked at him, and he went right over! He was so cool!"

As she spoke, her sapphire earrings and the small diamond in her nostril glimmered as they reflected light from the candle burning in the wine bottle on our table. The pride and happiness in her eyes far outshone the glitter of her jewelry.

When dinner arrived, Patrick scarfed his pizza and went through his salad like a runaway lawn mower. When he finished, he yawned several times and stared at the ceiling. No wonder Rebecca had left.

Jilly said, "So you used to ride for my granddad, right?"

"I was just an exercise rider in the mornings," I said, after finishing a bite of lasagna. "I was never a jockey or anything like that."

"Yeah, but you used to work horses out of the gate at Pimlico. That is so cool. And Granddad had some really good horses, right? Like, *stakes* horses."

"Jilly has school tomorrow," Patrick said abruptly. "We should head home."

Jilly and I exchanged a look just short of an eye roll.

When we got back to the house, she wanted me to meet Cody, but the way Patrick's lips compressed made me say, "You know what, Jilly? I'm starting to crash and should probably hit the pillows."

Her shoulders slumped and she threw me a sour look. "Yeah, sure," she mumbled, veering away from me and stalking down the hall.

"You see?" Patrick said before she was out of earshot.

"I guess it's not easy," I said quietly.

"You don't have a clue!"

*And you need to get one.* "It wouldn't have hurt to let her spend a few minutes showing me her horse, Patrick."

He made an impatient noise, "She has classes tomorrow!"

"There's more to life than school." I headed to my bedroom. "Good night, Patrick," I said, and closed the door behind me.

I awakened abruptly. The glowing clock on the night table read 2:00 A.M. Sitting up, I glanced at the sliding-glass door to the pool terrace. I'd left it open after closing and locking the screen. I stared into the night, listening. I could smell chlorine from the pool but heard nothing except the endless Florida breeze and the soft chirping of crickets. Ambient light and chilly damp air spilled into the room. Something had broken my sleep. A noise.

I eased off the bed and padded to the screen, straining my ears for a sound. A dim light flickered briefly inside the barn. When I'd gazed at the stable earlier, I'd noticed it had a center aisle that faced the back of the house and my bedroom. It was open and the light had come from there.

What was Jilly up to?

I knotted my nightshirt at my waist, pulled on a pair of jeans, and stepped into my Crocs. As I slipped my phone into a pocket, a horse whinnied anxiously in the distance, maybe from the next farm over. I shoved my Walther into the waistband at the small of my back, slid the screen open, and slipped out to the pool terrace.

Movement—outside by the rear of the barn. A shadowy outline of what looked like two people on a golf cart. The cart towed a wagon and rolled quietly away from the barn. I ran across the terrace, the lawn, and onto the drive leading to the barn.

What was this? Kids on a joyride? Stealing tack or Patrick's tools and equipment? Whatever it was, it wasn't right.

I sped down the drive, my rubber shoes silent. The cart had headed to the right on the far side of the stable, and it looked like the fastest way to catch up would be to run straight down the center aisle and out the other side. Plunging into the murk of the barn, I smelled a horrible, familiar odor before skidding in what had to be blood. I wound up on my hands and knees, staring at a dark lump on the floor.

God, no. "You sons of bitches!" I yelled. I staggered up, skirted the slick, sticky pool and ran out the back. In the distance I heard a couple of thumps. A truck engine started, but no lights came on. The sound of a motor rapidly faded into the distance.

Feeling helpless and sickened, I searched for a light switch and found it. *Okay, Fia, get a grip.* I flipped the switch.

Blood was everywhere. Cody's black tail like a paintbrush dipped in blood looked. I fought a wave of nausea. They had butchered him in his own barn, removing the large cuts of meat. I wanted to kill them. I grabbed my phone and called 911.

I told the dispatcher what had happened, exactly where I was, and to please roll in quietly because I didn't want my niece to see this. It would brand her brain. At least I could spare her that. What if I'd come to the barn with her earlier to meet Cody? Would I have seen something, noticed something? I should have come. Damn everything.

As I stood by the light switch, the smell of blood grew more metallic, the cloying scent bringing another wave of nausea. I had to get air. Dizzy, I moved toward the back entrance and froze.

A man dressed in camouflage with a gun holstered on his hip stood where the lighted aisle merged into the darkness beyond. He wore a bulletproof vest. Black greasepaint was smeared under his eyes.

My gun was in my hands and trained on his chest. "Stop. On the pavement, face down. Do it."

"Easy, sister," he said, sinking to his knees. "I'm on your side." Putting his palms on the concrete floor, he glanced at Cody. "I'm following the guy who did this."

"Except you're dressed like the killer. Pull that gun and toss it across the floor."

He did.

"All the way down," I said, trying to keep the nerves out of my voice. Please, God, don't make me have to shoot this guy. . . .

He shrugged. "Sure." He eased his hard-looking, six-foot frame onto the pavement. Beneath the greasepaint, dirt, and three-day stubble he was probably good-looking. He lay his right cheek on the concrete, never taking his left eye off me. "Was he your horse?"

"None of your business." Quickly, I stepped over to his gun and kicked it behind me, putting my body between him and his weapon. Lowering my 9mm to my side, I said, "Who are you?"

"Zanin. I run an outfit called PAL. We protect animals from this kind of crap."

"Sure you do."

"Think what you want," he said.

The anger in his voice and the tensed muscles in his forearms made me raise my gun again.

Headlights swept around the side of the house from the front yard. As the car rolled along the drive toward the barn, the outline of a light bar was visible on its roof. A Broward County sheriff. The car rolled to a stop outside the barn. The officer inside used his microphone, addressing us through his PA system.

"Ma'am, I need you to lower your weapon."

I did. His voice, blasting from the speaker in the front grille, had ripped open the night air. So much for hiding this from Jilly.

"Lay it on the ground nice and slow," he said.

I obliged and stepped a few feet away from the gun, praying Zanin, or whatever his name was, would stay put. I turned sideways so I could see them both.

The deputy, his service weapon drawn, climbed from his cruiser and walked toward me. He stopped as he took in the remains of Cody. When he carefully stepped around the pool of blood, his face turned a pale shade of green. I knew just how he felt.

Zanin raised his head from the pavement and squinted. "Rodriguez? If it's all the same to you, I'd like to get up now."

I stared at the name badge on the cop as he drew closer: Rodriguez. The deputy, who was neat as a pin with perfectly shined shoes, looked at Zanin, then at me. He grinned like something was amusing.

"Sure, Zanin. You're safe now. I'll keep this little gal covered for you, seeing as she took your weapon and put you on the ground."

Rodriguez was an ass, but at least the guy in the SWAT outfit hadn't lied about his name. The cold look in his eyes suggested he found Rodriguez's humor as annoying as I did. When Zanin climbed to his feet, the breeze coming through the rear of the barn carried his scent to me. Sweat, dirt, and testosterone.

Rodriguez still had his gun on me. He glanced at Zanin. "This guy, I know. Runs that Protect the Animals League. He didn't do this. But who the hell are you?"

I told him my name. "My brother owns this place. The . . . horse on the ground belonged to my niece, and the people who killed him just left." I gestured at the shadows behind the barn. "Out there. In a truck."

"They have a golf cart with them?" Zanin asked.

I suddenly felt very tired. "Yeah . . . they did."

"Damn it." Zanin turned toward the deputy. "I was tailing those guys out of the C-Nine basin. They went down one of those one-way tracks and disappeared. I knew they were gonna hit someone tonight."

I moved two steps toward him. "So you know who they are. Do you have a license number?"

He shrugged. "Unless you witnessed the slaughter and got a video, we can't do anything."

He was right, of course. But that didn't mean we couldn't put a little pressure on these horse-killing assholes. "But you do know who they are, right?"

"Yeah," he said. "His name is Luis Valera."

"That's enough," Rodriguez said to me, holstering his gun. "Let the police handle this."

"Except you won't," Zanin said quietly.

A shout came from the darkness beyond the parked cruiser, causing me to whirl that way. I heard a light pounding of feet and from farther back more shouting.

"Jilly, stop!" Patrick's voice.

Damn it. It had to be her footsteps approaching. As I ran to stop her, Jilly sped into the lights glowing from the rear of the cruiser. I sprinted toward her, blocking her path as she reached the side of the car.

"Cody!" she screamed, like she already knew what she'd find inside.

I tried to grip her arm, but she took me by surprise, shoving me, and kicking me hard in the shin with her cowgirl boot. As I fell to one knee, she raced by me, on course to collide with a horrific and indelible image.

Scrambling to my feet, I heard her scream. But it was a scream of anger, not anguish. Zanin had grabbed her shoulders, lifted her from the ground, and spun her away from the barn. But as he started to set her down, she kicked him in the balls, and Zanin doubled over with the pain. The second he dropped her, she ran into the barn.

Then the real screaming started.

# 6

Patrick, Zanin, and I sat at the McKee kitchen table working on double shots of iced Stolichnaya vodka. Zanin had just told us his first name was Kerameikos, making it easy to see why he went by his last name. His eyes were so deep-set and shadowed by thick, dark brows that even in the bright light of the kitchen it was hard to determine their color. My best guess was a very dark shade of gray.

Behind us, the refrigerator motor cycled off, leaving an intense silence in the room. Rebecca's decorator had been busy here, too, doing the kitchen in an orange and white motif that reminded me of a Dreamsicle. The table was inlaid with orange tiles and the obligatory gold accents hadn't been forgotten; the ornate metal weighed down the ceiling fixtures, knobs, and handles.

Zanin swirled the ice in his drink, stirring up the scent of the lime he'd squeezed into his glass. He wore his brown hair short, in an unyielding military style. His bulletproof vest hung on the back of his chair, leaving him in a sleeveless tee, and now that he'd washed the greasepaint off his face, he didn't look so tough—more the other way around, like life had been hard on him.

I'd bet my last bullet he was driven by an underlying need to help others. He'd insisted on being the one to clean the barn, telling me the members of PAL were used to it, that Patrick and I should stay with Jilly. Apparently, he kept plastic bags and disinfectants in the SUV he'd parked on Lead Pony Lane, telling me his outfit needed these supplies way too often, giving me an unpleasant insight into the world of PAL.

Patrick took Jilly back to the house, and Zanin produced a Nikon and took multiple shots of the scene. I used a hose and watched Cody's blood swirl through the grate and down into the floor drain. Zanin used his plastic bags to do the real dirty work, saying he'd take the parts that used to be Cody and bury them.

Shuddering at the memory, I pushed back from the dining table, went to the refrigerator for more ice, and poured another healthy slug of vodka into my glass.

The entrance to the dining room was at one end of the kitchen, with an access to the hall at the other end. Jilly was in her room back there, hopefully still asleep. Patrick had given her a Xanax, and when I'd come back from the barn, I'd stayed with her until her sobs stopped and she'd drifted off.

Her anguish had brought back the image of Dad's body stuffed between the wall and the back of the Dumpster outside his barn at Pimlico where I'd found him. The mental picture cranked up the pilot flame that burned in me, fueling it into a furnace. I'd never found justice for Dad. I wanted to hurt the men who'd done this to Jilly. And to Patrick. And Cody.

"Are you all right?" Zanin stared from across the table.

I nodded, sank into my chair, and sipped more vodka. The liquor had a nice cold bite, chilling some of my anger and easing my adrenaline crash.

"Now that we've all had a chance to decompress," Patrick

said, his gaze shifting to Zanin. "I want to know what happened out there. That useless Rodriguez didn't say much."

My brother could be so annoying. "For God's sake, Patrick. He had a domestic dispute call. Rodriguez had no choice but to leave."

Patrick waved me off with a "whatever" motion, never taking his eyes off Zanin. He'd always ignored what I said if it wasn't what he wanted to hear.

"Your horse," Zanin said, "was butchered by Cuban Americans who live in the C-Nine Basin. By now, they've delivered his meat to a specialty butcher shop in Miami."

Patrick shook his head as if denying the whole thing. "That's disgusting. It doesn't make sense. There can't be enough money to outweigh the risk."

"I'm betting the horse was young," Zanin said. "Maybe a little fat?"

Recalling Jilly's conversation at dinner, I said, "Cody was only three." An image struck me. Cody plump and happy in the paddock with Jilly that afternoon. "Oh, God. He was fat. Is that why they killed him?"

"Yeah," Zanin said. "They like 'em young and well-marbled. Brings the highest price, like beef."

I dropped my head into my hands. It was impossible to shut out the images. Glancing at him, I said, "Who are these people? And what's the C-Nine Basin?"

"It's the Wild West of Florida. Straddles the western edge of Broward and Miami-Dade counties, along one side of the Everglades. Mostly men live there, Cubans and Haitians and almost everything they do is outside the law—cockfights, horse slaughter, dogfights."

"But Patrick's right," I said. "It doesn't make sense. Horse slaughter is legal in so many places now."

Zanin gazed at me intently. "Think about it."

I cringed as it hit me. "It doesn't matter if it's legal because if those animals are old and tough . . ."

Zanin nodded. "They bring less money. The men in the C-Nine, they're renegades, squatters, really rough people. These guys build shacks and pilfer from electric lines. They don't care about right and wrong, especially when money in the form of prime meat is available just down the road. Believe me, the police are afraid to go in there."

"This is horrible." Patrick's voice sounded weak.

I stared at him. Tears glittered in his eyes. Was Patrick crying? My brother Patrick?

"Hey, man. I'm really sorry," Zanin said. "I shouldn't have lost Valera earlier."

And I should be comforting my brother, but I'd feel like a hypocrite if I did. Patrick had never cried when our dad died, or earlier when our mother had left us all for another man. Patrick had remained her little darling, and they stayed close. Me? I avoided the bitch.

So instead of comforting him, I glanced at Zanin. "Maybe we could do something about Valera."

Patrick forgot his tears and slammed a hand on the orange tile, causing the ice in my glass to rattle. "Forget it, Fia! We've had enough trouble. These people operate outside the law." He waved a hand toward Zanin. "He just said the *police* are afraid to go in there!"

"Somebody has to."

"Take it easy, you two," Zanin said. "Fia, he's right. People disappear in the C-Nine."

"I'm not saying it doesn't scare the hell out of me. It does. But I'll go in there if—"

"Listen to you!" Patrick shouted. "You may be a cop, but you have no jurisdiction down here. The Everglades are nothing like Baltimore. You have no idea what you'd be getting into!"

"You're a cop?"

Zanin had missed my little talk about that with Rodriguez. "Yeah, I am."

He shifted toward me, moving his body closer. The man needed a shower but there was some scent emanating from him that wasn't altogether unappealing.

"So why are you here? Vacation?"

"Something like that," I said.

His expression became thoughtful. "Maybe you could—"

"She's here to help me with Jilly. That is, if she hasn't forgotten why she came." Patrick made a helpless palms-up gesture to Zanin. "You see how she is? And Jilly is just like her."

A noise from the hallway made me turn. Jilly stood there, wearing pajamas printed with baby zebras. She looked confused, her eyes unfocused, her legs trembling. When I pushed my chair back and rushed toward her, her eyes opened wide, as if she were waking up. She started screaming. When I reached her and put my arms around her, the screams turned into wails and she clung to me like she'd never let go.

Stroking her dark hair, I glared at Patrick. "I haven't forgotten why I came here."

Patrick dropped his gaze to the floor, and my phone's familiar ringtone went off. I'd left it next to my glass on the kitchen table, close to Zanin.

Keeping my arms wrapped around Jilly, I said, "Zanin, could you check the ID?"

He slid a muscular arm across the table and looked at the phone. "Baltimore Police Department."

I squashed the impulse to grab the phone. "They can wait." Placing my hands on Jilly's shoulders, I set her back far enough to study her face. "You want to sit with us for a while?"

She nodded. Then her attention shifted to Zanin. "Who are you?"

"Most people call me—"

"You're that guy Zanin, the hero guy," Jilly said, "Everyone knows about you. You save animals from . . ." Her enthusiasm crawled to a stop.

As her voice trailed off, I steered her gently toward the table. "Come on, sit, and if you want, we can talk about what happened." I threw a sharp look at Patrick. "It would probably help all of us."

"You're the one with the training, Fia." But Patrick actually looked relieved. What rookie single parent would want to handle this mess?

Jilly eased into her chair, like an old woman might. Keeping her hands tightly folded in her lap, she looked at me. "How could they do that?"

I could sense the horrific scene playing behind her eyes. I wasn't about to coddle her with half-truths, so I gave her the short speech on humanity and greed, and told her they did it for money.

Her eyes widened and I saw a healthy spark of anger. "Are the police going to get them?"

I looked at Zanin. "Help me here."

He explained about catching them in the act. That animal cruelty was hard to enforce. "And think about it," he said, "Officer Rodriguez left the scene tonight because of a domestic dispute call. A person's life was likely in danger. That will trump an animal every time."

I nodded. "It's like that in Baltimore, too."

Zanin downed the last of his vodka. "You ever heard the old saying, 'The triumph of evil is made possible by good people who do nothing'? Fortunately there are a lot of people out there who stand up. I get more help from citizens than I do from cops. And when the police don't respond to their calls for help, I do."

Jilly put her palms on the table and leaned forward, a zealot's light igniting in her eyes. "I want to work with you!"

"Hold on there, warrior princess," Zanin said. "PAL rules won't allow it. You're too young."

Jilly slumped.

"But," he said, "it would be really cool if you'd organize a neighborhood watch."

"How?"

"Get together with the other horse people in the neighborhood. Tell them about Cody. Tell them everything. You'll get more volunteers that way. Let them help you put up neighborhood watch signs."

"Where do I get the signs?"

"Internet. You'll need the neighbors to put a little fund together. I've found it's not hard to raise money to protect animals."

I bet he was good at raising funds. For a moment I wondered if he took people's money to line his own pockets. Maybe I'd been a cop too long.

"Tell everyone," Zanin said, "to look for strangers in the neighborhood. Guys like Luis Valera ride around in daylight to identify their victims. If the neighborhood appears on high alert, he won't come here."

*He'll just go somewhere else.* I kept the thought to myself, because I could feel the positive energy flowing from Jilly.

"Yeah, I can do that," she said.

"I'll help you," Patrick said.

"Dad, you never have any time. You're always at your real estate office."

"Which is how I could afford to buy you a horse, Jilly."

I could smell a spat heating up.

Patrick paused, and exhaled. "I'll make the time, Jilly. Okay?"

She shrugged. "Whatever."

"All righty then," I said, forcing a bright smile. "Everyone will help." And then I'd make brownies and we'd all live happily ever after.

Patrick refrained from commenting, Jilly rolled her eyes, and Zanin gave me a lazy smile.

I stared at him. Here he was in the McKee kitchen, drinking booze, working his way into our lives. We needed to learn more about this guy.

# 7

When Zanin got up from the kitchen table to leave, it was already 5:00 A.M. I followed him out the French doors to the pool terrace where the smell of chlorine mingled with the scent of sand and damp soil. Behind the stable cupola, a false dawn hung on the gray horizon.

"Are you going to go after Valera?" I asked.

"I don't go after people," he said. "I just try to save the animals."

"But you were following this guy."

He rolled his shoulders and grimaced. "Look, I've been shot at, threatened, and beaten up. I can't afford to mess with Valera in his own territory. I followed him off the reservation so I could get the police on him before he killed again. But I lost him." He closed his eyes. "I shouldn't have lost him. . . ."

"True, but you're the only one who even knew he was on the prowl last night. No one *else* had a line on him."

I could almost see my consoling words bounce right off him. I knew about bulletproof guilt, and gave it up.

"Zanin, isn't there some way to stop this guy?"

He stared at me with blank eyes. "You say you're a cop. So you know PAL has to use the law. The bureaucrats have to be able to cite animal cruelty, slaughtering without a license, operating a business without a license, or something. I haven't been able to get close enough to this guy to tape anything. His place out there is big, and he's surrounded by some nasty electric fencing. I think he's using the place to slaughter animals. For sure, he's doing something illegal."

He raked the fingers of one hand through the stubble on his scalp, his frustration palpable. "Usually we can get someone in undercover as a laborer. Get videos. But Valera only works with family members. I'd guarantee the guy you saw with him was a brother, a son, or a cousin."

I flashed on the cart rolling away in the gloom, and the knowledge of what it carried sent a sick chill through me.

"It's been a long night," I said. "We should probably give it a rest for now. How can I reach you?"

He dug into his vest pocket and handed me his card. The red letters PAL were engraved on a black background. A circle with a black slash through it pictured a butcher knife dripping blood. PROTECT THE ANIMALS LEAGUE and an e-mail address were printed across the bottom.

I slid his card into my jean's pocket. "I'll call you."

He nodded and headed to the barn where he'd left his SUV.

I went back into the house and heard pop music playing softly in Jilly's room. Earlier, Patrick had told her she could stay home from school, before saying he'd try to snatch a few hours of sleep before he drove to his real estate office.

I entered my room and opened my laptop where I'd left it on a carved wooden desk.

When I Googled PAL, a site came up with descriptive text, ghoulish pictures, and graphic videos of animals being abused and slaughtered. I didn't want to look at them and instead clicked on news articles about Zanin.

Two stories praised him for being instrumental in shutting down illegal slaughterhouses in the C-9 Basin. He'd worked as an employee while secretly videoing the slaughter of horses, sheep, goats, and other animals. According to both articles, he'd used the legal codes against unlicensed businesses to pull in law enforcement. I liked having confirmation that what he'd said on the pool terrace was true.

Next I opened the Florida state government's site and read up on the statutes for animal cruelty. Like the cruelty codes in Maryland, they were pretty straightforward:

A person who unnecessarily overloads, overdrives, torments, deprives of necessary sustenance or shelter, or unnecessarily mutilates, or kills any animal, or causes the same to be done, or carries in or upon any vehicle, or otherwise, any animal in a cruel or inhumane manner, is guilty of a misdemeanor of the first degree, punishable by a fine of not more than $5,000, or both.

I was glad to read on and see that second-time offenders received stiffer penalties. I rubbed my temples, and shut down the laptop.

I walked from the desk and stretched out on the turquoise comforter covering my bed. Closing my eyes, I contemplated the fight of good against evil. As usual, it left me feeling powerless. Then, as they so often did, my thoughts darted to the man I'd killed. I could see his hands pulling the scarf tighter, Shyra fighting for air. I'd killed him and I still didn't know his name.

I jerked upright on the bed. *Move along, Fia.* I should find out who had called me from the Baltimore PD at 4:00 A.M. With a niggle of worry, I called up the message, saw Ladner's name, and listened.

"Fia," he said. "Lying to me about your visit to Shyra at Pimlico wasn't the smartest thing you've ever done. Gravelin just blindsided me. He knows. He's hot and wants your badge."

Anxiety bubbled in my stomach, made my face tingle.

"Listen," the message continued, "I've got a way out for you. Call me. I've got something going on this morning, but should be back at my desk by ten. Call me, damn it."

It sounded like he was involved in an early-morning operation, which explained the odd hour of his call, but not what he meant about a "way out." I replayed the message, then stared at the phone. I didn't want a way out. I just wanted to beat the IAD charges and keep my job.

I suddenly felt woozy. The shock of Cody's death, the fear and adrenaline that had coursed through me had taken a toll. I lay down again, closed my eyes, and at some point fell into an uneasy sleep.

I woke up a little after nine that morning. If Patrick had left the house, I'd slept too deeply to hear him.

*But where was Jilly?*

I scrambled out of bed and moved quickly through empty rooms. I couldn't find her. There was no note on the kitchen counter and Patrick's car was gone. Music was still playing in her bedroom, but she wasn't there.

I hurried to the French doors in the living room and looked out across the pool terrace. Jilly was sitting on the ground inside Cody's paddock. I hurried outside, slowing to a walk as I approached her. She wasn't crying, just sitting motionless, staring at nothing.

"Hey," I said. "You want some breakfast or something?"

Slowly, her glance lifted to me. "No." Her eyes held that distance that comes from seeing too much. It hadn't been there before.

"Well, how about you come in and show me where the coffee is?"

She frowned. "Yeah, okay."

When we reached the kitchen, she pulled out a bag of coffee and filters, and the action seemed to revive her mentally. I threw out the old coffee, and made fresh. The first sip, smooth and hot, went down like an elixir.

"Did you eat?" I asked her.

"Dad made me some eggs, but I threw them out."

At least Patrick had tried. I looked inside the cabinets and the fridge. "Do you eat yogurt?"

"Not that plain stuff Dad buys."

"It won't be plain when I get through with it."

I pulled out two bowls, a bag of walnuts and almonds, fresh strawberries and blueberries, and the yogurt. I found some granola and a jar of honey. I put it all together, stuck a spoon in each bowl, and slid one across the table to Jilly.

"Eat."

She scowled at me but took a bite.

"You're lucky your dad keeps such good food in the house," I said.

"Oh, yeah. I'm *really* lucky."

If she'd been a cat, she would have hissed at me. But she was eating, so I zipped my lips, spooned in a few bites of breakfast, and sipped my coffee. A glance at the wall clock showed it was close to ten, almost time to call Ladner.

My pulse started hammering in my ears and I pushed my bowl away. I could hear my dad saying, "No good deed goes unpunished." Damn it, I'd done the right thing. Was I supposed to let that guy *kill* Shyra?

"What's with you?" Jilly asked.

"Nothing. I have to make a phone call."

She shrugged. "Whatever."

At least she was spooning down the yogurt at a good rate. I took my phone through the living room, out onto the terrace, and called Ladner.

"It's me," I said when he answered.

"Fia, you need to come up to Baltimore and meet with Gravelin and this guy from the TRPB, name's Gunford Jamieson. It could be an out for you. A good one."

"What? I don't want an out. I want to be a cop! What does the TRPB have to do with me?"

Ladner coughed as if my outburst had made him choke on his cigar.

"Could you shut up a minute? I told you, Gravelin is gunning for you. You pissed him off with that flip remark you made. Not to mention you ignored his direct command to stay out of the case. You're not helping yourself."

Beyond the barn, a ragged cloud drifted across the horizon and shut out the morning light. I could smell a dampness in the earth beyond the terrace. Ladner's voice had become so sharp and loud, I held the phone away from my ear, and still heard the next words clearly.

"You know what the TRPB is, right?"

I pulled the phone back, feeling like a grade-school kid presented with a pop quiz. "The Thoroughbred Racing Protective Bureau," I said, trying not to grit my teeth. "They work to keep racing clean so the public's confidence doesn't go down the drain any worse than it already has. What's that got to do with me?"

"Jamieson called me yesterday. He's the TRPB VP. They want to hire you."

They wanted to hire *me*? Why? I didn't want to work for the racetrack. Did I? My trip to Pimlico's barns had raised painful memories of Dad's murder. I shook my head and started to say, "No way." But Dad had died at the track. Maybe I could find some sort of explanation or at least closure for his death.

Over Cody's barn, the cloud on the horizon drifted just enough to let the sun's rays hit the brass on the stable's cupola.

"Fia, you still there?"

"Yeah, I'm here. What do they have in mind?"

There was a pause while Ladner took a pull on his cigar. "Undercover work. But you gotta come up here and see this guy. He's not hiring you without meeting you. But the main thing is, if you agree to work for them, I think Gravelin will close the investigation on you."

"He wants me out that much?"

"Listen, once things cool down, you can come back."

*Yeah, and then I'd rise to police commissioner.*

Still, the bureau was a watchdog for the integrity of American horse racing. Since I can be a bitch and have met a few racetrack lowlifes I wouldn't mind biting, the TRPB job might suit me.

"Ladner," I said, "thanks for looking out for me. I'll come up there, if only for you."

"Let me know when you book a flight. I'll set up the meeting."

I slid the phone in my pocket and stared at the pool's surface that glittered like wet diamonds. I'd been in the same rut for almost five years, a beat cop, going nowhere. Maybe I should take the job. But this guy Jamieson must have a real problem to be so urgently in need of a new undercover agent.

What had happened to the last one? And why did he want me?

# 8

On the first of December, I caught a late-afternoon flight and left the warmth of Fort Lauderdale behind. Two hours later, the plane descended onto the frozen runway at Baltimore-Washington International Airport. After riding the light rail downtown, I walked to my apartment on the second floor of a row house not far from the Mount Street police station.

Some of the houses I passed had blank-eyed boarded-up windows. The rest were secured by barred windows and doors. No sane West Baltimore resident would live without their protection.

When I reached Fulton Street, an icy wind whirled down the gray sidewalk, causing me to pull the hood of my black anorak tightly around my face. I'd always worn a lot of black when out of uniform. Doesn't show dirt, goes with everything, and looks excellent with white-blond hair. And there is something tough about the color that's always appealed to me.

The wind bit into me deeper, and I broke into a jog along the sidewalk, my carry-on luggage bouncing behind me as it hit cracks and the humps caused by tree roots.

By the time I reached my building the light had faded to the color of three-day-old city snow. After grabbing my mail out of the letter box, I lugged my bag and laptop upstairs, relieved to find the door to my apartment was still securely locked. My place had been robbed before.

When I pushed through the door of my apartment, I felt a sharp ache for Buster, the part Maine Coon cat I'd had until the infirmities of old age had taken him a month ago. After the vivid warmth of Florida, the stark emptiness of my environment shocked me. Why did I live like this?

Had the rage caused by my father's murder blinded me to anything beyond police work and fighting the bad guys? At Jilly's age I'd been so happy. I'd had friends at school, friends on Pimlico's backstretch. I'd adored my dad and his dry sense of humor, not to mention his love for the spirited, sometimes magical horses. My shared fascination with these incredibly strong but fragile creatures had bonded me to my dad like a horseshoe nailed to a hoof.

I could have called a girlfriend and gone out for dinner, but instead I microwaved a box of frozen lasagna, poured myself a vodka and tonic, and watched a rerun of *Law & Order: Special Victims Unit*. Buster's empty spot on the couch beside me was another lonely reminder of things lost.

At eight the next morning, my supervisor Ladner walked with me into Detective Gravelin's office in the Internal Affairs Division on Kirk Avenue. I had asked Ladner to be my personal representative during the meeting, and he had accepted.

Gravelin rose from a battered desk and led us down a corridor into an overheated interview room with dull green walls, a long metal table, and half a dozen scarred wooden chairs. A man, maybe in his sixties, sat in one of the chairs that faced the entrance. I'd never seen him before, but Ladner nodded at him. Someone from IAD?

A tremor started somewhere deep inside me and I took a breath and exhaled slowly, determined to control the fear.

Gravelin seated himself at one end of the table where a case file, probably mine, lay in wait for the meeting. Ladner and I sat opposite the stranger, and Gravelin spread open the file. Even though Ladner had left his cigars at the Mount Street station, the familiar smell still clung to him and I found it comforting.

Gravelin did not introduce me to the stranger, instead he switched on a recording device and after flipping through a few pages of my file, he spoke for the record, giving his name, the date, time, place, my name, and the charge against me.

"Officer McKee, you have previously been read your rights regarding a charge of excessive use of force. Is that correct?"

"Yes, sir." My foot started jiggling. I pressed it hard against the carpet.

Gravelin picked a document off the top of the stacked papers and stared at it, his lips compressed.

"It seems the Baltimore state's attorney's office is not inclined to bring charges against you in this matter. The autopsy report on your John Doe revealed large amounts of meth and steroids in the blood system, which corroborates your claim that the man was beyond reason."

I breathed a mental sigh of relief. I was not going to be prosecuted. I'd known they had no case, but still . . .

As Gravelin looked at me, some emotion caused the mole beside his nose to quiver. His mouth grew tighter.

"Make no mistake. You are still under investigation by this office! Your repeated tendency to overstep police powers concerns me. After being ordered off the John Doe case, you defied a direct command from both me and Detective Ladner by interrogating Shyra Darnell." His gaze shifted to Ladner. "I've said it before, and I'll say it again. We don't need her type on this force!"

He stared at me like I was something that had crawled out of the sewer. Men like him probably hated my double earrings and short hair as much as any crime I might have committed. He struck me as the kind of guy who wanted women to have long hair and wear knee-length skirts, preferably in the kitchen.

"With those concerns in mind," he continued, "and because Mr. Jamieson here thinks you could be useful to the Thoroughbred Racing Protective Bureau, you should seriously consider any offer he may have for you. I'll leave you three alone to sort this out."

The room was so hot I was sweating.

Gravelin glanced at my boss. "Ladner, let me know the outcome. It would be in everyone's best interest if McKee left the department."

I watched Gravelin walk from the room and shut the door behind him. What were the chances of the TRPB wanting me after *that* introduction?

Ladner leaned forward and switched off the recorder. He glanced at the man who must be Jamieson and said, "Gravelin's an ass."

Jamieson stretched a hand to me across the table. "Gunford Jamieson," he said.

I shook his hand. It was cool and slightly gnarled, but the man had an excellent handshake, firm and strong. A faint scent of Old Spice aftershave clung to his skin, startling me. The scent my father had used. Pale red strands left from the glory days streaked his faded hair. The knowing look in his eyes told me he'd seen a lot, much of it not good.

"Jamieson spent time with the Miami police department," Ladner said. "He knows all about IAD officers, don't you, Gunny?"

Jamieson nodded. "So tell me, Ms. McKee. Would you shoot the strangler again if the same situation presented itself?"

No point in pretending. "Yes, sir."

It must have been the right answer. The two men smiled at each other like they'd both won a bet.

Jamieson gave me a long, speculative glance, then nodded. "The TRPB may have a position for you."

A jolt of excitement shot through me, surprising me. I *wanted* this job?

Jamieson continued. "I hear you're good at undercover work. That you used to ride for your father at Pimlico. We have need for an agent who can pose as an exercise rider at Gulfstream Park down in South Florida. Does that interest you?"

I stared at the drab wall behind Jamieson, mentally piercing it, seeing the gray streets outside and the steel bars on my apartment.

"Yes, sir, that is something I'd very interested in."

"You have a brother who lives down there, correct?"

"Yes, Patrick McKee. He's in real estate." But Jamieson probably already knew that. He'd probably done enough due diligence on me to know where I shopped online, what bank I used, and who my friends were.

Ladner leaned toward Jamieson. "I told you it makes a good cover, Gunny, Fia having family near the track. She's got the training and she can ride."

"What's going on at Gulfstream?" I asked Jamieson.

"Horses that shouldn't be winning races are cleaning up at long odds."

"What do the tests show?" I asked, knowing they would immediately run blood and urine tests on the winning animals.

"That's the problem," Jamieson said. "Nothing comes up positive. Someone's got a new drug."

*Every crooked horseplayer's dream. An untraceable performance enhancer.*

"Not good," I said.

Jamieson leaned back into his chair. "No, it's not." He gazed at me a moment. "Okay then, Fia. Why don't you take a few days to get things in order here, then I want you up at the Fair Hill office for some basic training and paperwork. How long do you think it will take you to get in shape to ride?"

I hadn't ridden much in the last five years, but I was fit from running and regular gym workouts. Still, the cardiovascular demands of galloping multiple sets of fresh Thoroughbred racehorses were tremendous.

"I could be ready in less than two weeks," I said. The TRPB offices were on the grounds at Fair Hill, which happened to be one of the nicest training tracks in America. It would be a great place to get my sea legs back. "Can I leg up at Fair Hill?"

Jamieson's smile went right to his eyes. "That's the plan."

Back at my apartment, I paced around the small living room trying to mentally juggle things in place. In five days, I had to report for duty at Fair Hill. They had a place for me to stay there and though I'd make use of that offer, it might be smart to continue the rent on my Baltimore place until I knew what the future held. I had paperwork to fill out with the Baltimore PD. I had to get my car up from Florida.

My pacing took me to a window overlooking Fulton Street. Below, a skinny girl, her hair in cornrows, carried a baby stuffed into a puffy pink jacket. The young mother's coat was tattered, and a sockless big toe stuck through the front of one of her sneakers. Her cornrows made me think of Shyra Darnell. Where was Shyra? I continued staring at the girl and it hit me. *She doesn't look any older than Jilly.*

I squeezed my eyes shut. With just one wrong decision, Jilly could be the girl walking away from me on the street below. I grabbed my phone to call Patrick, and flinched when it rang in my hand. The caller ID read Patrick McKee.

"Hey," I said, "I was just going to—"

"Jilly's run off to the C-Nine Basin with that guy Zanin!"

"What? She told you that?"

"No, she left a note on the kitchen table. They've gone to look for Valera."

"Are they both *crazy*?" This was insane.

"Fia, you gotta get back here!"

"Did you call the police?"

"You *are* the police," he yelled.

"You're the one who told me I have no jurisdiction down there."

*Why was I arguing with my brother when Jilly was missing?*

"I'll get the next flight," I said. But you've got to call Sheriff Rodriguez!" I hurried on before he could interrupt me, "I've got a number for Zanin. I'll call him, but first read me Jilly's note."

"Hold on," he said.

I heard the sound of his footsteps fade and return before he came back on the line.

" 'Dad, I'm going with Mr. Zanin to find the guy that killed Cody.' That's all it says."

"Okay. Do you recognize it as Jilly's handwriting?"

"Yes. Why wouldn't it be her handwriting?" His voice rose in panic. "You think somebody took her?"

"No," I said quickly. "Just making sure."

"Damn it, Fia. You're scaring me."

"Just call Rodriguez." I ended the connection, grabbed my wallet, and ripped out the card Zanin had given me. I entered his number on my phone. Damn Zanin. What was he thinking taking Jilly into that no-man's-land?

# 9

Zanin's cell rang six times before it sounded like it switched to call forwarding. A woman answered, "Animals League."

"I need to speak to Zanin," I said. "It's urgent."

"Sorry, he's in the field."

"I really need to speak to him."

"He's not available."

"Okay," I said. "What's your name?"

"Betsy."

"Listen to me, Betsy. Zanin has my fifteen-year-old niece with him. He's taking her into the C-Nine Basin. If I can't talk to him, maybe the Broward County sheriff's department will have better luck."

Silence, then, "Does your niece have dark hair, with a diamond stud in her nose?"

My pulse quickened. "Yes. Her name is Jilly. You *saw* her?"

"Yeah, earlier. And she is *not* with Zanin. We get kids like her all the time. Dying to fight the good fight."

"So Zanin took her with him?"

"Absolutely not! You aren't *listening* to me. He sent her on her way before he left. I heard the whole thing. He told her what he tells all the wannabe young warriors, 'Keep your eyes and ears open, be our radar, but keep yourself safe.'"

I stared at the vehicles parked on the street below my apartment window. What would I have done when I was fifteen? "But you say Jilly left your office before Zanin did?"

"Yes."

"How do you know she didn't stow away in the back of his SUV?"

"*Zanin* would never let that happen."

"*You* don't know Jilly," I said. "Please, you need to contact him."

"He's deep into a reconnaissance mission. I told you. He's unreachable."

"You can't even text him or send some sort of radio alert?"

"No."

"That's the dumbest thing I've ever heard!" I shouted. "What will you do if he goes missing?"

The voice on the phone hardened. "Aside from the one in his cell phone, he has a GPS tracker sewn into his bulletproof vest, and one hidden in the buckle of his belt."

I heard her breath suck in.

"Oh, crap. Nobody's supposed to know that!"

"No one will hear it from me," I promised, then gave her my and Patrick's cell numbers. "If Zanin becomes *reachable,* please get him to call my brother or me." I thanked her and disconnected.

Calling US Air, I discovered a noon flight. I had an hour. Ladner knew I'd taken the job with Jamieson and that I wasn't expected up at Fair Hill for a few days. I was lucky the timing had worked out. I threw everything into my carry-on, ran from my apartment, caught a cab on the corner, and told the driver, "Cash reward if you can get me to BWI in twenty minutes."

At three that afternoon, I'd retrieved my Mini from Fort Lauder-dale's general airport parking and was heading south on 95 with my windows rolled down. Warm salt air and the smell of the sea blew through the car. I checked for messages but had only one from a woman at the Fair Hill offices of the TRPB. Nothing from Zanin or Patrick.

Now, as I sped down the highway, crossing over an arm of the Intracoastal Waterway, whizzing past docked boats and waste-landlike swamps, I used the Mini's Bluetooth to call Patrick.

"Fia," he pounced, "have you heard anything?"

"No. Have you?"

"Nada. The sheriff's department won't do anything. Jilly hasn't been missing long enough."

"I told you that." Yet I'd been hoping they might put a track on Zanin's phone. Not that they would tell me. "Where are you?"

"The office. What are you going to do?"

"Find Jilly," I said.

Patrick's snort of irritation echoed through the Mini's speakers. "How? You have no idea where you're going."

"Wrong. I have friends in the Baltimore PD, remember? They ran Luis Valera through the system and got me an address. OnStar should get me within shouting distance."

Outside the Mini's passenger's window, palm trees and tele-phone poles zoomed past. I decided not to mention Valera's ugly police record to Patrick.

"I have to call Zanin's office," I said. "I'll be in touch." I dis-connected, and called the PAL office.

Betsy answered. No, she hadn't heard from Zanin.

"Can you at least tell me the make and color of his SUV?" My only recollection was that is was midsized and dark.

"I don't think he'd like that," she said.

"Betsy, I'm a Baltimore city police officer, so you might want to cooperate, because Zanin's going to dislike the idea of your obstructing justice a whole lot more than a simple description of his SUV! Jilly's still missing. If she's not with Zanin, I need to know it so we can search elsewhere."

"All right, *all right*. It's a black Chevy Tahoe, okay?"

"Okay," I said more gently. "Please call me if you hear anything."

"Sure," she said, her sarcasm leaking out the Mini's speakers like snake venom. "You have a nice day."

*Fia McKee, specializing in lies, threats, and making new enemies.* I pressed harder on the accelerator and called OnStar.

When a male operator came on, I relayed the address and halfway held my breath. My cop buddy in Baltimore had said the intersection of Flamingo Road and 178th Street wasn't visible on his satellite map.

"I'm sorry," the OnStar guy said. "I'm not finding that location. The streets are listed, but the system's not giving directions."

We settled on the intersection of Okeechobee Road and 137th Street. He sent the directions, and I sped south on 95, before exiting onto Hollywood Boulevard and traveling west past miles of tile-and-stucco housing developments, shopping malls, and garden centers stuffed with palms and flowering bushes.

After a drive that seemed endless, the road changed into Pines Boulevard. Stopping at one of the larger gas stations for fuel, soda, and the restroom, I bought a Rand McNally Map of Florida. OnStar was pretty cool, but I wanted something on paper so I could *see* where I was heading. Sitting in the car, I sipped a cup of iced Diet Coke and poured over the map. I found 137th Street, which appeared as a tiny squiggle trailing into nothing.

Not promising. Back on the road, the heavy traffic thinned. After passing under Interstate 75, the road narrowed to one lane, finally dead-ending at North Okeechobee Road. Across the pavement a one-lane sand track led into a flat, empty distance.

After swinging south onto Okeechobee, I rode alongside a narrow canal paralleling the highway. Beyond it was an endless landscape of skinny, denuded tree trunks, thrusting skyward like broken knives. Maybe they'd been sprayed with chemicals to keep them off the electric lines that stretched endlessly to the west.

Continuing south, I passed more landscaping companies, seedy-looking trailer and fishing camps, and airboat tour sites. There were no nice homes, no hotels, no shopping malls.

A sensation of crossing a dark threshold touched me as Okeechobee passed over Snake Creek Canal and I officially entered the C-9 Basin. A cloud bank was building on the western horizon, gray, ominous, and heading my way. I wanted to find Jilly and head for home.

Fifteen minutes later, OnStar announced that 137th Street was a mile ahead. The road was marked by a small dented county sign, and after turning, I drove slowly down a pocked gravel road hoping to find a place to ask for directions. The clouds were overhead now, the light dim and unsteady. I passed a palm tree nursery on the right with no visible office or humans. Properties barred by chain-link fences advertised five- or ten-acre lots for sale.

Ahead, a large tarp covered the outside of a metal fence, hiding whatever was on the other side. I'd never been one to resist curiosity and eased the car to a stop. It wasn't like there was any traffic on the road. I slid my gun into the waistband at the small of my back and got out. The air was warm, humid, and dusty. When I smelled horses, my head lifted like a dog, testing the airborne scent.

Walking to the end of the tarp, I peered through a narrow gap between the blue plastic and thick waxy bushes. There were five or six mixed-breed horses inside a dirt lot. They appeared well fed and in good shape. One of them was a paint like Cody. Why were they hidden? *Stolen? Slaughterhouse potentials?*

"What you want?" a harsh voice asked.

I whirled to face a thickset man with a poorly trimmed beard and moustache. He held a machete at his side.

I smiled and gave him my best dumb blond look. "I heard you have horses for sale."

"You heard wrong." He stared at my car. "You from Maryland? You don' belong here. This property private."

*"Lo siento,"* I said, telling him I was sorry. "This is 178th Street, right?"

He shook his head.

*"Lo siento,"* I repeated, *"puede digame dónde está?"* Could he tell me where it was?

He rolled his eyes to the heavens as if dealing with me required help from above. *"Dos millas,"* he said. Using the machete, he pointed in the direction I'd been heading. The blade was dirty and crusted with something reddish brown.

"Two miles." I nodded and smiled. *"Gracias!"*

Still facing him, I eased away. You don't turn your back on a man like that. After edging sideways, I hopped into the Mini, fired the engine, and bumped away on the potholed road, hating to leave the animals behind. When I found Zanin, I'd ask him about the horses.

First, I had to find out what had happened to Jilly.

# 10

The clouds overhead thickened, and the vegetation closed in, almost swallowing the road as I crawled forward searching for 178th Street. I rolled my window down and listened. Air, heavy with moisture and the scent of vegetation, seeped into the car. With relief I saw a trailer camp ahead to the right.

A closer view caused my hands to grip the steering wheel.

Six or seven dogs growled at the Mini. Their lips curled back to reveal jagged, yellow teeth. With heads low and hackles up, they rushed the car, their chains rattling behind them until the slack caught against metal stakes, making them choke. Straining to get at me, they snapped their teeth. I doubted the county's animal control came into a place like this.

Two chocolate-skinned men with dreadlocks stood by a dilapidated double-wide, their malicious stares more intimidating than the fangs of the dogs.

I should have rented a dented-up farm truck instead of driving a Yuppie mobile with out-of-state tags. Not a good place to ask for directions. I kept going.

Two swamps, three jungles, and a half-dozen fenced-in shacks later I had a new appreciation for West Baltimore. After passing through a well-kept palm nursery, I saw a different street branching to the right. I had to stop the car and get out so I could squint up at the county street sign riddled with bullet holes. I made out the numerals 178.

I got back in the car and checked my cell, relieved to see I had service in the jungle. I tried calling Patrick and Betsy. Both efforts went straight to voice mail. Spreading out the Rand McNally map, I traced the new street with my finger, hoping I might notice something more encouraging. The track still trailed into nothing.

I angled the Mini into the lane, grateful for the car's small size. The rutted dirt track was so narrow the average car couldn't have turned around. Horses would fare better. I shifted the Mini into low gear and crept ahead, avoiding puddles of water with unknown depths.

To my left the ground dropped away and turned into a swamp with cypress trees and other water-loving plants I didn't know the names of. Something large and reptilian moved through the muck. To my right the ground was higher and lined by a heavy fence of chicken wire. Ducks, chickens, and geese scratched in the dirt. One white gander honked in alarm as the Mini crept past. Their dusty farmyard scent drifted into the car along with the overripe smell of stagnant water.

About a hundred yards farther, another narrow track curve onto the higher ground on the right. A hand-painted sign read, FLAMINGO ROAD, PRIVATE PROPERTY, KEEP OUT.

Had I arrived at Luis Valera's?

I rolled to a stop before a large hog pen someone had built on the corner. A sour stink rode the air outside the Mini. I flinched, my heart pounding as huge pigs squealed and stampeded the fence. They stopped short of the barrier, their snouts filthy.

Coats of coarse, matted hair covered their skin. Large tusks curved and sprouted from their jaws. *Feral hogs.*

They grunted and raked the ground with long, cloven hooves. I grabbed my gun. In addition to heavy wooden boards, the pen had solar-powered fence chargers with thick lines of electrified wire attached to the top of each board. Without it, I had no doubt the hogs would have trampled the fence and crushed my car like a tin can.

I stared with disgust as smaller pigs fought over a goat carcass farther back in the pen. With their alpha buddies preoccupied, the lesser pigs tore frantically at the carcass until the big boys reversed, charged, and ran them off.

*Nice place you got here, Valera.*

I looked beyond the pen. Flamingo Road curved around a bend and disappeared.

"What the hell are you doing here?"

I gasped. *Zanin.* "Damn it, you scared the hell out of me." How had he snuck up on the side of me like that? I ran my eyes over him. Probably the camouflage clothing and the green and brown greasepaint smeared on his face

"Keep your voice down," he muttered. "Maybe put the gun down, too?"

The hogs grunted, squealing as they made a rush toward Zanin, again stopping short of the electrified fence.

I kept my gun trained on him. "Where's my niece?"

He looked confused. "What are you talking about?"

"She's missing. Last seen at *your* offices. Ring a bell?"

"*Jilly?* I sent her home."

"She didn't make it."

Zanin leaned his neck to one side like he was trying to work a crick out. "Damn," he said. "You thought she was with me?"

"Is she?"

"No. She's a nice kid. I'd never bring her out here."

"Where's your Tahoe?" I asked.

"She's *not* here," he said, a sharp edge to his voice.

I believed his innocence and lowered my gun, but not my theory. "It would be just like her to stow away in your SUV. At least that's what I would have done when I was her age."

Something that was almost a grin brushed his lips before apprehension chased it away. "We can't stay here. Pigs are like watchdogs. If they don't shut up, someone will come. These people wouldn't think twice about killing us and using the pigs for disposal. They eat everything, even the bones."

I shuddered.

"Drive down 178th Street." He gestured in the direction I'd been heading. "Go about a half mile, and look for an abandoned barn on your right. The ground's solid, you can drive behind the barn. You'll see my Tahoe. I'll meet you there."

He jogged a short distance away on Flamingo Road and melted into the heavy brush.

I put the Mini in gear and eased away from Flamingo Road and the horror hogs. They gave a few good-bye squeals, probably disappointed to see me go. A short way down the road, I passed a Latino man leading a burro loaded with broad leaves hacked from some kind of plant. The burro ignored me. The man sent a long suspicious stare, and I understood why Zanin had chosen to trek unseen through the brush.

After a stretch dense with plants and pines, the view opened and I spotted the dilapidated barn and drove across a weedy field of Bermuda grass. When I reached the wooden structure, I drove behind it, and pulled up next to Zanin's Tahoe where he'd left it parallel to the road. I appeared to have arrived first. He must still be creeping through the tangled vegetation.

I got out, walked to the SUV, and leaned in close to the back of the vehicle, cupping my hands around my eyes to see through the darkened glass. A tarp covered most of the contents of the rear compartment. A few things were visible—some jugs of water, a horse lead, and a box of vet wrap, gauze, ointments, a big bottle of Vetericyn wound spray, and a can of bug repellent.

I stared at the tarp. Something about the hump it formed behind the backseat was familiar. The cloth rose up and down ever so gently.

"Jilly, I know you're in there." I wrapped my knuckles on the window. "Jilly!"

She gave it up and pushed the tarp away from her head, her expression defiant. I tried the passenger's door. Locked. Even though it was only in the mid-seventies, she was lucky for the cloud cover or she would have roasted in that black Tahoe.

"Open the door," I said.

She glared at me and didn't move. Just then the screen of bushes and pines stirred nearby and Zanin slipped into the open. I scowled at him and pointed at the Tahoe. He walked quickly toward me.

"You've got a hitchhiker," I said.

"What?"

"Jilly is in your SUV. You want to unlock the doors and get her out?"

The whining sound of a rapidly approaching engine made us turn to the road. The vehicle wasn't in sight yet.

"Jilly, cover back up!" I yelled.

Zanin ran at me, grabbed my shoulders, and pushed me to the ground. "Go with me on this," he said, pinning my shoulders to the grass and dirt, lowering his body to mine, covering my mouth with his. His weight made my gun press hard into the small of my back.

I knew what he was doing and why, but the instinct to fight him off was too strong. As I struggled, a Jeep careened off the road and bore down on us.

"Shit," Zanin said. "Fia, slap me."

I obliged, smacking him as hard as I could. He laughed, caught my hands, and pushed me back to the ground.

The Jeep stopped and two men got out who might have been Haitian, African, or mixed Latino. They both had rifles.

Zanin sat up and rolled off of me. "Whas the problem, *amigos?*" he asked, slurring his speech as if he'd had too many beers.

One of the men moved closer, towering over us. "Get up."

He must be the one in charge. A leather thong circled his neck. A beaded amulet with a tiny black and ivory skull hung from it. The man pulled his lips back in a distorted smile. His front teeth were missing and I could smell a sour odor coming off him.

Zanin grinned. "Hey man, can't a guy have some alone time with his woman?"

"Not on *our* property. You should do *la chica* at home."

"Dude, her *husband* probably wouldn't like that. Know what I'm sayin'?" Zanin winked.

"You full of shit, man," the guy with the skull around his neck said. "You got that camouflage shit on your face!"

"What can I tell you, man. The bitch likes it kinky." Zanin's smirk was so lewd, I smacked him again.

"You bitch!" He pushed me back on the ground and dropped his weight on me. His eyes and mouth found mine, so did an electrical connection. Now I had a gun and an erection pressing against me.

Skull Man swung the barrel of his rifle against Zanin. "*Escucha!* I told you to get up."

"Yeah, sure," Zanin said, still slurring like he was hammered, and rubbing his side where the gun had struck him. So low I could barely hear, he said, "Santerias." He rolled off me.

The only thing I knew about Santerias was that they sacrificed animals for their religious ceremonies and that was enough.

"I like your woman," Skull Man said, his lips stretching to a grin. "My boss say, 'If she like pig so much, she meet them.' But," he said, leering at me, "I think I meet her first. Then we go to see my boss and she meet pig."

The other man laughed wildly like a hyena. He stepped closer. He wore loose burlap pants and no shirt. His feet were bare. Someone had painted white symbols on his chest.

I truly did not like the way this was going.

Zanin raised himself onto his knees, grabbing my wrists. "Get up, baby." He slid me roughly along the ground toward him. A rock, a stick, or something dislodged the Walther from my waistband.

The guy with the symbols yelled, *"Pistola!"*

In slow motion, I watched him flip his rifle so he held it by the barrel. He slammed the butt into Zanin's head. Skull Man kicked my gun away just as my fingers touched it.

Zanin appeared unconscious. Skull Man laughed, picked up my Walther and shoved it into his waistband before jerking me roughly to my feet.

I came up fast, smashed my palm into his nose, used the momentum to twist away and then slammed an elbow back into his neck. He went down choking, but the man with the painted symbols had his rifle pointed at my chest. He did his hideous hyena chuckle again.

In my peripheral vision I saw something creep from behind the Tahoe. I held up open palms to the man holding the rifle. "I have money. I will pay you."

"I don't want your money."

"Hey, dick face," Jilly said from behind him.

The guy turned. She sprayed his face with bug spray. She hit the side of his head with the can and took the rifle.

Skull Man was still on the ground, so I rushed forward, kicked his windpipe, and jerked my Walther from his waistband. Then I smacked his head with the gun and knocked his lights out.

I glanced at Jilly. We were both shaking.

"You," I said to the shirtless Santeria, "help me get him into the SUV." I pointed at Zanin, really glad to see him trying to sit up. "*Now,*" I snapped at the guy. "Jilly, carry those rifles." She did and with the reluctant help of Hyena, we managed to get Zanin into the backseat of the Tahoe.

"Where are your keys?" I asked Zanin.

"Pocket." He fumbled at his jeans. I brushed his hand away and snatched up a set of keys.

"Fia," Jilly said, "give me your keys."

"*You* can't drive."

She looked at me like I was as stupid as a stick. "Of course I can drive. You can't leave your car *here!*"

She had a point. I gave her my keys.

*Stupid as a stick Fia McKee contributes to the delinquency of minors.*

I got behind the wheel of the SUV and cranked the engine. Jilly ran to the Mini and threw both rifles inside. As the Hyena man gazed at her, I could feel the weight of his malevolence. Jilly gave him the finger and fired up the Mini.

We gunned the vehicles across the field and fled for the distant highway.

# 11

We sat at the orange-tiled table in Patrick's kitchen. The four of us ate Chinese food from cardboard cartons delivered by a man from Wu Fong's Chinese Emporium. Steam and the smell of garlic rose from my plate as I ladled another serving of shrimp and broccoli onto fried rice.

When Zanin pushed a carton toward me, I stared at him. "I can't believe you're eating pork."

"Me, either."

"Why wouldn't he eat pork?" Jilly asked.

"You didn't see the pigs." I pushed the offending carton back at Zanin.

Patrick and Jilly sat at opposite ends of the table, carefully not speaking to each other, avoiding another eruption of angry words.

When we'd rolled in the driveway and Patrick had seen Jilly driving my car, he'd exploded. It had only gotten worse when Zanin crawled out of the Tahoe pressing his hand to the lump that oozed blood from his scalp.

I rubbed at my forehead, hoping to ease the ache that pounded behind my eyes. Probably nothing compared to what Zanin must be suffering. Jilly had given him a Ziploc bag of ice, and he was pressing it against the lump on his head.

"You really should go to the ER," I said. "You were out cold."

"I'm fine." He concentrated on forking up another bite of sweet and sour pork.

"You don't look fine," Jilly said.

Patrick set his water glass down with a bang. "I can't believe you people won't call the police."

I shook my head. "We've been over this. Do you really want warrants for assault with a deadly weapon issued on Jilly and me? And trespassing? Because that's just what those guys will have a magistrate do if we don't leave them alone."

"She's right," Zanin said. "People like Valera know how to play the system. He's probably got a stable of criminal defense attorneys."

Patrick curled his lip with disdain. "So you're just going to let his people beat you up?"

Jilly eyes had been darting back and forth, following the verbal jousting match. She raced in. "Dad, you don't know what you're talking about!"

I shot her a warning glance, but she was already in full stride.

"I creamed one guy's head with a can, and Fia beat the shit out of the other one!"

"Damn it, Jilly. Do not use that language in this house."

She glared at her father. "You just said 'damn it.'"

"That's enough," Patrick roared. He glared at me. "My daughter hit one of these guys? We *have* to call the police. They'll come after her!"

"No," I said, "they won't. They have Zanin's license number and my Maryland tags. No direct lead to this house."

"They'll come after *me*," Zanin said.

At least Jilly hadn't metioned that I'd almost been raped and fed to feral pigs. I rolled my can of cold Coke back and forth across my forehead and took a breath before my next thrust.

"Listen to me, Patrick. If you file a warrant, these people will know who Jilly is and where she lives. They'll file a warrant for assault with a deadly weapon."

"It was only a can of *bug* spray," Jilly said.

"Doesn't matter," I explained. "A can of bug spray is a deadly weapon. Under the law it doesn't have to be a gun or a knife, it can be anything that can be used to kill someone." I rubbed my neck. The knots back there were giving birth to baby knots.

Patrick stood up, "You are *so* wrong. I'm calling the police right—"

"Here's how it works!" I shouted. "They will file a warrant against Jilly. They'll tail her so they know where she is. On a Friday afternoon they will tell the deputies where to find her, remind them of the outstanding warrant, and make sure she is picked up. I see this happen all the time."

Patrick started to protest, and I held up my hand. Time to go for the jugular. "How do you know Valera doesn't have a sheriff in his pocket? They pick her up on a Friday afternoon. She'll be held over in *jail* until an arraignment on *Monday*. You want to risk that?"

Patrick sat down, elbows on the table, his head in his hands.

"She's right," Zanin said. "Sometimes the law is the perpetrator's best friend."

"Well, that's just *stupid*," Jilly said.

"Yeah," I said, "but that's the way it is."

Apparently the subject had been beaten to death. Except for the scraping of forks on stoneware plates, the room was silent as we scooped up the last bites of Chinese food.

Zanin pushed his chair back and eased himself upright. "Patrick, thanks for the meal."

"Sorry I yelled at everyone," Patrick said, looking at if he meant it. "I'm just so worried."

"It's okay, Dad." Jilly gave him a tentative smile.

Standing, Patrick took the three steps between him and Jilly and rested his hand on her shoulder. He glanced at Zanin and me. "Thanks for getting her back here safely."

"Sure," I said.

I walked Zanin out and we stood under the portico for a moment. The earlier clouds had developed into a hard rain and the Florida breeze was wet and chilly.

"You sure you can drive?" I asked, noticing he was still pressing his bag of melting ice to his head.

"I'll be fine. I've been through worse, but I'm sorry Jilly got mixed up in this."

"She'll be okay," I said. "McKees are tough."

"That they are."

His stare lingered so long I could feel heat flush my cheeks.

"We're not finished with Valera yet," he said.

"No, we're not."

"Keep in touch, Fia." He dashed through the rain, fired up the Tahoe, and left.

I liked this man, but did I need to get involved? Especially now? Besides, I had questions about him. Like how did he make a living rescuing animals? Did he have some ulterior motive? *And when had I become so cynical?*

A gust of wind swept rain into my face. I wheeled and hurried back inside.

When I walked into the kitchen, cookie crumbs littered the table and Patrick and Jilly were reading their fortunes. They set the tiny papers down without comment.

"Maybe things can get back to normal now," Patrick said. "Jilly, you've learned your lesson, right?"

She rolled her eyes.

"I want you to concentrate on school and getting those grades back up," he said.

*Patrick, leave it alone.*

"Fia and I will be checking to make sure you're at school when you're supposed to be."

*I hate being volunteered for things. He'd always pulled this crap.*

"No more with the class cutting, Jilly," he continued, oblivious to the rebellion building on his daughter's face.

"May I be excused?"

"No, you may not. You can sit there and listen for a change. It's about time—"

"Patrick," I said. "I have to head north tomorrow."

"What?" he asked.

Jilly's eyes widened. "No, you can't."

"I have to. I've been offered a new job."

"Can't it wait?" Patrick sounded almost desperate.

"I'm sorry, but it can't." I glanced at Jilly.

She narrowed her eyes and glared at me.

"But I'll be back in about two weeks."

"*Two weeks?* I don't believe you. You're just like Mom. You *won't* come back." She pushed back from the table so violently her chair crashed to the floor. She kicked it three feet across the tile and ran from the room.

"That went well," I said, reaching for my fortune cookie.

"How can you joke about this?"

"Would you rather see me cry?" I broke open the cookie and read the little slip of paper. "A journey awaits you. Beware of danger."

"Lovely," I said, and bit into the cookie.

In the morning, Jilly was quiet and distant as Patrick rushed off for an early closing on a house he'd sold.

"Let me drive you to school," I said.

"I can take the bus."

"I know that, but this way I can see you for a little longer. Once I drop you off, I'm getting on Ninety-five."

"Whatever."

It was as close to a yes as I was going to get.

The Mini was loaded for my trip north and she had to hold her backpack on her lap with my tote bag. The sun was out, but a few drops of water still glistened on the hood of the car as we drove out.

It had rained hard all night, and I wondered if the chickens and geese near Flamingo Road were wading through standing water in their pen. The pigs could drown for all I cared, but they were probably wallowing happily in goat remains.

The image forced a little sound of disgust from me.

"What?" Jilly asked, as I turned onto the county road.

"I was thinking about yesterday."

"That was so wild." Her face brightened with excitement.

"And dangerous."

She responded with an eye roll.

"Your school is off Griffin Road, right."

"Yeah."

I swung onto Griffin and headed east. "What else do you love?" I asked.

"Huh?"

"You love horses. You like sapphires. How about music, boys, movies, that kind of stuff?"

In my peripheral vision, she was giving me a look. "I like Zanin."

I almost snapped at her. Almost said, "Forget it," but she'd already stiffened, anticipating my angry response. So instead, I asked, "Why?"

She blinked, then stared at her lap. "He's like this iconic hero, the way he rescues animals. And he's cute."

Three cars ahead, a school bus stopped to pick up some kids and the traffic ground to a halt. Jilly raised her eyes to mine. "I know he's too old for me." She dropped her gaze and shrugged. "Besides, he likes you."

"Me?"

"Oh, puh-leeze. I saw the way he kissed you yesterday."

"You did?"

"*Everybody* did."

"That was just a show for those thugs," I said.

"Not the *second* time."

This kid didn't miss anything. I closed my eyes and remembered the pressure of Zanin's hard body against mine.

"You're blushing, Aunt Fia."

"What are you?" I asked, returning my attention to the road. "A detective?"

"I'd . . . I'd like to be," she said.

The red lights ceased flashing on the school bus, the little stop sign folded back, and the traffic rolled forward. I glanced at Jilly.

Her eyes were wide and her mouth formed an O, as if her declaration surprised her.

"You wanna be a *cop*?"

"I think . . . yeah. I'd like to be in law enforcement."

*Patrick was going to love this.* "Mull it over a little," I said. "If you decide you really mean it, I'll help you in any way I can."

A few minutes later I pulled up in front of her school. She gave me a quick hug, hopped out of the car, and disappeared into a wild herd of teenagers. For a moment I understood Patrick's fear and frustration.

I swung out of the school drive and turned the Mini toward 95. I wasn't looking forward to the cold north of Baltimore, but that was the least of my problems.

What were my chances of making it with the TRPB?

# 12

I stayed in a cheap motel in South Carolina that night, and continued north early the next morning. When I climbed out of the car just outside Richmond, a cloud bank was forming to the north. An icy breeze whirled past, hurrying me into the Love's Travel Stop for hot coffee and a snack.

Back on the road, I zigged east off 95 onto 301 north, quite pleased with myself for avoiding 95 into D.C. and the Washington and Baltimore beltways, which I've always believed should be pictured in the dictionary under "traveler's worst nightmare."

By the time I found a place to park on Fulton Street in Baltimore, sleet and freezing rain had crusted over part of my windshield. By the time I dragged my bag and laptop inside my building, I was shivering. After lugging the stuff upstairs, I stopped dead when I saw the door to my apartment. It was open.

I snatched the gun from my tote bag, dropping everything else on the landing. I listened. Nothing. I kicked the door wide open and stared. Though my apartment was tiny, someone could be hiding behind the kitchen counter, in the bathroom, or bedroom. I darted inside, did a fast search, and found no one.

But they'd been after something. My drawers and cabinets were pulled open and stuff was strewn on the floor. I couldn't imagine what they'd been looking for. My two most valuable possessions were my gun and my car. The gun was always with me and the Mini didn't fit in a drawer.

Unless they'd been looking for a computer, which I didn't have. *Damn it.*

I cranked up the heat on the wall thermostat and called the police station. I may be out of favor with IAD, but I still had friends at Mount Street. The station sent two people right over from crime scene to dust for fingerprints.

A small guy with a pockmarked face came in first when I opened my door. I didn't know him, but was glad to see the tall, full-bodied figure of Barbara Symesky behind him. She'd worked a number of crimes scenes I'd called in, and we'd occasionally gone out for coffee and burgers together. She'd been the one to tell me about Luis Valera's police record.

The two agents got to work, and a while later Barbara said, "You know how it works, Fia. It will take a while to get the print results, but I'll call you."

"Thanks," I said, rubbing the back of my neck where my knot buddies were blooming again. "Nothing seems to be missing."

The guy with the bad face said, "You think this has something to do with that guy you killed?"

"No." *Did it?* "Probably just someone looking for drug money."

He gave me a skeptical look. "People looking for a fix don't usually bother with gloves."

"He's right," Barbara said. "What about a computer?"

"Laptop," I said, pointing to the case still on the floor.

She stared at me for a beat. "You need anything, Fia, you call me. Right?"

"Sure."

"Wait a minute," the guy said. "Is this yours?" He was leaning over near my TV couch, staring at something on the floor. Using tweezers, he picked up a small orange bead.

"No," I said, "that's not mine." But something about the bead made me think of Shyra Darnell.

"I'll take it to the lab," he said. "See if they can get anything off it." He dropped the bead into a plastic evidence bag.

They packed up and started to leave. Barbara's hand was on my doorknob when I said, "There is one thing."

"What?" she asked.

"I'd appreciate *any* information you could find on the victim from that night. The woman who disappeared, Shyra Darnell."

"You got it," Barbara said.

I thanked them, and after they left, I went to work cleaning up the mess from the intruder and the fingerprint dust. By the time I finished, I had as much strength as a dust rag. I pulled a pizza from the freezer and slid it into the microwave. As the machine clicked and whirred, I remembered the microwave in Shyra's room at Pimlico.

In my mind, I inventoried the scant belongings in her tiny room. I closed my eyes, concentrated, and saw the altar. And the strings of beads around the necks of those porcelain saints. I couldn't recall their color.

Why would Shyra have come to my apartment?

# 13

A week later, at Fair Hill's training track, Rosario Jones gave me a leg up on the big gray mare, Luceta. By now, my muscles had finally stopped screaming though those first few days I'd galloped horses, I'd been so cold, stiff, and sore I hadn't been sure I'd make it.

Regular doses of ibuprofen and late-afternoon toddies of hot tea with lemon, honey, and bourbon had been my best friends.

Rosario, a jockey-turned-trainer, studied me from beneath the fur trapper's hat he wore every day. He had a full salt-and-pepper beard, and with the fur upholstery on his head, he reminded me of a lop-eared rabbit. I knew his mother was Mexican and figured it was his Latino half that needed the hat to ward off the biting wind.

He favored hunter green and a bright rose red for his stable colors. His buckets, wire gates, and tack boxes were all done in the dark green. The flashy rose color lit up his horses' blankets and stable bandages, the color incongruous in the gray, frigid landscape.

The TRPB had sent me to him, informing me I'd work for him as an exercise rider. After two weeks at Fair Hill, I'd be going with him to Gulfstream. I'd had one conversation with the whiskered trainer behind closed doors. After that, my connection to the agency was never mentioned.

Rosario's glance as I sat on Luceta was thoughtful. "This horse is gonna be a bit fresher than what I've thrown at you so far. She's only about six weeks out from racing." So far, Rosario had only given me older horses coming off layups. Those animals had been seasoned and fairly quiet. With Luceta under me, I felt the power and eagerness of youth.

A blast of icy wind rushed down the aisle, blowing wisps of hay, a candy wrapper, and an almost empty container of poultice with it. Luceta snorted, raised her front legs into the air, and tried to bolt down the barn's dirt aisle. She rushed forward a few steps before I got her under control. Instead of trying to turn or stop her, I let her walk on.

I called back to Rosario, "I'll just give her a turn around the barn."

"Good idea," he said. "And hold on to that martingale."

I glanced down at the mare's withers. Instinctively, I'd already hooked one finger securely into the leather martingale that circled the filly's neck. I was glad that old habits die hard. If the mare reared up, that hold on the martingale could keep me from going off backwards.

Luceta and I completed one circuit along the dirt aisle that ran outside the stalls of the rectangular barn. Rosario watched as we returned.

"You think you can two-minute lick her a mile?"

Either the horse wasn't very valuable, or Rosario had more faith in me than I did. Letting someone who hadn't regularly galloped horses take one for a two-minute lick was risky. At thirty miles an hour she could run off. I might not be fit enough to stop her.

"Sure," I said.

"Then jog her to the mile pole and break her off."

"Okay."

I took a mental deep breath and urged Luceta along the trail that led from Rosario's barn to the big Fair Hill Training Center track. The mare's head came up when she stepped onto the dirt where Kentucky Derby winners like Animal Kingdom and Barbaro had trained.

I eased her into a jog and felt her muscles pumping with blood, saw her veins pop out on her neck as her immense cardiovascular system fired up. Racehorses always seem to know when you mean business.

As Luceta reached the mile pole, I sat lower in the saddle, picked up the reins, and chirped once. She took off, and I steadied her to the quick rhythm of a two-minute lick.

The wind tore at my face mask and goggles as we whipped down the backstretch. Into the turn, the wind hit the right side of my face, burning it with cold. As we rolled into the stretch the gusts blew us along from behind like Luceta was a sailboat and I was her mast.

When we hit the wire, I stood in the stirrups and slowly eased her speed to a canter, then a jog. I knew I was grinning like a fool. I'd forgotten the amazing high that hits me when I let a horse cruise and discover we function as a single entity.

Rosario stood at the gap in the rail to the barn path. He glanced at the stopwatch in his hand and nodded approvingly. "You've got a good clock in your head."

"Thanks," I said, enjoying the warm steam rising off Luceta's body. It was so cold at Fair Hill, even the manure in the stalls was half frozen. The warm, horsey smell reaching my nostrils from Luceta was wonderful.

"I don't know what you're grinning about. You've got five more horses to get out this morning." But Rosario was smiling.

Later I downed a cheese sandwich in my room on the

backside, changed clothes, and walked over to the TRPB offices
housed in a large stone and wood building that overlooked the
training track's first turn. I liked the building's steeply pitched
roof and the numerous plate-glass windows that made for a sunny
interior. Since they keep the front door locked, I headed around
to the back and used a card key to gain entrance.

I'd looked up the history of the bureau and discovered FBI
Director J. Edgar Hoover, an avid racing fan, had a hand in forming the TRPB back in 1946. Spencer J. Drayton, formerly an FBI
agent and administrative assistant to Hoover, had been selected
to head the new organization. Apparently Drayton had mod-
eled the TRPB along the lines of the FBI and brought in several
FBI colleagues to assist him. I didn't see myself fitting in all that
well with the strict bureaucratic codes of the FBI and hoped
the organization had lightened up somewhat since 1946.

Inside, I walked down a long hall with offices on either side
and stopped at the room I supposedly shared with an agent who'd
been out in the field since before I arrived. If it hadn't been for
the framed pictures of him, his wife, and his kid, I might have
doubted he existed. His phone never rang, and his in-box was
empty.

Mine wasn't. A handwritten note rested on the papers I'd
accumulated from my afternoon studies with an agent named
Brian who was teaching me the ins and outs of the TRPB. The
note was from Jamieson: *See me as soon as you get in.*

I'd learned that everyone who'd been at the bureau a while
called Gunford Jamieson "Gunny." I planned to stick with "Mr.
Jamieson" for the immediate future.

I hung my anorak on the coat hook and hurried to his office.
I hadn't spoken directly with him since I'd arrived and was a little
anxious about our first meeting.

When I stepped inside, he fixed cop eyes on me and pointed
his pen at the chair facing his desk.

"Sit."

"Yes, sir." Resisting a nervous urge to run my fingers through my short hair, I sat. Miraculous second chances don't come often, and I was determined this one would work.

Jamieson twirled his pen. "You know I'm sending you to Gulfstream."

I nodded, once again considering my good fortune. Gulfstream Park was a beautiful track, a winter mecca for horse racing fans. The big weekends at this tropical track attracted the finest horses, best trainers, top jockeys, and big money.

My new boss opened a folder on his desk and studied the contents a minute. I noticed an economy-sized bottle of Pepcid Complete on his desk. The faint scent of my father's aftershave drifted past when he tapped his pen on the file.

"I want you to keep an eye on a trainer named Michael Serpentino. He heads up a racing syndicate called BetBig." He paused a few beats. "You don't know anyone down at Gulfstream in Florida, do you?"

"No, sir. Not anyone that would recognize me now. My dad only trained horses in Maryland and I lost weight after he . . ." Jamieson *had* to know my father had been murdered. But he couldn't know how my world had stopped, hadn't seen that moment of rage and grief when I smashed the china horse my father had given me and chopped off my long dark hair. "Anyway . . . my looks have changed."

The cop look eased. "I hear the riding is going well?"

"Yes, sir."

His gaze dropped as he hesitated a moment. "You should think about . . ."

I leaned forward. "Yes?"

"Never mind."

I watched his cop face slide back into place.

"I'm sending you down next week. You'll be working as an exercise rider for Rosario. You two will be in the same barn as Serpentino. You'll need to stay under the radar, keep your TRPB

ID hidden. Rosario knows nothing about Serpentino. Keep him out of this."

I nodded.

"Serpentino likes to hang out at a posh restaurant on the third floor of the grandstand at Gulfstream. It's called Christine Lee's. We think he's conducting business there that is not in the best interest of racing. He also has horses in his barn for his syndicate owners, horses that will suddenly run the race of their lives. Serpentino and his cronies cash some huge bets when that happens."

"This is what you meant when you said horses were cleaning up at long odds?"

"Exactly. And since you're adept at undercover work, you need to spend time there. See what you can overhear."

A little wave of excitement rippled through me. "I can do that," I said. "I can turn into a dumb blond party girl who knows nothing about horses except how to bet 'em." I had wigs, glasses, and outfits that could change my identity in an instant. I was starting to like this gig—going double undercover in the track's best restaurant.

"McKee," he said, pointing his pen at me, "no need to look like the cat that swallowed the canary. You are going there to *work*. And don't *do* anything. Just watch, listen when you can, and don't let Serpentino know it."

"I think I can manage that," I said.

His expression hardened. "Listen to me. If you carry any kind of weapon, you're done. Got it?"

I flinched. "Yes, sir. Absolutely." Even with my background in law enforcement and horse racing, I was lucky he'd taken me on. But though I might be grateful, I wasn't thrilled about working unarmed, and had no intention of letting my pistol stray too far from my hand.

Gunny slid the file across the desk to me. "Serpentino isn't the only one dosing his runners with an untraceable substance. But he's a good place to start."

I picked up the file.

"Okay then, Fia. You study that," he said. "Run your own background check on Serpentino and his known associates. See if anything new comes up."

I knew the information available through the TRPB's massive server was immense and I could still use some pointers. "May I borrow Brian to help me?"

"No. You've had the crash course. I'd suggest you start digging." His hand slid to the bottle of Pepcid but he didn't touch it.

"Yes, sir."

He pointed his pen at me. "Make sure the first time you meet Serpentino, you already *know* him."

A while later I hunkered down at my desk with a fresh cup of coffee to read the contents of the folder. Before I could start, my cell rang, the ID telling me it was my friend, Officer Symesky.

"We didn't have any luck with those fingerprints," she said, when I answered. "Whoever ransacked your apartment didn't wipe the place clean, because *your* prints were all over it. But, since we didn't find any other prints, I figure the scumbag wore gloves."

*Another mystery unsolved.*

"Damn. I really hoped we'd get an ID on this person. I still think it was Shyra Darnell."

"Wish I'd been more help, Fia."

"Thanks for trying," I said. We ended the call, and I turned back to the folder Gunny had handed me.

Michael Serpentino was a native Floridian of Cuban descent. His father had owned a chain of restaurants with branches throughout the state. The old man had sold out to a conglomerate ten years earlier for twenty million, which explained how son Michael had so easily stepped into the role of racehorse trainer.

Most start at the bottom, apprenticing to an established

trainer, working their way up slowly. Often, the apprentices were related to or had an association with their tutor. Like most businesses it wasn't what you knew, it was who you knew. But money had oiled the way for Serpentino.

I booted up the PC. A wealth of information was at my fingertips if I could find it. I felt like such a newbie! I typed in Serpentino's name and got a hit. Only it was the same story I'd seen in Jamieson's file. But I studied it. Serpentino had started his racing syndicate, BetBig, two years earlier, buying horses and obtaining owners at a suspiciously fast clip.

Hearing footsteps in the hall, I looked up. Gracie, Gunny's assistant, tapped her knuckles on my office door frame. "Having any luck?"

"Um, not yet." I liked Gracie. Competent to a fault, she had a softer, sisterly side that had welcomed me into the organization. Her neat bob and conservative look were pure TRPB.

"Can I sit for a minute?"

I nodded and she grabbed a side chair. "I've read your file, Fia. You're sharp as a knife. Gunny's not worried about you handling the *data*."

My right foot started to jiggle. "Thanks. So . . . what *is* he worried about?"

"Gunny's good with the rules, and managing the guys. Not so much with the females. He's old-school."

I remembered his earlier hesitation. "He's not happy with my look?"

She leaned one elbow onto my desk. "If I had your cheekbones and big eyes, I'd be tempted to cut my hair like yours. But the color's a bit electric. It could stand out too much at Gulfstream. And Christine Lee's is somewhat conservative."

"I'll be wearing a wig there. But I'll tone the color down for the track."

Gracie's responding smile warmed her eyes, so I continued.

"It's short because a guy almost killed me when he was able

to grab my hair. Besides, it's good with the wigs I wear—I mean wore—for vice work with the Baltimore PD." Only, with it super short, I liked the added bling of electric blond streaks.

"And," Gracie said, still smiling, "one set of earrings is enough."

I touched one of the gold rings I wore near the top of each ear. "I'll take these out."

"Good."

Outside the office window, the cold had browned and shriveled the grass. On the wall next to my desk, the forced air heating blew a warm gush, spreading a scent of paper and dust. By now, my foot jiggled like a pot ready to boil over.

"Gracie, to be honest, I'm a little surprised I got hired on."

She shrugged. "I'm not. Gunny likes brains. He also needs horse racing knowledge. There aren't too many like you. And"— she swiveled her chair, glanced into the hallway, and lowered her voice—"you never heard it from me, but he liked the way you nailed the strangler."

*Old-school.* I nodded. "Thanks, Gracie."

She slipped out, and I went back to Serpentino on my PC after taking a strong sip of java. I wanted to see if I could find additional information on the trainer.

*Whoa. Who knew there could be half a dozen Michael Serpentinos in the world?*

But I'm good at finding things and after I got my rhythm, I realized that the information I'd read in Gunny's folder had been gathered through noon of the day before. I kept going, sorting by date and time. Nothing new on Serpentino, so I entered the name of his company, BetBig.

The path of the company's partners was convoluted. Syndicate members came and went faster than shareholders on the New York Stock Exchange. People bought in, they got out. The horses BetBig owned changed names and faces as fast as a merry-go-round. So did the people who supplied them.

*Nice place to hide criminal activity.*

The previous afternoon BetBig bought a colt named Dixie Diamond for $250,000. Antonio Morales was listed as the seller. I'd seen his name before. I entered it. Morales showed up five times. Always involved with BetBig purchases of more than $200,000. *Interesting.*

A preliminary background check on Morales revealed dual Mexican and U.S. citizenship, but no dirt. He was a banker heading up the Miami office of a Mexican bank.

I studied his photo. Morales had light hair for a Mexican, almost blond. He reminded me of something or someone. It would come to me.

But there was another face I needed to see. I didn't care that its owner wasn't damaging the integrity of horse racing, or that I probably shouldn't spend company time looking him up, because this man murdered horses and broke young hearts. I typed in "Luis Valera."

*Oh, was he ugly.* Scar tissue around his right eye kept it from opening all the way. His long nose had been so badly broken, it looked like a fist full of clay had been smashed between his cheekbones. The eyebrow above his good eye rose up high into his forehead and formed a question mark.

I glanced down and read the stats under his photo. Thirty-six years old, five-eight, two hundred and fifty pounds.

He carried the weight on a squat frame, the muscles on his arms appearing strong under a layer of pudgy flesh. He had bags of fat under his eyes, and a precisely clipped mustache above an ordinary mouth. Dark hair and dark eyes that showed brutality rather than intelligence.

"Luis," I said, staring at his face on the computer screen. "We should go out sometime."

I attached his photo to an e-mail and typed a message. "Jilly, here's a picture of Valera to use for your neighborhood watch flyers." I sent the e-mail. Then I printed a copy of the photo, which I folded and put into my tote bag.

I shifted back to the computer. There had to be more information about Michael Serpentino, and I intended to find it. But first I typed in Kerameikos Zanin. This man had gotten close to my brother, my niece, and me. I wanted to know what I was dealing with. No arrests, no warrants. The guy appeared to be squeaky-clean with donations from do-gooders providing him an income. I breathed a sigh of relief and turned back to Serpentino.

# 14

I stood in the doorway to Jilly's room, tired from the trip south cramped in the Mini from which I'd just emerged after ten hours of driving. Jilly lay on her bed wearing a purple tunic and black leggings. She was reading a fantasy novel with a picture of a winged horse on the cover.

She set her book down. "So how are you going to see Zanin if you have to be at the track every day?"

"I'm not *seeing* Zanin, but I am expected to show up at work."

"But we have to take care of Valera. He'll kill other horses. Or don't you care anymore?"

*Hadn't I sent her his picture?* "Jilly, *we* are not taking care of Valera. I'll talk to Zanin, but I just got here. How are you, anyway?"

"Fine." She picked up the book.

I almost asked her how school was but it was such a stupid, aunty question, I cut myself short. "Has the neighborhood been safe?"

She perked up. "Yeah. Zanin's flyer idea was cool. And

Valera's arrest photo was *awesome*. Now, everyone knows what he looks like. I think he looks like a *pig*. And we're using a Twitter feed to send out alerts."

"Good job," I said, thinking she was like a high-strung filly. You couldn't restrain her. You had to distract her.

"Dad's even learned how to use Twitter."

*Go, Patrick.* I searched for something else to say and settled on her novel. "If you see a horse that looks like the one on that cover, bring him down to Gulfstream."

She leaned forward. "Can I come to Gulfstream? I mean, like on a Saturday?"

"It's fine with me," I said. "I'll have to ask Rosario if it's okay. It's his barn."

"That would be so cool. Maybe I can ride!"

"That's not likely," I said quickly. "At least, not right away." Why had I added the last part? She couldn't gallop horses before she was sixteen and she didn't have the faintest idea how to anyway. But her smile gave me a glow I hadn't felt in a while.

Besides, having her at the track could help with my cover of being a local Florida gal. Yeah, right. *What was I thinking?* I could already see the headline, FORMER COP CHARGED WITH RECKLESS ENDANGERMENT: NIECE USED FOR UNDERCOVER POLICE WORK.

"We can talk more about this later," I said. Maybe I should back out of this, yet the last thing I wanted to do was set Jilly up for another disappointment.

The next morning, Rosario watched as I rode Luceta toward him at his barn at Gulfstream Park. Like most racing stables, the rectangular barn held about sixty stalls, thirty per side, backed up, with doors facing out. Wood posts supported a roof overhang that sheltered the dirt aisle running outside the stalls. The short ends of the rectangular building had rooms for tack, storage, or a cot for a groom. The section of barn housing a trainer's horses and supplies was commonly referred to as his "shedrow."

Rosario's had green plastic flowerpots filled with miniature red roses hanging from the edge of the roof overhead. The
hot rose red that had been so out of place in the frigid gray at
Fair Hill fit perfectly with the Florida warmth and sunshine.

Rosario had left his fur hat up north and trimmed his beard
to a mustache and goatee. I hadn't known he had a full head of
hair, hadn't even recognized him when I'd arrived that morning. Even minus the hat, with the soft gray streaks in his hair
combined with his bright eyes and the way his nose wrinkled,
Rosario still reminded me of a rabbit.

I'd just breezed Luceta for three-eighths of a mile in good
time, and though we'd both worked up a gleam of sweat, neither
of us blew hard enough to put a match out. That final week of
riding in Maryland had accomplished the job for me.

Apparently Rosario agreed since he'd brought a string of
twelve ready-to-go racers to Gulfstream and left the horses that
still needed legging up with his assistant trainer at Fair Hill. I'd
be riding horses that were sharp and anxious to run.

"She looks good," he said, studying Luceta as I walked her
past him. "I got a new one that shipped in last night, a three-
year-old Not for Love filly. Her name's Last Call for Love and
she has a lot of speed. But she's quirky. Her previous trainer
couldn't do anything with her. Said she doesn't like to train."

Dad had conditioned a horse by Not for Love. I was pleased
we had one in our Gulfstream barn but wasn't thrilled about a
horse with a screw loose. I rode Luceta into her stall, slid off, removed her saddle and bridle, and let the groom, Julio, lead her
away to cool out on the shedrow.

When I emerged from the stall, Rosario gestured me toward
him. "Why don't you see if you can get Last Call to gallop a mile.
I'll have to lead her out for you."

*Just what I needed, a horse that refused to walk to the track.*

"Okay."

I followed Rosario down the aisle breathing in the warm air

and the scents of hay, grain, molasses, and roses. A hint of liniment drifted past, tangy and sharp in the salty Atlantic breeze.

As we approached her stall, the new horse thrust her finely made head over the stall gate. She glared at us, pinned her ears, whirled, and disappeared into the depths of her stall.

"She's flighty," Rosario said.

I refrained from saying, "Really?" and instead said, "But pretty."

Stepping up to her gate, I stared. She was a dark blood bay with a blaze widening into a big pink splash over one nostril. She had a white sock on her right front and another on her right hind leg. Very attractive. But it was the Not for Love confirmation that made her beautiful. Rounded and muscular, with sturdy, strong-boned legs.

The only thing I'd hold against her was her weight. She was too thin. I judged her to be under sixteen hands, but when she walked closer, back to the stall gate, she was tall. Nature had put her together so well, so compactly, it made her appear small at first glance.

"Did her dam have Northern Dancer in the pedigree?" I asked.

He gave me a sharp look. My dad *had* taught me a thing or two.

"She's the last foal out of an old Minstrel mare," he said.

Giving her two crosses of the great Northern Dancer. No wonder Rosario was willing to take her on.

When we got the tack on her, and led her from the stall, she plunged out like she'd just left the starting gate. Then she stopped dead. Rosario gave me a leg up, and Last Call stood like carved marble, refusing to budge. Rosario had taken my whip away, saying he'd been told if you smacked her, she got worse. *Like Jilly.*

I leaned forward and stroked her silky neck, trying to see if I could get her to relax. She didn't. The muscles in her neck were as tight as lug bolts.

"I don't want to get into a war with her the first day here," Rosario said.

"We could try a carrot."

He got one, broke off a little piece, and offered it to her. When she condescended to nibble the small piece, Rosario and I exchanged a glance.

He stepped back and stretched his arm out, offering another bite slightly out of reach. She leaned toward the treat, but couldn't get close enough. She rolled forward onto the front edge of her hooves until she was forced to take a step or fall down.

She got her next bite and once she'd taken three steps in this manner, she gave it up and walked along with Rosario.

He led her down the bridle path to the track, walked her out onto the deep, sandy surface, and let her go. I urged her forward and she promptly froze.

Rosario shook his head. "They don't sell enough carrots in Broward County to get this filly around the track."

"Maybe we'd better use the pony," I said, thinking an equine escort might prompt her to be less contrary.

Rosario threw a hand up in frustration, glaring at Last Call, before stalking off to get his stable pony.

Fortunately, Rosario had planted us next to the outside rail where we were away from the horses galloping in the center and the speed demons working the inside rail.

I felt idiotic sitting on a horse statue as the rest of the world went by in a whirl of motion and color, with the sound of air pumping from their lungs. I got a few comments from other exercise riders like, "Enjoying the view?" and one smart-ass who galloped past and yelled, "This dirt is for horses, not potted plants."

By the time Rosario jogged up, mounted on his big palomino stable pony, my face felt a fine shade of red. I wanted to throw something, but instead forced a deep breath.

Rosario slipped a lead strap through the ring of Last Call's bit and hauled her off with the help of his pony who bumped her shoulder hard to get her moving. Rosario and the palomino got Last Call around the track, at least putting a slow gallop into her. I went along for the ride, like a kid on a bike with training wheels.

As we headed back to the barn, Rosario glanced at me, his lips pressed tight. "We're gonna have to do better than this, or she's outta here."

"Maybe she isn't happy. Which might have something to do with why she's too thin."

"You think I don't know that?" Rosario's voice knifed at me with sarcasm.

Maybe better to remain silent. I remembered how Dad had always said, "A happy horse is a winning horse." It seemed to me he'd had a horse with a similar temperament.

"We'll think of something," I said, patting Last Call's neck.

After the morning's work, I went to find the TRPB rental on Second Street in Hallandale Beach. Just a couple of blocks from the track, I found a pink stucco house with an orange-tiled roof and three South Florida palms out front. The bureau used the property for overnight visits from traveling agents, so except for me, it would mostly be empty.

I'd been allotted a small room with a double bed and a bath down the hall I'd have to share with anyone else who showed up. With Patrick's house thirty minutes away, the rental provided a place to clean up and change near the track. But since they'd asked me to, I planned to stay with Patrick and Jilly. Nonetheless, today I had a special use for the rental.

I washed off the morning's sweat and shampooed my hair in the bath's tiny shower stall, careful not to bump my elbows against the Pepto-Bismol pink tiles inside its narrow confines.

Back in my room, I opened the black duffel bag I'd left on the edge of the bed, pulled out an expensive, red shoulder-length wig, a pair of tortoiseshell reading glasses, a short black dress, and some strappy, high-heeled sandals. My arsenal of makeup included a paint-on lipstick that lasted for at least twenty-four hours, providing a way to enlarge my lip outline, making it bigger and fuller. Green contact lenses were an excellent addition to the kit.

I set my bag of makeup next to the clothes and glanced at the clock. Post time wasn't until one, and getting up at four thirty after a ten-hour drive had left me ragged. I lay down next to my disguises and closed my eyes.

I thought about my Florida undercover work. One of the hardest things was remembering who your false persona knew and didn't know, especially when doing double undercover work.

Kate O'Brien would need to be focused when she walked into Christine Lee's.

# 15

Wearing the red wig, dark eye makeup, the short dress, and heels, I walked into the bar at Christine Lee's, ignoring the heads that turned in my direction. After perching on a bar stool and allowing my hem to slide up my thigh, I leaned on the granite bar top, let my grandmother's big diamond rings sparkle, and smiled at the bartender.

He was about my age, bald, with a soul patch and a diamond stud in his ear. His gaze dropped to my rings, and I could almost hear him estimating the size of his tip. Behind him, a wall of mirrors reflected bottles of whiskey, vodka, fine wines, and the gleaming glasses that lined the bar's display shelves.

"What can I get you?"

I ordered a club soda and cranberry juice, then glanced at the diamond on my middle finger. My paternal grandmother had never liked my mom. She'd left me all her jewelry when she died, including the huge gentleman's diamond pinky ring that my great-grandfather had won in a poker game in Cuba. Patrick and my mother had been furious when the ring came to me.

Smiling at the memory, I spread the *Daily Racing Form* open on the smooth counter and retrieved a pen from my patent leather purse. I glanced at the second race in the *Form* through the prescription-free tortoiseshell glasses perched on my nose. Two horses' names made me think of Jilly. I circled them. Toocool Forschool and one named Diploma.

Breathing in the scents of liquor, sliced lemon, and expensive perfume, I surveyed the rest of the room. Behind me, a betting counter fronted a wall with half a dozen overhead monitors simulcasting races from around the country. To my right, the dining room's tables and chairs spread to a glass wall overlooking the racetrack two stories below.

There were maybe fifty people in the room, but I didn't see the trainer Serpentino. Checking through the *Form*, I noticed he had a horse in the fifth, his only runner for the day. Maybe he'd come up for a drink afterward. Though not thrilled about the long wait, the surroundings beat the hell out of a parked surveillance car and a Thermos of lukewarm coffee.

Two men strolled into the room, and my blood kicked up. One of them was the Mexican banker and racehorse owner, Antonio Morales, the guy involved with Serpentino's syndicate, BetBig. He grabbed a chair at a table just behind me and sat down.

I studied his reflection in the mirror. Golden brown hair, a fine linen suit, and manicured hands. He might be Mexican, but his blood probably originated in Spain. He had the refined bones of a European beneath the skin of a handsome but dissipated face. I suspected he pursued his pleasures a bit too hard.

The image of the second man appeared in the mirror. He was so good-looking, I almost sucked my breath in. He caught me staring and smiled.

I bent over my *Form*, made mindless doodles with the pen, and inventoried what I'd seen. About six-foot-one, intense brown eyes with thick lashes, dark, perfectly arched brows, strong cheekbones, olive skin, and the kind of lips you dream about on a long, restless night.

The bartender set my drink down and I took a sip, wishing it could be vodka. I heard a waiter at the table behind me and looked up again. In the mirror's reflection, I watched Morales's companion walk toward me. I turned to stare and my stomach contracted. Beneath his black jacket, he had wide shoulders that tapered down to a narrow waist and hips. Up close, his full lips promised sensuality, but his nose was a bit too sharp. Thankfully, it was hawklike and stopped him from being absurdly handsome.

"Calixto Coyune," he said, extending his hand. "Forgive me, but my friend and I would be honored if you would join us, *se-ñorita*. Unless you are . . . waiting for someone?" His voice stroked like fingertips, his speech educated. Maybe Cuban.

"Kate O'Brien," I said, taking his hand as briefly as possible. Better to avoid physical contact with this one. "I'd love to."

I had no intention of passing up the opportunity to sit with Morales. He was one of the people I wanted to know more about. If I kept my eyes away from Calixto's, I would be fine. Men with his kind of sexuality should wear a warning label.

I slid from my stool and joined them, taking the chair next to Morales, setting the *Form* and my drink on the table. Morales's eyes slid up and down my body. He seemed to like what he saw. Push-up bras usually have that effect on men. The short skirt and muscle tone from galloping the horses did the rest.

After we exchanged names, Morales, whose features were open and friendly, grinned at Calixto. "Kudos for convincing this pretty one to join us."

His accent had a Latin flavor, but, of course, it would. He worked for the Miami branch of a Mexican bank. The blond streaks in his light brown hair made me suspect the hands of a beautician.

Calixto had a cagey smile that revealed a set of even, white teeth, but never reached his eyes. Definitely harder to read than Morales.

After the waiter brought the men their drinks, Morales raised his glass. "To beautiful women and to good luck."

I smiled, and the three of us clinked our glasses together. The smell of their scotch and bourbon drifted past me, along with expensive cologne, and that undefinable scent that emanates from a man in his prime.

"Do you have a horse running today?" Calixto asked me.

"Who, me? No, I just like to bet 'em."

"You should own one," Morales said, his gaze resting on the rings on my hand.

I grinned. "I wouldn't mind owning a racehorse," I said. "I mean, who wouldn't want one of those?" I gestured at a monitor where the horses were going to post for the second race. Their gleaming coats, polished hooves, plumed tails, and tossing heads painted a magical picture.

"Tell her about BetBig," Calixto said.

I grew quiet inside, and waited.

Morales gave Calixto what could have been a warning glance, before leaning back in his chair. "That's an opportunity we might discuss later."

"I love to bet the ponies." I gave them my eager-to-be-foolish smile. "Betting *big* sounds exciting."

"So, who do you like in this race?" Calixto asked.

Not the time for me to press about the syndicate, so I glanced at my *Form* where I'd circled Toocool Forschool. He had good speed figures, was running a shorter distance than usual, and wore first-time blinkers.

"I like the change of equipment on Toocool Forschool," I said.

Morales glanced at his copy of the *Form*. "He's in over his head. Pletcher has one in there that will win easy."

He referred to one of the leading trainers in the country whose horse, Larceny, was the favorite in this race.

"Bet you're wrong," I said.

Calixto grinned. "She has a point about first-time blinkers."

"My friends," Morales said, "it's time we went to the window."

I stood, drained my drink, and set it on the tray of a passing waiter. Morales and Calixto didn't need to know it was alcohol free. I took a last look at the *Form*, studied the horse named Diploma, and decided he wouldn't earn his today.

At the betting counter, I left an extra window between me and my new friends. They didn't need to hear my careful little bet. After confirming Toocool Forschool had drawn post position four, I leaned in close to my teller and pulled six bucks from my wallet.

"Two across the board on the four horse," I said, letting the teller know I wanted to place two dollars on three separate bets—a win, a place, and a show. It was a cheap, nonglamorous bet. No doubt my two new friends were putting big money into exactas, trifectas, pick sixes, and who knew what all.

But all they had to know about me is that I went to the window and bet. And that I drank vodka. After slipping my bet ticket into my purse, I went to the bar before Morales or Calixto could, and ordered myself a glass of tonic water with Rose's Lime Juice. Looked just like a vodka tonic.

I walked to the two men standing on the bar's plush carpet, their attention on the monitor. It was quiet in the room as Toocool Forschool broke on top, attained an early lead, and led up the backstretch by five.

I'd never understood how people could enjoy watching the action on a monitor, when just outside, the real thing was playing in the open air—the jockey's yelling, the horse's lungs audibly pumping massive quantities of air, with the fans on the rail screaming for their pick, their bones vibrating from the pounding, metal-shod hooves thundering past.

Toocool Forschool was still on the lead going into the turn, and I began to feel a low hum of a bettor's excitement.

"He'll fold before the wire," Morales said. "Larceny will get the win."

Morales could be right, but I was pleased about my hunch on the blinkers. With nowhere to see but straight ahead, a lot of horses run faster, like Palace Malice's Derby effort where, with first-time blinkers, he ran one of the fastest miles in Derby history. Except the Derby was a mile and a quarter, and the horse hadn't held to the wire. But the race we were watching was only six furlongs.

Toocool Forschool was driving hard for the wire, when Larceny rocketed up behind him, moving alongside and pushing his nose up to my horse's neck. Toocool Forschool dug in, but Larceny kept coming, and the two drew head and head. Larceny was gathered up, ready to take that last winning stride as Toocool Forschool's body stretched long and low, his stride extended fully. They hit the wire just like that, and my horse won by a whisker.

"Gotcha!" I grinned at Morales who scowled.

Calixto's mouth twitched in an almost smile, and I swaggered over to the betting window to collect my earnings. If I'd been a rooster, I would have crowed. Still, I stuffed the money into my wallet, hiding the meager number and denomination of bills.

When I returned, my buddies were already studying the next race. I sat, letting my skirt ride high, and took a swig of my new drink. From the table, a vase of fresh-cut purple flowers emitted a sweet and pungent scent.

"You were right," I said to Morales. "Larceny was the better horse. The wire just got there too fast." I placed a hand on his arm, letting it linger a moment too long. "So what do you do when you're not betting the races?"

By now, he was well into his whiskey. My attention caused him to preen a little. "Banking. Money is my game."

*Other people's money.* "You're an interesting man," I said.

Next to him, Calixto watched us, then looked away as if bored. He wore his sideburns narrow, trimmed to a length slightly shorter than his finely made ears that lay close to his head. Beneath his black jacket, his starched white cuffs were studded with gold cuff links engraved with double Cs that had nothing to do with Coco Chanel.

Time for a sip of cold tonic. I forced my attention back to Morales, letting my eyes widen, my lips part. "So who do you like in the third, Tony? May I call you Tony?"

This time it was his hand on my wrist that lingered too long. He slid his copy of the *Form* between us and leaned toward me so we could study it together. Only his mind wasn't on the third race.

"Tell me more about yourself, Kate. I'm sure I haven't seen you before. No way I would have missed *you*."

My turn to preen and play out a little line with a hook on the end. "This is my first visit to Gulfstream. I came down from Philly for the meet." I paused, letting him think I was hesitant about my next words. One thing I'd learned about working undercover was to go with the truth as often as possible. Keep the stories close enough to home so you can remember them.

I lowered my voice and forged ahead. "I finally got my inheritance from my grandmother." I waved my rings at him. "I thought she'd *never* die."

Morales seemed amused, but a look flashed through Calixto's eyes like he'd stepped on a snake.

"Oh, dear." I took a long sip of my drink. "That didn't sound right. What I meant is she was so *old* and had Alzheimer's. All that money slipping away to uninsured long-term care. Drove me nuts!"

"I understand," Morales said. "Foolish to waste good money on someone who doesn't even know what day it is. Life is meant to be *lived*."

"Exactly," I said.

We smiled at each other. Truth be told my grandmother was

as sharp as a tack the day she died, I'd called her faithfully every week, and we'd loved being together and talking about Dad. I'd never given her jewelry a thought, which is probably why she left it to me.

Calixto pointed to the monitor where Toocool Forschool and his beaming connections were crowding into the winner's circle. "If Antonio and I are lucky in the fifth, you can join us for the photo."

"Absolutely," Morales said.

I leaned forward excitedly. "You have a horse in the fifth? Wow. I'm impressed!"

I grabbed the track program and flipped to the fifth race. Antonio Morales wasn't listed, but BetBig Stables had a horse named Primal running in the race. And oh, looky there, Michael Serpentino was the trainer.

I rounded my eyes. "Tony, is this horse, Primal, yours? Are *you* BetBig stables?"

He answered my first question. "Yep. And Primal's got a great shot to win. You should bet him."

I stared at the program. "He's a long shot. What do we know that the oddsmaker doesn't?"

Morales grinned. "It's a horse race. Anything can happen, right?"

Calixto stared at me, his expression speculative.

Was my last question too spot-on?

"Wow," I said, and took a sip of my drink. "I'll place a bet on him. Are you going down to the paddock?"

"Antonio doesn't mingle with the *criados* unless he wins," Calixto said.

"*Criados*? You mean, like, lowlifes?"

"Exactly like that," Morales said.

"You are *my* kind of people." With a giggle, I upended my glass.

Our waiter came and placed a fresh round of drinks on the

table. My buddies must have hooked him while I was cashing my bet.

"I ordered Grey Goose for you," Morales said. "Was I right?"

"*Yes*. Thanks."

I took a sip from the fresh glass. Jesus, what had Morales ordered? Straight vodka?

"I'm going to powder my nose." Smiling at Morales, I took a large swig from my glass and walked to the ladies' room. Inside, I spit the liquid into the sink.

When I returned, lunch menus had arrived. The waiter brought rolls and I coated my stomach with bread and butter before taking a small sip of Morales's rocket fuel.

By the time we finished lunch, the horses were parading in the paddock for the fifth race. I resisted the urge to go down and see the animals up close where I could smell them, hear them snort, and feel the mist from the fountain spraying in the center of the paddock. Instead, I stayed in my seat and studied the runners' statistics on paper more closely.

Primal had run eleven times. Been in the money three times, almost winning a cheap claimer at Penn National. Michael Serpentino had claimed the horse out of that race for $5,000 two months earlier and this was Primal's first start for his new trainer. Serpentino had put him in today for a $25,000 tag, a huge step up in class from his last start for only a nickel.

Even though Serpentino's horse was running against other maidens, those horses had better speed figures and had shown a boatload more talent in their previous starts than Primal had. No wonder he was a forty-to-one long shot. Maybe Serpentino had injected Primal with some other kind of rocket fuel. Something more powerful than the stuff in my glass.

If I bet two dollars across the board and the horse won, my take would be more than a hundred dollars on a six-dollar bet. Like insider trading.

Morales headed for the restroom, and I rose from the table and walked closer to the monitor, looking for the groom wearing the apron marked number six, Primal's number. Until the numbered saddlecloths were placed on the horses' backs, only the groom's number indicated the identity of each animal.

I spotted Primal. He looked like a wet, hungry rat compared to the other animals striding around the paddock, all of them well-rounded and muscular. Anyone could see Primal was out of his league. I felt sorry for him. A solid dark bay with no white markings, he looked thin, nervous, and slightly bug-eyed. Still, Morales wanted me to bet his horse, and if somehow Primal came in, I'd better have a ticket to cash.

His odds had increased to sixty-to-one by the time I bought my usual cheap ticket and planted myself before the monitor to watch the race.

Morales came back from the restroom, and I knew he'd hit himself up with something. Probably cocaine, seeing the way he wiped one finger under his nose. His eyes held a wild intensity, and with quick, impulsive strides, he headed for the betting window. When he and Calixto finished laying their money down, they joined me before the monitor, their attention on the coming race. The odds had dropped to thirty-to-one. My guys had thrown down some serious money.

The broadcast's audio came on. The bell rang and the gates crashed open. The horses broke evenly, with a gray surging to the lead, followed by two chestnuts. Primal lay fourth on the rail, another gray close on his flank, the rest of the twelve horse field crowded behind. Morales's little rat scrambled to get his feet under him. He appeared confused, as if he wasn't sure where the cheese was.

As the field flew up the backstretch, Primal traveled with an alarming lack of consistency, his legs climbing in the air, losing precious ground. Suddenly, he pinned his ears, lowered his belly to the dirt, and took off like a rocket.

"Holy shit," I said.

"Oh, yeah!" Morales yelled.

I stole a glance at Calixto. Motionless, he watched the race through narrowed eyes.

Primal shoved his head between the hindquarters of the two chestnut horses and plunged through the hole, quickly leaving them in his dust. He drew even with the gray who dug in and tried, but was no match for the smaller bay. Primal scurried forward faster than a rat abandoning ship, opened up by five lengths, and hit the wire a clear winner.

"If I hadn't just seen that, I wouldn't believe it," I said.

"Believe it!" Morales yelled. He let loose a high, wild laugh. "Come on." He rushed through a door in the dining room's glass wall, and dashed down the outside stairs to the track apron and winner's circle below. He pumped his fist in the air, shouting and whooping the whole way.

Reaching the apron, Morales busted through a crowd of racing fans, pushing one man to the side. Calixto hurriedly apologized to the guy who snarled, "The son of a bitch should watch where he's going!"

I smiled pleasantly and followed in Calixto's wake, reaching the winner's circle, a half-moon of rubber pavers surrounded by a green hedge. With a start of recognition, I realized the tall, thin man standing at the entrance was Michael Serpentino, Primal's trainer; the real reason I'd come to the grandstand. His dark hair was shaved close to his skull, like in his picture, and he had a long, thin neck.

A man in a ball cap, his face red with anger, yelled at Serpentino.

"You expect me to believe that horse isn't juiced? You shot him up with something! I'll make sure they triple test him, you piece of shit. I hope they rule you off!"

Serpentino ran his tongue over his lips, then shrugged.

"I hope they do check him out. He'll test clean because I didn't give him anything."

*What a liar.*

Morales, who'd been shifting his weight from one foot to the other, rushed at the man with the ball cap, getting in his face. "We had the best horse, Parker. Get over it. Fucking crybaby."

Calixto seemed to grow even quieter. There was something focused about his silence that frightened me. I hoped there wasn't a fight. It would draw too much attention, might even blow my cover.

Parker made a disgusted sound, spun on his heel, and strode away. Over his shoulder, he shouted, "This isn't over. Not even close."

Morales laughed, pranced into the winner's circle, and did a little dance. He glanced up. "Hey, here comes our horse! Everybody, get in here."

A groom was leading Primal into the enclosure. Calixto and I hurried inside, and stood next to Morales.

"This is so cool," I said to him. "I want a piece of this pie. I want *in,* Tony."

"Antonio, I believe she's a player," Calixto said.

"Sure, doll. Whatever you want."

I faked a happy smile at Morales, when I really wanted to scream at these men to do something for the poor horse.

Primal was heaving from his effort, stumbling as the groom led him toward us. He stopped and the groom jerked hard on the horse's lead. Serpentino shoved at Primal's hind quarters with both hands, pushing him forward, positioning him for the picture.

When they got him settled, Primal's head hung almost to the ground, and the jockey managed a weak, nervous smile for the win shot.

The photographer called, "Okay, everybody ready?"

I smiled, the flash popped, and Primal groaned. His bony frame shuddered.

"Shit!" The jockey flung himself from the horse.

The animal's knees buckled and he collapsed onto the pavers. By the time I knelt beside him, Primal was dead.

# 16

When I returned to Patrick's house, I disappeared into my room, booted up my laptop, and sent an encrypted message to Gunny, telling him about Primal and the events leading to the horse's death.

"I am particularly interested," I typed, "in receiving the necropsy results. Will request a copy from Brian." I signed off before sending my query to the TRPB tech, wondering what drug, if any, the postmortem tests would find in the horse.

After hooking into the TRPB site, I looked up Calixto Coyune. I'd been right about his accent. He was Cuban American, his father having fled Cuba in 1958, where he'd left a wife and two children behind. The father divorced the woman within a year. Apparently he'd come to Miami with a lot of money and connections because he snagged a top American fashion model. The resulting marriage had produced Calixto. No surprise the son was good-looking and well dressed.

*Did he ever wonder about his two half siblings in Cuba?*

Interesting that both Calixto and Serpentino were Cuban American. Calixto was on the board of the lucrative coffee company his father had started in 1960 in Miami. The father was well into his eighties, and I assumed Calixto would be the heir. What a spoiled brat.

The Florida Division of Pari-Mutuel Wagering listed Calixto as a current owner of three racehorses. He had an address on swanky Fisher Island. No further information was available, which raised a red flag. What was the man hiding?

A glance at the clock suggested it was time to stuff these men in a mental file and go to bed. But sleep eluded me that night. I couldn't stop the images of Primal running his heart out, his legs buckling, and finally the trailer with the winch they'd used to drag his body from the winner's circle.

Angered and disturbed by the images, I threw back the turquoise comforter and left the bed to stare out the plate-glass window. The ambient light lit the surface of the pool, and I could see the outline of Patrick's barn in the distance. The only sound was the chirping of crickets.

So far, I'd accomplished nothing. Cody and Primal were dead at the hands of greedy humans, and I'd been unable to save them. My new job was to protect the integrity of horse racing, which was fine. But I wanted to protect the animals. I admired Zanin for what he did and the directness of his approach.

I paced across the room and back to the window where the dark shapes of palms and tropical shrubs shifted and swayed in the night breeze. What kind of man was Serpentino? He looked like a snake with his long, thin neck and the way he darted his tongue over his dry lips. If he had administered a drug that forced Primal to run beyond his ability and die at our feet, Serpentino was worse than a poisonous snake.

Recently, the trainer had been out of town, and though he had stalls on the back side of Rosario's barn, I hadn't seen him before the race, only his assistant trainer. Maybe Serpentino had been out shopping for drugs and more horses he could run to death.

"Damn it." I would nail that son of a bitch for what he'd done. And Antonio Morales. What a piece of work he was. And what was the deal with Calixto?

Sometime later, I fell asleep and drifted into uneasy dreams where I followed Serpentino through pines and thorny scrub brush. He led me past stagnant, swampy water, taking me down Flamingo Road. I couldn't stop the journey. Something dark and terrible lay ahead. Something nameless. I jerked out of the nightmare and sat up. Short of breath, my muscles in knots, I was relieved to be awake in the safety of my room.

In the morning, I shook my mind clear of dead horses and bad dreams, warming my cold hands around a steaming mug of hot coffee. I checked my laptop for messages, but it was so early, Gunny hadn't replied to my e-mail of the previous evening.

I arrived at Gulfstream before sunrise and rode Luceta out in the first light of dawn. The temperature had dipped into the low fifties, but the early sun had so much strength, it wasn't long before it warmed my back right through my protective vest and nylon jacket.

When I finished with Luceta, Rosario's other exercise rider, a woman named Meg Goffman, rode out with me on the colt Money Honey. When Meg and I rode our horses past the barn closest to the track, they stopped short to stare at a brown and white companion goat tied outside a stall.

"You'd think they never saw a goat before," Meg said.

"Especially that goat," I said, "since it was there yesterday and the day before."

Meg booted Money Honey forward and we left the goat behind, riding the horses past the last barn and onto the trail leading to the track. The horses hooves churned the sand beneath us and the rising warmth brought its earthy scent to my nostrils.

For a moment, I wondered about the person who'd named Last Call for Love and what events in their life had made them choose that name. But it was time to focus on the present. We still had two more sets to gallop that morning.

The horses stepped onto the track, heads up, bodies quick and bouncy beneath us. We eased them into a trot, then a gallop. At the mile pole, we racheted up the pace to a two-minute lick and sped away down the track.

When I'd opened Last Call's stall gate she came out in her usual explosive style, then refused to go to the track until dragged along by Meg and the palomino pony. Though we got her around the big oval, the use of the pony sadly restricted both the pace and fluidity of Last Call's movements.

Now I watched her gaze longingly over her stall gate, testing the barrier's strength by pressing her muscular chest against the metal wire. To be honest, the tight, honed muscles under her coat surprised me, considering her limited exercise. Who knew how good she'd be with normal training? But to accomplish this, she needed to be more agreeable and willing.

Dad had convinced me that some horses demanded special treatment and damn well knew when they received it. Thinking about this, I watched Last Call's behavior in her stall. She still pushed against her gate, pinning her ears and snaking her head back and forth. Clearly, she hated being locked up.

I walked to the small block building opposite our shedrow that management had provided us for storage. I'd seen an extra stall gate leaning against the wall in there. After flipping on the light and digging through supplies, I found the gate and wrestled it free from a stack of buckets and tack boxes filled with stable bandages, brushes, combs, hoof picks, and polish. I carried the gate to the filly's stall, set it down, and walked back to where our groom, Julio, sat in a lawn chair by the storage building.

Finished with his morning duties, he was relaxing with his first beer of the day. Dark stubble already peppered his jaw. One cheek wore a smear of dirt and dried poultice streaked the front of his pant's legs with white. I felt guilty asking him to go back to work and pulled some dollar bills from my pocket.

"Julio, I have to make some adjustments to Last Call's stall. Would you take her for a few loops around the shedrow?" I pushed the money toward him.

"*Sí.*" He waved the bills away. "*Pero, no es necesario.*" He drained his beer, tossed the can into a trash barrel, and stood. He found a lead shank and led Last Call from her stall. After she finished her customary exploding exit, Julio walked her away down the shedrow, with her hooves leaving tracks in the sand he'd watered and raked to the smoothness of glass. Overhead, the miniature roses swayed gently in their planters.

I stuffed the ones into the pocket of his jacket that hung on a nearby hook, knowing he would have to rerake the sand to avoid Rosario's wrath.

As I watched Last Call amble around the corner, it was obvious that without tack, and knowing she wasn't going to the track, she enjoyed a promenade along the shedrow. She probably liked one-upping her neighbors still locked in their stalls.

I zipped into the storage shed and grabbed two large screw eyes and a long screwdriver before darting back to Last Call's stall. As I worked the sharp end of the screw into an old hole in the door's frame, a faint whiff of raw wood reached me.

Sliding the shaft of the screwdriver through the loop of the screw eye, I twisted the shaft and wound the screw tightly into the wood. After fastening the second one, I picked up the gate and slid its two pins into the screw eye loops. Now a gate hung from each side of the door frame. I swung the two gates together, as if closing them, and when they met, they formed a V out into the shedrow.

When Julio appeared around the corner with Last Call, I said, "Put her in."

He did a double take. "What you doing?"

"I'm giving her a room with a view."

Julio shook his head. "Rosario, he won't like."

"Let me worry about Rosario."

Looking doubtful, and muttering something in Spanish, Julio led Last Call into her stall, then retreated. I snapped the gates together with metal snaps and held my breath, scared to death she'd bust the V open and run loose on the grounds.

She marched into the V and stopped. She looked right. She looked left. She snatched some hay from her hay net and stood looking out her "window," munching contentedly.

I forked a bunch of straw into the V to give her front feet more cushion to stand on, then sat on a hay bale that lay against the wall outside her stall. I sat there until the loudspeaker called for the first race. I wanted to see how she'd react when another horse walked by on its way to the races. If she bared her teeth and lunged, I'd have to undo my handiwork before complaints were lodged with management. Heck, grooms might lodge complaints anyway, as their horses were likely to spook at a horse standing partway out of its stall.

The door to Rosario's office in the block building opened and the trainer stepped out. "What's this supposed to be?"

I hadn't realized he was still at the track.

"Who put those gates together?" He did not sound pleased.

"I did. It's part of my make-her-happy plan."

"You had no right to—"

Rosario stared as one of Serpentino's grooms led a horse toward Last Call's stall. The horse was bridled, wearing racing bandages on its legs, and was wound up like a top with pre-race nerves. The groom led his horse past Last Call, and our filly stood like a statue, a regal queen regarding her subject.

"I don't know about this," Rosario said.

"But *look* at her." The filly was nodding her head up and down, her expression more content than I'd ever seen. "She *loves* it."

"Huh," Rosario said. "I hope she's worth the trouble. I was going to send her out of here in two days." He paused and stared at the filly. "Put a couple more snaps on those gates. I don't want her getting loose."

"Absolutely," I said. "Rosario? I have another idea."

"God help us. What?"

"I've been thinking about the round pen Serpentino has on the other side of the barn. If he'd let us use it, we could put the tack on her and let her explode in there every day. Might do her good."

"You learn that from your dad?" Rosario asked.

"Yeah. Everything I know about horses, I learned from him."

"He was a damn fine trainer. All right, Fia. See what Serpentino says."

*Perfect.* Now I had a reason to talk to Serpentino, spend time on his shedrow, maybe get to know his grooms, and find out what went on over there. Not to mention save Last Call from a very dim future.

"I'll talk to him," I said.

As Rosario walked away, the message chime sounded on my phone. A text message from Zanin: "We need to talk."

I called his number. It went directly to voice mail. I left him a message that I'd try to reach him later.

I waited until the next morning to talk to Serpentino, when I knew he'd be overseeing his operation on the other side of our barn. Most tracks have a half-hour break in the middle of morning training to allow maintenance time to water, grade, and smooth the track surface. Gulfstream was no exception, and as soon as I dismounted and handed my last pre-break horse over to Julio, I walked to the other side and introduced myself to Serpentino.

I could see in his eyes he did not recognize me as Kate O'Brien. But I hadn't expected him to. Searching his face, I saw no trace of kindness in his features.

I forced a smile. "You won the fifth yesterday. Congratulations!" Somehow, I managed enthusiasm while keeping a straight face.

He nodded. "What can I do for you?" His gaze swept away from me to one of his horses being hosed by a groom on the pavement outside. His expression made it clear he had better things to do than talk to some other trainer's exercise rider.

"We have a filly that could really benefit from using your round pen. Maybe twenty minutes a day? Is that something you might consider?"

He responded with a long, calculating look. "Why would I want to?"

"We can pay. If it's not too much."

Serpentino turned and gazed at the horse finishing its bath. The groom shut off the hose and began smoothing excess water from the horse with a plastic scraper. The young Latino glanced up at me and smiled. He didn't look more than sixteen or seventeen. He had nice brown eyes and a gold horse head ring in one ear. I smiled back, picking up a fresh liniment smell that he must have added to the horse's bathwater.

"*Hola,*" I said, nodding at him. I felt Serpentino's eyes on me and shifted my attention back.

"Fifteen bucks a pop," Serpentino said. "Cash."

Rosario probably wouldn't agree to this, but I'd take it out of my own pocket if necessary. Last Call had a lot of ability. I wanted to set it loose.

"It's a deal. Thank you, Mr. Serpentino," I said with respect I didn't feel.

He nodded curtly and glanced at a vet truck that was driving up to the barn. He walked toward it as the groom led the horse onto the shedrow to walk until his coat dried. When the vet truck stopped, Wendy Warner got out.

Except for that quick glimpse of her at Pimlico, I hadn't seen her for many years. She had aged over the years with lines on her face and pouches under her eyes I didn't remember. When she'd met my dad Wendy had been divorced after one failed marriage. About five feet, seven inches tall, she had light brown hair and slightly bucked teeth, which gave her full lips and a nice smile. She still had broad hips and capable hands. I waited until Serpentino finished his conversation with her before hurrying over.

"Wendy! Hi." She looked at me like she was trying to place me. "It's Fia," I said. "Fia McKee."

"Oh, wow!" She rushed forward and hugged me. "I haven't seen you in so long, not since—"

"I know. Those were bad times." I'd forgotten how large and pretty her eyes were. Still a pleasing shade of green.

"You must really miss your dad. God, we all miss Mason. But you look great," she said. "Love the blond hair."

I shrugged. "I needed a change." To switch the subject from my dad, I said. "So, have you moved to Florida for good?" Why was she working for the likes of Serpentino?

"Now that the Gulfstream meet runs for so long, I like to stay warm and work here during the winter. I'll transfer up to Pimlico in the spring. By then, most of the big trainers and good horses have headed north anyway."

"I guess business is good here?" I asked, nodding at Serpentino's shedrow.

"You know how it is. You take what you can get." She took in my riding clothes and lowered her voice. "You aren't exercising horses for Serpentino, are you?"

It sounded like she didn't think much of him, either, and I was glad to hear it. "No. Rosario Jones. On the other side."

"Oh, great. He's a good guy. But what happened? I heard you were a cop."

I shrugged. "Nah. It wasn't right for me. Now I'm doing what I really love." I glanced at my watch. "And I'd better get back to it before the break ends."

We said good-bye, and as I turned to leave, Serpentino stood in the doorway to his office, watching us. Flicking his tongue over his lips, he stared, his expression icy and without emotion. The guy made my skin crawl. I beat it for the good side of the barn.

# 17

When I arrived at Patrick's house later that afternoon, the sun was radiating heat onto the paved drive. The sprinkler system fought back, spraying the grounds with water while the fresh scent of jasmine drifted to me from the purple flowers bordering the front of the house. Jilly met me at the door, her eyes bright with excitement.

"Zanin just called," she said. "He's in the neighborhood and wants to talk. He asked if he could come by. I told him you're usually home by now and to come on over."

I'd never connected with Zanin after that text message I'd received, and though I wanted to talk to him, I was tired and dirty and had planned on a shower and a nap. The sound of tires rolling up the drive told me that wasn't going to happen. I glanced over my shoulder and saw his black Tahoe.

The car stopped, and he climbed out, wearing jeans, work boots, and a sleeveless black tee. He carried a nine-by-twelve envelope.

He looked good, and I wished I'd had time for that shower.

After we exchanged greetings, Zanin waved the envelope at me. "I brought some photos of Valera's place. I can't make a whole lot of sense out of them. Thought you might want to take a look."

"Sure," I said. "Let's go inside."

We went to Rebecca's Dreamsicle kitchen and sat at the orange-tiled table. Jilly offered to get us glasses of iced Cokes, and when Zanin's phone pinged, he studied the screen, apparently reading an incoming text.

As Jilly busied herself at the refrigerator, I wondered how often she talked to her mother. Should I call Rebecca and see what her plans were for Jilly now that she'd apparently left her husband and daughter for another man? Was that a role I wanted or would even be allowed?

Weird, the way history had repeated itself for my brother. I hoped that for Jilly's sake, Patrick could remain on the same good terms with Rebecca that he had managed to maintain with our mother. Personally, I felt like smacking Rebecca, who could get in line behind my mother, but then I didn't know Rebecca's side of the story.

Jilly set a glass of Coke in front of Zanin, and stared at the unopened envelope on the table, intense interest shining in her eyes. I was grateful Zanin had provided an outlet for her grief over Cody, and a way to channel the pain into positive action, but I wanted to make sure the action remained positive. She didn't need any more altercations with Santeria thugs.

Zanin set his phone down and picked up the envelope.

"I snuck out to Valera's the other night with a Canon that shoots pretty well in the dark. Fia, take a look at these," he said, spreading four photos on the table and sliding them toward me. Jilly hurried around the table and stared over my shoulder.

The photos showed what looked like a tree nursery, planted outside three sides of a long building. "What is this?" I asked. "Is he growing something like marijuana?"

"I don't know," Zanin said, "but he's taken over more empty

land and fenced it in with electric fence. He's up to about fifty acres on his place now. There used to be a shack with some squatters living in it where those trees are. God knows what happened to them."

I pointed at the photo with the clearest shot of the plants. "Can you identify the tree?"

"Not really."

"What would trees have to do with killing horses?" Jilly asked.

"Good question," I said. "Are there many horses or other animals on the property?"

Zanin pressed his lips together and glanced at Jilly. "There's a small herd of horses there now, but they have grass and water, so there's nothing illegal or inhumane going on."

"Until he *kills* them!"

The shrillness of Jilly's words startled me. I twisted in my chair to where she stood behind me. "Easy, Jilly. We'll stop them if we can. You wanna be a cop, you gotta learn to keep a cool head. Right?"

She rolled her eyes and shrugged. "Yeah, I guess."

"Guess nothing," Zanin said. "There's been times if I'd gone off half-cocked, I'd be dead. What animals do you think I could help then?"

If God had spoken, I didn't think Jilly would have paid more rapt attention than she did to Zanin's words. No eye roll. Instead she straightened her spine and said, "You're right."

I stared at one of the pictures where Zanin had zoomed in on the trees. I pointed at what looked like a spiderweb hanging along the outside of the plants. A tall chain-link fence appeared to support it. "Is that some sort of netting? Is he raising birds or insects on those trees?"

"Good. You see it, too," Zanin said. "We need more light for clarification, but going out at night is risky enough. Trespassing on his place in daylight . . ."

"You might disappear forever," I said. This was crazy. The local police wouldn't go to Valera's. We needed a Navy SEAL team for God's sake.

"Don't they make night cameras that show body heat and stuff?" Jilly asked.

"They do," Zanin said, "except I can't afford a good thermal imaging camera. But I could rent one for a night. It would help to know if there is any kind of heat inside that netting. And its shape."

"Suppose they're raising something cold-blooded like cobras for poison?" Jilly asked. "I read they give cobra venom to race-horses so they don't feel pain. Thermal imaging couldn't see them, right?"

No flies on Jilly.

"It depends," Zanin said. "If a snake was basking in the sun and the nighttime temperature dropped faster than the snake's body temperature, you could see them."

We were wasting time. "It doesn't matter anyway," I said. "The tracks test for cobra venom and frog juice. There's no point in cultivating those drugs."

"Frog juice?" Jilly's face took on a puzzled look. "What's that?"

If she wanted to be a cop, she might as well know how low humans were willing to sink to make a buck.

"There's a South American tree frog that secretes a substance called dermorphin. It can be as much as a hundred times stronger than morphine," I said. "Crooked trainers had a great run with it at Remington Park in Oklahoma until a lab in Colorado developed a test for it."

Jilly's eyes took on that zealot gleam I'd seen before. "That's disgusting! You're saying they, like, *milk* snakes and frogs? Give it to racehorses so they won't feel their injuries, and then they *run* them?"

"That about sums it up," I said. "Except frog juice is even 'better' because it gives a sense of exhilaration and euphoria."

"Man, I could use some of that," Zanin said.

"Don't joke. People use it."

They both looked at me like I was crazy. "People ingest *frog* juice?" Zanin asked. When I nodded, he said, "*Damn.* I hadn't heard that."

Jilly sat up straighter in her seat. "Please, Zanin, if you go into Valera's with that thermal thing, I want to go with you."

Zanin and I exchanged a glance. "Let's see how this plays out," he said. "If I need help, I'll let you know."

Jilly knew a refusal when she heard it, but instead of sulking, she looked at the pictures some more. "What do you think he uses the building for?"

"Well, Warrior Princess, that's what I intend to find out."

From the glow on Jilly's face, it appeared she liked Zanin's use of the nickname. He glanced at me. "Fia, keep the pictures. Maybe with your police connections you can get wind of something new on the drug scene."

"Except," Jilly said, "Fia's working at the track now, not for the cops."

Zanin stared at me. "You left the Baltimore PD?"

"Think of it as a leave of absence. But I still have connections and ways to find out things."

With raised brows, he gazed at me before drawing out the word, "Oh-kay." He shrugged. "I'll find a way to get into Valera's during daylight. Beyond learning what he's doing with this nursery, I need pictures of the horses on the property."

Jilly's face darkened with pain. "God, they could be somebody's horse—like *Cody*."

Then something else occurred to me. "Don't they have missing horse Web sites?"

"Yeah," he said. "Facebook pages, too."

"Couldn't you post pictures?"

"If I can get them," Zanin said, "I'll post on every site I can find. If someone could ID even one horse, we could get the police in there."

No flies on Zanin, either. I hoped his words hadn't fired Jilly's imagination too much.

"Cool," she said.

Zanin stood. "I should get going." He paused a beat. "Fia, walk me out?"

Jilly scowled when I said, "Sure," and stood up to follow him out of the kitchen. I remembered how exclusion by my elders infuriated me when I was a teen, but I welcomed an opportunity to talk to Zanin without feeling the need to tread carefully around young ears.

After we crossed the living room, Zanin stopped in the cool, tiled foyer by the front door.

"You're not in any trouble, are you?" he asked.

"What?"

"With your job?" When I just stared at him, he said, "It just seems weird you'd go from working for the Baltimore PD to the racetrack. It's none of my business, but I thought maybe there might be something I could do to help."

"I'm not in trouble. I used to work at the track," I said, and filled him in with half-truths, telling him about my life with my dad, the murder, and that I'd decided to take a break.

"Sometimes I feel like I only got into law enforcement as a way to go after the bad guys, maybe seek some sort of revenge. I'm reconsidering some things now, you know?"

"I do," he said. "I used to be in real estate."

"No *way*."

"Yep. I was after the big bucks. But I've always loved animals and did volunteer work for the SPCA when I could. When the economy burned up after 2008, the Florida real estate market crashed with it. I spent more and more time at the SPCA. One day they invited me along on a rescue mission."

He shook his head. "What an eye-opener. So many abused animals at this place out in the C-Nine. But it was this horse someone had left tied up to a tree that got to me. He was starving, almost dead. I was able to save him and the feeling that gave me is like nothing else I've ever experienced. So, yeah, I know all about reassessing."

When Zanin made time-to-go noises, I said I'd follow him outside. Though the sun's heat on the terrace had eased as the day grew late, I headed for the shade of a date palm away from the house.

"So what's on your mind?" he asked.

"I didn't want to say this in front of Jilly, but someone juiced a horse up pretty bad at Gulfstream in the fifth race yesterday. He won. Then he collapsed and died in the winner's circle."

"Oh, God."

I wanted to talk about it more, but caught myself. I shouldn't appear to be overly knowledgeable about drug problems at the track. This conversation should be saved for Gunny.

"It was awful," I said. "I'm having trouble getting it out of my mind. But there's something else I wanted to mention."

"What's that?" he asked.

"Jilly. I remember how I was at her age, and I see the hero worship in her eyes when she looks at you."

He stiffened. "I would never hurt her!"

"I know, I know. It's just that she's too much like me. The way she lit up when you talked about getting into Valera's and taking pictures of his herd. I'm afraid she might try something like that on her own."

His eyes widened. "She wouldn't, would she?" He thought for about a half second. "Yeah, I can see her doing that. No way I want that to happen."

"Exactly," I said. "She's lost her horse, school will be letting out for the holidays, and—"

"She needs to be kept busy."

I nodded. "I'm going to see if I can get her work as a groom during the school break, or find her a new horse, or *something*."

"You really care about her, don't you?" he asked.

"Yeah, I guess I do. Which is funny because before I came to Florida I never even *thought* about her."

He grinned. "Well, she's branded you now."

"Yeah," I said, suddenly swept with raw emotion. "I'd do *anything* for her."

Zanin hesitated like he wanted to say something more, then straightened and took a step back. "Okay, Fia. You stay safe. Let's keep in touch about this stuff."

He climbed into his Tahoe and drove away. His brake lights flashed red before the curve in the drive, and his SUV disappeared into the landscaped jungle.

I hurried inside, anxious to call Gunny and figure out what I could do to bring down that bastard Serpentino.

# 18

In the sanctuary of my room, the lure of a hot shower quickly beat out my resolve to sleuth. I succumbed to the delicious pleasures of lavender soapsuds and steaming water jets that drummed on my back and eased tense muscles. After changing into clean clothes, I booted up my laptop, where I found a message from Gunny saying, "Call me."

Beneath it was an e-mail from Brian, sent about the time I'd been talking to Serpentino and Wendy Warner.

Fia, preliminary necropsy results due in tomorrow.
Sounds like you were in the right place at the right time.
Stay safe, Brian.

I'd known it was too soon for toxicology results on Primal, but still, I felt frustrated. Grabbing my cell from the desk, I called Gunny, who answered on the first ring.

"Fia," he said, "that was an interesting report you sent last night. I appreciate your thoroughness, but I want you to back off

Morales. Serpentino is your target. Even with him, keep a *distance*." He paused a beat. "You should never have been in the winner's circle with those people." His tone sharpened with impatience. "Now they have your *picture,* for Christ's sake."

Struggling to keep the frustration and hurt from my voice, I said, "Sir, I went in undercover as Kate O'Brien. I've used her before. She's solid. I spoke to Serpentino earlier today, and he did *not* recognize me." Damn it, I wasn't a novice. I took a quick breath. "Mr. Jamieson, I still believe the opportunity was too good to pass up."

"Your instructions were to watch *Serpentino*, not his connections."

"But—"

"Do you remember me telling you to watch him, listen, but not to *do* anything?"

"Yes, sir." I heard a rattling sound and pictured his hand reaching for his plastic bottle of Pepcid tablets. But how the hell was I supposed to get info on Serpentino without getting close to his associates? I rose from the desk chair and paced the room with the cell phone crushed to my ear.

"Fia, listen to me. Focus on information you can cull from the backstretch. And I repeat, listen and watch. Next time an *opportunity* presents itself, you check with me first. You haven't been here long enough to run your own show. Is that clear?"

I gritted my teeth. "Yes, sir." A voice could be heard in the background, as if someone had entered his office.

"Wait a minute." The connection blanked as he put me on hold. I sank onto the edge of the bed, rubbing my forehead. I sighed softly and repeated my mantra, the jockey instructions I'd so often heard Dad give before a race, "Sit chilly and wait for an opening." I was in no position to argue with Gunny.

I stared out the window. The palm fronds swayed gently poolside as the daylight faded toward evening. I exhaled slowly.

Gunny came back on the line. "Fia?"

"I'm here."

"You're clear on procedure?"

I could hear him tapping a pen on his desk. Could almost see it. He was also chewing on something; probably his antacid tablets. "Yes, Mr. Jamieson. There is something else I'd like to mention."

"Go ahead."

I recounted my conversation with Serpentino from earlier in the day, that I had the use of his round pen, and would try and worm my way into his shedrow through his stable help. The groom that had smiled at me seemed a good place to start.

"That's more like it," Gunny said. "Okay, then. You keep on course like that and get back to me with anything new."

"Yes, sir," I said and ended the call. Was this the same guy that liked the fact I shot a perpetrator? I wasn't crazy about this side of Gunny—patriarchal and filled with admonishments, seeking to control. Maybe there was more of that conservative FBI influence in TRPB policy than I'd hoped. Standing, I tossed the phone on the bed and left the room.

A half hour later, Patrick, Jilly, and I sat on the pool terrace. Blooming flowers and chlorine perfumed the air while we ate the pizza we'd ordered for dinner. I was inhaling bites of hot cheese and tomato loaded with mushrooms and green peppers. I finished one slice and grabbed another. When I realized I wanted more, I trudged to the kitchen and snatched an apple off the counter to satisfy my hunger. I might be galloping horses every morning, but there's only so much junk food a woman over thirty can handle without paying a hefty price.

Apple in hand, I ran into Patrick in the living room on my way back. I stopped. "Jilly seems to be doing well."

"She is. Hasn't skipped class since the day she snuck a ride with that Zanin guy." He started to brush past me, but stopped. "Having you here has really helped, Fia. So . . . thanks."

"You're welcome." This was as good a time as I'd probably get, so I rushed ahead. "Have you thought about getting her another horse?"

"I have."

"And?"

"What do you think I should do?" he asked.

I did a mental double take. My God, were we having a family moment?

"I think you should," I said. "Get her back up on the horse, so to speak. She took a horrific emotional fall when they killed Cody."

"Yeah, you're right," Patrick said, suddenly grinning. "Let's see what she says!" He rushed toward the pool with the enthusiasm of a kid. It was nice to see.

Jilly was finishing the last slice of pizza. She licked her fingers, wiped her hands on her napkin, and glanced up at us.

"Jilly, you ate the whole thing," Patrick said, his tone accusing.

"Well, *you* guys didn't want it."

Didn't take Patrick long to get off course. He could be so annoying.

"She can afford to eat the last slice," I said. "If she was any skinnier, she'd disappear."

He shrugged, and we sat at the table with Jilly. I munched on my apple and Jilly stared at the fingernails on one hand, then started picking at a hangnail.

"Don't do that," Patrick said.

"Wasn't there something you wanted to ask Jilly?" I asked, throwing Patrick a meaningful look.

Jilly tried to bite the hangnail off, and I almost added my own sharp reprimand.

"May I be excused?" she asked, already pushing away from the table.

"Sure," said Patrick. "But before you go, I was wondering if you wanted another horse?"

She stood up fast. "Are you *crazy?* Why would I want another horse? That guy will kill it, just like he did Cody." She jerked her palms up, whirled, and rushed into the house.

Patrick dropped his head in his hands, and I took another bite of my apple. We were silent a few beats, then I said, "I'm sorry that didn't go better."

"I don't know what to do with her. Christmas vacation's coming up and God knows what will happen if she's sitting at home every day."

"Doesn't she have friends she can hang with? Do you know their parents? Can't you arrange some stuff for her?"

"Her two best friends both have a horse and they go riding every day. I'm really busy at the office right now. I just . . ." The look he gave me was so pleading, I wasn't sure if I wanted to smack him or hug him.

"Listen. I'm pretty sure Rosario could use another hot walker and someone to help with stable chores at the track. I can probably get her a job, and she could come with me to the track every day during the break."

Patrick's eyes grew wide. "Really? Suppose she doesn't want to?"

"She already told me she'd love to go to the track. And believe me, by the time I'm through with her, she'll be too tired to get into trouble."

I'd never seen anyone look more relieved. Patrick's shoulders dropped, and he seemed to almost go limp. "That's great, Fia. This is really wonderful!"

Now what had I gotten myself into? Did this qualify as something I needed to check with Gunny about? I would have to call him to make sure.

"Jilly will be fine," I said, staring at the expensive pool Rebecca had demanded Patrick install and pay for. Damn that bitch, anyway. What kind of woman abandons her daughter to run off with another man? *One like your mother,* an inner voice taunted.

"I'll try and work it out, Patrick. I should know by tomorrow. Please, don't say *anything* to Jilly until we know."

"For God's sake, Fia. I wouldn't do that. You must think I'm really stupid!"

He was so touchy. "No, I don't think you're stupid." I stood up. "I've got some stuff I need to do on my computer," I said by way of excusing myself. Then, like Jilly, I fled for my room.

# 19

That night, I sank into sleep like a brick dropping into a murky pond. When I surfaced, a question clung to me, niggling and itchy. *What kind of drug grows on trees?*

Rolling over to glance at the clock, I saw it was almost four thirty, my wake-up time. I stretched, wondering what Valera was up to inside those fifty acres. If he was tinkering with drugs—which seemed right up his alley—what was the product? Who was the buyer?

I shoved the covers back, hearing my boss's words, "Your instructions were to watch *Serpentino*." I climbed out of bed, grabbed a carton of yogurt on my way out, and headed for Starbucks.

By the time I got to Gulfstream, I was wide-awake and relieved to see Last Call for Love hadn't busted loose overnight.

"You're staying right here," I said to her, and while Meg and I exercised Rosario's other horses, I left Last Call to contemplate her life from her room with a view. When Meg and I were done, I saddled and bridled the recalcitrant filly, hoping to get her into

Serpentino's pen. I was careful to run the stirrups up the leathers; slide the straps through the metal, and tuck the reins safely behind. Didn't want her stepping on them. She could rip her mouth or even flip over backward in reaction to the pain. I'd seen it happen.

With Julio's help, we got her into the round pen. I stepped back. Tense, she stood still, pinning her ears at me. Might be the first time she'd been turned loose wearing tack. She looked pretty flashy with her rose pink saddle towel and exercise bandages on. I clucked. She didn't budge. I leaned over, picked up some sand and tossed it at her hind legs.

She exploded straight up in the air, all four feet off the ground, the rose pink saddle pad heading for the sky. When she came down, she bucked and crow-hopped around the pen like a rodeo horse. I had a great respect for her hind legs and did my best to keep a distance. When she finally stopped, her nostrils were wide, her veins had popped out on her skin, and her tail waved like a banner behind her. I could smell her sweat. She snorted and took off again.

"Yee-haw! Go, Last Call!" I laughed with glee, loving that my plan had worked.

Rosario appeared at the corner of Serpentino's shedrow to observe the performance from a distance. After a moment, he nodded at me and called, "Good job, Fia." He turned and left.

Last Call stopped, and I shook my head. "I don't think so." I threw more sand at her fetlocks and she exploded again. "You gotta work a mile."

Serpentino's young groom eased up to the chain-link fence that encircled the pen. He watched the filly's antics, but kept glancing over his shoulder as if afraid he'd be caught loafing. Each time he twisted to look back, his gold horse head earring glittered in the late-morning sun.

"*Hola,*" I said. "*Como se llama?*" Asking his name.

"*Me llamo Angel.*"

I nodded. The name fit him. His brown eyes were lovely. And kind. With a rush of flying sand, Last Call tore past where I stood, and Angel laughed. "She very pretty!"

"Angel! What the fuck?" Serpentino stood on the aisle of his shedrow, glaring at the boy.

Angel cringed, and I could see the fear in his eyes. "It's my fault, Mr. Serpentino," I said quickly. "I *asked* him to come watch."

The man ignored me, continuing to stare at Angel. "Get over here. You got two more stalls!" Angel scurried toward him and disappeared down the trainer's shedrow. Then Serpentino's cold eyes shifted to me. "If you want to use this pen, don't fuck with my help."

"No, sir," I said.

"Where's my money?"

I put my hand in a pocket and pulled out a ten and a five, letting him see it.

"Leave it on my desk." He gestured at a room behind him that must have been his office.

"Yes, sir. I will." An older groom with a thick mustache pushed a wheelbarrow along the barn aisle. He smirked, apparently finding my predicament amusing.

Serpentino nodded, then glided away, his movements smooth, his tread soft and quiet. He was probably on his way to hiss at Angel. I'd bet my paycheck the kid was an illegal alien. No better than a slave.

I turned back to Last Call, who'd been watching the human exchange. I got her going again and when we were finished, she was lathered and blowing. Her rose pink saddle towel had darkened to maroon from her sweat. *Perfect.* I used my cell to call Julio, who came over and led her to the other side, where he'd give her a bath and cool her out. I took the money from my pocket and walked to Serpentino's office.

After placing the bills on his desk, I scanned the room. It

seemed ordinary enough, the desk littered with the usual condition books from various racing offices, overnight sheets, and tubes of the expensive anti-inflammatory gel, Surpass. A training chart, marked up with different colored pens was pinned to a corkboard, and a metal supply cabinet stood against a nearby wall.

I took two quick steps to the door, looked outside, saw no one, and reached for the cabinet's handle. Locked. I noticed a feed bill on the desk and, after another glance out, I lifted the paper to see what else I might find.

Wendy Warner's vet bill lay beneath, dated the day Primal ran. A quick search of the pre-race drugs administered to Primal revealed nothing unusual. But I doubted Wendy would be involved in something like that, and if she was, she'd hardly list an illegal drug on her bill.

My best bet lay with a groom like Angel. The boy might have assisted Serpentino if the trainer had administered a drug. Clearly, I needed to gain the boy's trust. If not his, then another of Serpentino's employees. Though I'd prefer to steer clear of the smirking man who'd pushed the wheelbarrow, who knew? He might hate his boss enough to leak useful information.

My gaze flicked back to the cabinet, but remembering how quietly Serpentino could move, my pulse quickened with fear. Better to leave before he caught me snooping around his office. Though curious about the cabinet, I had no probable cause, nor evidence to convince a judge to issue a search warrant. It was too early in the game. I slipped from Serpentino's office with my nerves wound tight, and returned to my side of the barn.

When I rounded the corner, Last Call was standing quietly in her V gazing out over her domain. Her coat was smooth and glossy, telling me that Julio had done his usual good job. The groom was kneeling at Last Call's front legs rubbing them with liniment. Rosario held her halter, keeping her still.

"How is she?" I asked.

"Best work she's had in my barn. You really pumped her up."

He nodded happily. "And her legs are as cold and tight as my ex-wife's."

I grinned. I hadn't known Rosario had been married. In fact, I didn't know a whole lot about him. But no doubt Gunny did.

"Good," I said. "A couple of days of that and maybe she'll be loose enough to train. I'm going to the kitchen. Anyone need anything?"

Rosario shook his head, but Julio glanced up. "Beef burrito and a Coke?" he asked, thrusting some crumpled bills at me.

Waving the money away, I said, "I got it," and headed up the path leading to the groom's quarters and the "kitchen" or track restaurant.

Gulfstream boasted about the most attractive quarters I'd ever seen for grooms and hot walkers. Ahead of me, a rectangular, white concrete building rose high above the fluffy palm trees that surrounded it. Balconies and walkways for the backstretch help surrounded the structure and an emerald green roof crowned the top. At the base of the building, I opened a glass door and stepped into the noisy track kitchen. Steam rose from cookers behind the counter and the Latinos who ran the café were busy stirring pots of beans, rice, and taco sauce. Mingling with the zesty tomato scent, I caught whiffs of fries, bacon, and coffee. I almost drooled.

The track security offices were safely tucked behind a wall in this room just in case the backstretch help broke into food fights in the kitchen. Apparently, the security guys took the threat of crime seriously, since their offices were protected by a locked steel door with a thick, bulletproof window.

I ordered a burrito for Julio and a grilled ham and egg for myself. I grabbed two Cokes, mine Diet, from the cooler, collected the paper bag holding my two orders, and peeked inside. My ham and egg sandwich was on top. They'd even added a grilled tomato. It smelled so good, I almost chewed on the bag but decided to wait until I got back to the barn.

When I stepped outside the kitchen, a huge eighteen-wheeler

was easing up to the stable gate where the duty guards inspected incoming and outgoing vans and trailers. This was the only entrance to the backstretch and the guards regularly checked papers and vet certificates, making sure they were in order and matched the animals on board.

With air brakes hissing and a hot scent of diesel fuel, the big rig ground to a stop. A uniformed guard left his air-conditioned cubicle to speak with the driver. Both the rig's cab and trailer were painted with the Coastal Horse Transport logo, a common carrier used to ship horses up and down the Atlantic seaboard.

I glanced at the paper bag in my hands. The scent of hot food emanating from inside was relentless and temptation prevailed. I pulled my sandwich out and took a large bite. *Delicious!*

Through the open windows of the van, I could see horse heads and a couple of grooms as I took another bite from my sandwich. The raised ramp in the middle of the van gave the grooms a ledge to rest their elbows on and look out at their surroundings.

I stared, then scuttled backward, almost choking on my sandwich as I ducked behind a palm tree. The guard waved the rig in, and the driver shifted the big engine into first gear. With a grinding of gears and a rumble, the cab lurched forward and the trailer moved slowly past, carrying maybe ten horses, a male groom in a ball cap—and the woman I'd killed a man for. I stared from the shadows of my palm tree as Shyra Darnell rolled back into my life.

# 20

Ducking from Shyra's line of sight was pure instinct. When in doubt, hide and regroup. This is a corollary to "sit chilly and wait for an opening." After the van passed, I left the cover of the palm tree and followed.

Rigs like the one rumbling ahead of me tend to move slowly through a track backstretch and usually avoid making deliveries during training hours. You had to think of it from a horse's point of view. A huge, scary monster with horses in its belly. It could cause a racehorse to spook, get loose, and run wild through the grounds, at risk of severe injury or death. I'd known it to happen.

While Shyra's van followed protocol and crept along, I trudged behind, considering the life of transport grooms. They travel for hundreds of miles, often staying overnight in the delivery location before working a return trip the next day. But if Shyra was in the middle of a turnaround trip, she'd leave immediately.

It wasn't difficult to keep up with the rig as I worked on the second half of my sandwich. I planned to have a little chat with Shyra when the van stopped to deliver its load.

I swallowed my last bite of ham, wiped my fingers on the front of my black jeans, and pulled a bottle of Diet Coke from my vest pocket. My other pocket held Julio's soda and I felt guilty I was making him wait so long for his lunch.

The Coastal truck stopped five barns past Rosario's and the driver left the rackety diesel engine running. Why do they do this so often? I'm convinced it's a rule for a secret diesel lovers society of which I am not a member.

A moment later, grooms emerged from the barn. They held lead shanks and headed for the van. I slipped between a Dumpster and a red pickup parked close to the Coastal rig's cab. Standing behind the pickup's side-view mirror, I could watch while remaining partially hidden.

Shyra and the guy with the ball cap helped the grooms unload the horses. When they got the animals safely down the ramp and into the barn, Shyra walked to the cab and spoke to the driver.

I'd forgotten how wide her shoulders were. She had done her hair in cornrows again. Her almond-shaped eyes showed less wariness and more strength than I'd seen in Maryland. When she finished talking to the driver, he nodded, and she headed for a nearby block building that housed showers and toilets for backstretch help.

The driver climbed from his cab, and he and the ball cap guy raised the ramp, locking it into place. Shyra entered the restroom, and the door slammed shut behind her.

The two men climbed back into the cab, and the rig ground into gear, rolling forward and blocking my view of the restrooms. Were they leaving without Shyra? Surely she'd hop in at the last minute.

I left the shelter of the Dumpster and ran alongside the moving trailer until I could scoot past its departing bumper. I made a beeline for the block building, opened the door, and before even checking the shower and toilet stalls, I knew the place was empty. *Damn it.* Shyra had eluded me again.

I ran to Rosario's barn, and breathing hard, I thrust the luke-warm burrito and Coke at Julio. "Sorry. I'll be back in a minute." I took off for the stable gate, certain I would get there before the van. I did, and when it pulled up at the guardhouse, I ran to the cab, climbed to the ledge outside the driver's door, and stuck my head in his open window. The cab smelled like Cheez Doodles and peanuts. The driver's belly suggested he had a fondness for both.

Plastering on my best how-ya-doing smile, I said, "Hey, my friend Shyra told me she'd be on this van and I was supposed to meet her. Did I miss her?" I looked at him expectantly.

"Shyra? She came down with us from Baltimore, but she was scheduled to get off here."

"Darn," I said, grimacing, letting my frustration show. "I can't find her cell number. Do you have any way I can get in touch?"

"Sorry, I don't. You could call the office. They'll be able to help you. I think she might have a place here in Hallandale." He glanced at the guy in the ball cap and dark glasses. "She tell you anything?"

"Nah," he said. "She don't say much."

"Okay, thanks." I realized the gate guard had moved closer, impatiently shifting from foot to foot, doing a lot of exaggerated sighing. Hopping off the ledge, I gave him a nod, and headed for my barn. I found a number by Googling Coastal Transport on my phone, and called.

When I reached the woman who handled groom schedul-ing, she listened to my spiel. There was a brief pause, then, "I can't give out information about our employees."

Telling her my name was Fia McKee and that I worked for the TRPB wasn't a viable option.

"But she's my friend," I said, letting a little whine into my voice. "I *promised* her I'd meet her this afternoon."

"I guess you'll just have to wait for her to call you, won't you?"

The woman hung up, and I stared at the phone. I felt like biting it. Instead, I called Brian at the Fair Hill office. I'd sic him on her. He answered on the second ring, and I told him I needed info on Shyra Darnell. That she was wanted for questioning regarding a death in Baltimore, and that she'd just shown up at Gulfstream.

"I'm on it," he said. "I know someone at Coastal."

We disconnected, and I headed to my barn, where I checked with Rosario to see if he needed me to do anything before I left for the day.

"No. We're good, but look at your filly."

Last Call wasn't visible in her V, so I hurried to her stall and peered inside. She was stretched flat out, sound asleep on her bed of straw. I could feel my lips curl in a smile. Rosario joined me and we both watched the filly a moment.

"That's the first time," he said, "I've seen her lay down to rest."

"She didn't need to before. She wasn't doing anything."

My phone chimed, and easing away from Rosario, I answered.

"Fia, I got an address for you on Shyra Darnell. Coastal has her in a rental in Hollywood."

Hollywood was less than fifteen minutes from Hallandale. I made a mental note of the address. "How long has she worked for Coastal?"

"Only about three weeks," Brian said.

"That fits. Thanks, Brian." I ended the call and headed for my Mini. After phoning Shyra's address to OnStar, I took off, curious to see Florida's version of Hollywood.

My directions took me to Hollywood Boulevard, a wide street divided by a paved median strip studded with flowering trees and bushes. Butterflies and bees darted around their blossoms. Outside the street's storefronts, palms sprouted tall and green in the warm, humid air. The one- or two-story buildings were made of cinder block or concrete, their walls spread with smooth stucco in shades of pink, turquoise, or cream.

The aroma of garlic, fried fish, and the ever-present scent of ocean water rode the breeze. The strip featured billiard halls, pawnshops, pottery stores, restaurants, and boutiques filled with tacky beach clothes. A lot of the stuff looked more like hooker wear than street wear. *Welcome to Hollywood.*

Following directions, I swung off the boulevard onto a side street, cruising for about a mile as the view became progressively seedier. One-story rentals with names like the Roosevelt were cut into six or eight units, boasting two small windows, a narrow front door, and a rusty through-the-wall air-conditioning unit. Chain-link fences and sparse vegetation surrounded these concrete buildings.

OnStar's female voice announced, "Your destination is one hundred yards ahead on the right." As I drew closer, the location turned out to be an abandoned lot.

"You have arrived at your destination," the voice said with happy authority.

I stared at the empty lot and its broken pavement, strewn with trash and scraps of rusted metal. "Brilliant," I said.

"*Thank* you for using OnStar!"

I made a rude gesture at the speaker, then drove down the street a block before pulling a U-turn and parking against the curb. As a Baltimore cop I'd learned fake addresses were often familiar to the person who issued them. Sometimes the location is even close to home. I would wait a while, just in case.

An hour later, the sun's heat was roasting my Mini and my cold Diet Coke was a desperate memory. My longing for a toilet was about to win out over surveillance when Shyra strolled past the abandoned lot toting a small bag of groceries.

I didn't want her to recognize me and rabbit again, so I opened the Mini's console and grabbed my hat-with-hair, an excellent disguise I'd ordered. Brown bangs and a short bob were neatly attached to a ball cap, far more comfortable in the heat than a wig. I shoved the ensemble over my cropped hair and watched Shyra as she headed my way across the street.

When she hooked a right at the next corner, I grabbed a newspaper from the backseat, left the Mini, and jogged after her, slowing as soon as I had her in sight. Staying on the opposite side of the street, I watched her step up a broken walk to a squat, concrete building cut into little units. A sign indicated she'd arrived at the Ocean Arms. When she paused to fiddle with her keys, I stopped and pretended to study the paper like maybe I was looking for a rental.

Shyra's block featured a Laundromat across the street from her building. I stopped outside this pink concrete building, breaking into a sweat as the hot exhaust from dryers engulfed me. Inside, trade was brisk, with customers stuffing machines with dollar bills and dirty laundry or folding clean shirts, pants, and towels.

Shyra went into her residence and shut the door. I jogged around the block and down the alley that ran behind the building. There were no rear exits and the windows were tiny. Maybe I had her this time. I stuffed the paper and the hair hat into my tote, hurried back to her door, and rang her buzzer. She didn't answer, so I shoved my thumb against the buzzer and held it.

"Open up, Shyra, I know you're in there."

The door wrenched open. Shyra's eyes blazed with anger and her large hands held a baseball bat level with my head.

"Whoa, whoa," I said scrambling backward. "There's no reason for that."

"Why are you hounding me like this? You got no right!"

"I'm not a cop anymore. I got fired because I killed that man. I'm galloping horses in the morning at Gulfstream. I saw you, and . . ."

Her expression had become more wary than angry. Slowly, she lowered the bat to her side. "What do you *want*?"

"I lost my job because of that man. I told you. I never killed anyone before. It's eating at me. I want to know who he was, and why he was trying to kill you."

My plea was so genuine, it seemed to halfway convince her. She stepped back from the door.

"You best come in. You running up my AC bill."

Her setup was better than the Pimlico hovel. Two closed doors in the back probably led to a bedroom and bathroom. A couch, a small table with two chairs, and a fake wood cabinet filled the front area along with a tiny kitchenette in one corner.

She turned to set her baseball bat on the floor and lock her front door, and I stared at the same bronze figure of Christ I'd seen in her room at Pimlico. The savior was still mounted on a dagger, only this time Shyra had stuck the blade into a flower vase and added fresh white flowers on either side. The familiar porcelain figures of saints, draped with strings of beads, stood next to the vase.

The altar meant enough to her that she'd brought it with her. I stepped closer to the chest and zeroed in on the beads. Some were orange, like the one left in my apartment.

I shifted back to her. She stared at me with an expression that was cold and hard. I gestured at the icons. "Your figurines are pretty. Are they Catholic saints?"

"You didn't come here to ask me about my religion. It's none of your business, anyway."

"Shyra, cut me some slack here. Maybe I just want to know more about the person I killed a man for."

She crossed her arms over her chest. "Now you just tryin' to make me feel guilty."

"Have you ever heard the saying that if you save someone's life, you are responsible for them?"

"What if I have?"

Could *this* be the reason I'd been so anxious to find this woman? "In an odd way," I continued, "I do feel responsible for you." My words rang with surprising truth and Shyra seemed to hear it.

She dropped her arms, pulled out a chair at the little table and sat. She waved at the other chair, so I sat, too.

She stared at her porcelain saints and shrugged. "My family follows the Santeria religion. That's the kind of altar most of our people have in their homes."

I forced my mouth to close, my mind to chill. "I think I've heard something about that religion. Doesn't it come from Africa?"

"It does. But came by way of Cuba and Puerto Rico before Florida."

*Florida?* Was she from Florida? If I hadn't just put my cop face in place, I'd be scraping my jaw off the table.

She nodded. "Lots of us Santerias down here. It's a good faith. We practice herbal and spiritual healing. What you call a holistic approach."

I nodded, wondering if she'd hand me a Santeria brochure before I left.

"We believe in the connection between the heart, mind, and the body."

I didn't ask her about animal sacrifices. "That sounds pretty cool. So, are you from Florida?"

"Grew up over near Hialeah."

*The closest town to the C-9 Basin.* "Are you safe now, Shyra? I mean, that man is gone. Nobody else wants to harm you, do they?"

She stared at her strong hands that lay flat on the table, raised her eyes to mine, then dropped her gaze back to her hands. "No. I'm all right now. I was just real scared at the time and didn't want to talk to nobody."

"That was a scary night," I said. "But when I saw you at

Pimlico and offered my help, you said *nobody* could help you. That I didn't *know* him. So, who is 'him'?"

"Woman, you like a dog with a bone. I still know this bad man, but he ain't blaming me no more, so we don't need to talk about that."

I felt like I'd hit a wall and wanted a way to blast through it. "Does this bad man know the guy who tried to kill you?"

The fear I'd seen before momentarily shadowed her eyes. She shook her head. "I appreciate what you did for me, but it's better I don't talk about this anymore."

"Please, Shyra. At least tell me about the dead man. He can't hurt you now."

Her shoulders dropped and she sighed. "His name was Emilio. He was stealing from . . . someone, so I told on him, and he tried to kill me."

"Does Emilio have a last name?" If I had his full name, I could find out the rest.

She shook her head. "You don't need to know that. But I'm telling you, the man you killed was a very bad man. He did something terrible, so don't go feeling guilty about him."

Sounded like she knew a lot of bad men. I suddenly wanted to know that she had work and would be safe. "So are you working for Coastal now?"

She stood. "I don't know what I'm going to do. But we ain't friends, and I don't want to see you again. You understand?"

"Sure," I said and though I rose to leave, I had one last question for her.

She unlocked her door, pulled it open, and stood back to let me out. I stepped into the doorway, then turned back to her. "Shyra, someone broke into my apartment in Baltimore. They left an orange bead behind. Like those." I pointed at the ones on her dresser. "Was it you?"

Her eyes widened and she looked over my shoulder, not

meeting my gaze. "Are you crazy? I don't know what you're talking about!"

"I think you do."

"I *don't*. Now get out!" She shoved me with those big hands
and I stumbled through the doorway onto her stoop and caught
myself on the railing.

The door slammed, and I heard her lock click into place. She
was lying. What the hell had she wanted in my apartment?

# 21

When I returned to Patrick's after my Hollywood adventure, I checked Kate O'Brien's e-mail account and felt a nervous tingle to see a message from Antonio Morales.

In addition to this account, I had Kate O'Brien business cards displaying the e-mail address and listing her as a resident of Philadelphia. Three days earlier at Christine Lee's, Morales had asked how to reach me, and I had given him one of the cards.

I clicked his message open.

*Kate, enjoyed meeting you and am eager to invite you into the BetBig partnership! This is a terrific opportunity for you, and we would love to have you join our family. Be assured that what happened to Primal was a freak accident, something that has never happened to our stables before. I will be at Christine Lee's on December 22 for the whole racing card. Let me know if you can join me and we can discuss you becoming a valued partner of BetBig. Yours, Tony*

It was clear as daylight the guy was after my money. He seemed the type that would steal my diamonds and anything else he could get his hands on.

Thinking about his offer, I turned away from the computer, and looked through the open sliding door as the day slipped toward dusk. Patrick's Polaris robot motored about the pool, gurgling and bumping as it kept the blue water crystal clear. Too bad the Polaris company didn't make an electronic fly I could stick on a wall at Gulfstream. I'd love to spy on some of the thugs I'd been meeting.

Morales wanted to see me the next day, but before I met with him, I needed permission from Gunny. I called him and got his voice mail. Out of the office until December 26 and in case of an emergency, I should call his secretary, Gracie. *Holidays could be such a pain.*

Standing up, I paced the room. Meeting with Morales was a way to get closer to Serpentino. Couldn't I avoid cameras and stay just long enough to confirm my association with BetBig? I needed to find out more about the operation and its trainer, Serpentino. Of course, this could be done over the phone, but I wanted to see Morales's eyes when I asked my questions.

But remembering how angry Gunny had been the last time, I decided I'd better call Gracie. She picked up, and I relayed my thoughts about Morales. I also mentioned that I wanted to get Jilly a temporary job with Rosario during Christmas break.

"So," I said, "what do you think?"

It was cold up there in Maryland, and I could hear the heater by her desk kick on followed by the blowing of hot air.

"Let's take the last part first," she said. "I'm sure Gunny will have no problem with your niece working there for a few days, but meeting with this man Morales I'm not so sure about."

"Gunny wants me to track Serpentino, Gracie. What better way to learn about him than coming in as owner Kate O'Brien?

As Fia, I can watch him on the backstretch, and owner Kate can meet him in the clubhouse. Creates a nice two-pronged attack, don't you think?"

Gracie paused a few beats. "It sounds like something Gunny would go for." Another hesitation, then, "I'm not going to call him. The man really needs a few days off, and I don't think this qualifies as an emergency." Her voice sharpened. "But just the meeting at Christine Lee's, okay? Do not go anywhere with this man, or make more plans until you've had a chance to talk to Gunny. You understand this?"

"Absolutely. Thanks, Gracie."

"I mean it, Fia. Promise me you'll be very careful."

"I promise. Gracie, you're a peach."

"You won't think so if you piss me off!" But she sounded amused as she hung up.

Turning back to my keyboard, I sent an e-mail to Morales saying I was looking forward to seeing him the next day. I hoped that Brian could get me Primal's preliminary necropsy results from the TRPB before I met with Morales.

After looking through my closet for something Kate could wear, I grabbed a short leopard print skirt and a black top and added them to Kate's bag of disguises for the next day. Gathering my dirty clothes and Kate's dirty clothes, I carried them to the laundry alcove off the kitchen. A double life has its drawbacks.

In the morning, Rosario asked me to work Luceta five-eighths out of the gate. He'd arranged for the mare to go with three horses trained by a fellow in the barn next to ours. I was a little nervous and excited about busting out of the steel contraption. It had been five years, and things can go very wrong in there.

Rosario rode his pony out with me so he could watch Luceta when she broke. We walked on to the track the "right way," or counterclockwise, the direction that horses race in.

When we reached the wire, Rosario pulled up his palomino gelding.

"Jog her the wrong way to the gate. I'll meet you there."

I nodded, turned Luceta around, and eased her into a trot, taking her the long way around. Rosario walked his pony in the opposite direction, and by the time Luceta and I met up with him, my mare was warmed up and ready.

I stared at the giant metal machine as I circled Luceta outside. Glancing at Rosario, I said. "Is Luceta okay in the gate?"

"She'll be fine. Not so sure about that one."

I followed his gaze. A bug-eyed, chestnut filly pulled back against an assistant starter who was attempting to lead her into one of the gate's stalls. She reared and jerked the strap from the assistant's hand. She rose to the sky, and when her rider realized the filly was going over backwards, he bailed. He cleared, barely avoiding her withers as they crashed beside him, driving more than a thousand pounds of weight into the dirt.

My hands shook, and I stroked Luceta's neck, more to calm myself than her. She acted interested, not alarmed.

The fallen rider scrambled to his feet and leapt to one side as his filly rolled over, thrust her front legs out, then rocked to her feet. The starter grabbed her reins, walking her a few steps to check her action. He threw a questioning look at the rider, who said, "Give me a leg up. The bitch needs to learn."

Rosario and I exchanged a glance. The rider was using his anger to fuel his courage. He remounted, the starter led the filly into the gate, and it was my turn.

Luceta marched in like a pro and ignored the lunatic next door, who stood so stiff and tense, I was afraid she'd explode again. I wanted to get out of there before she did. A moment later, the crew led the last two horses into their slots.

I gathered the rubber-covered reins, crossing them over Luceta's neck. I held the cross with one hand, and grabbed a handful of her gray mane with the other.

The sudden clang of the bell rocked me as the metal gates crashed open. Luceta fired out like she'd been poked with a cattle prod.

My heart raced and my spirits soared. I kept a long hold on the reins and sat chilly. Not asking, seeing what she wanted to do. And she wanted to do plenty. She was not liking that the chestnut who'd flipped and had just streaked out of the gate like the devil was on her tail. Luceta ran head-to-head with her down the backstretch. I stole a glance back. We front-runners had opened a good two lengths on the others.

My internal clock said we hit the first quarter in twenty-one and change, probably faster than Rosario wanted. I sat like a block of ice, hoping to relax Luceta. The crazy chestnut filly's rider stood in his stirrups and leaned back, letting his weight pull on her mouth. She fought him until we'd run a half mile, then she grew tired and her stride shortened.

Luceta left the chestnut behind, but I could hear the remaining competition closing. Those two horses drew abreast as we headed into the last furlong. Their riders were whipping and driving, and though I never asked her, Luceta refused to be out-finished. We all hit the wire in a dead heat.

"Photo finish!" the rider next to me shouted as the three of us stood and began to ease our horses. "Hold all tickets."

I grinned at him, then left him behind as Luceta galloped out with big ground-eating strides. It took a while to pull her up, and when I finally eased her to a jog and reached Rosario, my boss was grinning like a little kid in a candy store. Could there be a better time to ask him if Jilly could have a job?

After the morning training hours, which garnered a bullet work for Luceta, a job for Jilly, and an excellent round pen rampage by Last Call for Love, I drove to the TRPB house. I hid my Mini in the garage, and once inside the rental's pink stucco walls, I enjoyed a shower and a nap. Then I gathered up Kate's wearable lies.

Studying my reflection in the bathroom mirror, I decided the fake ruby earrings looked deliciously tacky with Kate's red and black leopard skirt. After arming myself with the glasses, the wig, and my diamond rings, I left the house and hurried to the corner where the cab I'd called idled by the curb. I could have driven but didn't want anyone seeing Kate in a car with Maryland tags that were registered to Fia McKee.

My cabby had a heavy Russian accent and after glancing at me in the rearview mirror, he approached the grandstand's main entrance via a drive through the Village at Gulfstream Park. Kate must have struck him as a woman who'd like a whirlwind tour of Gulfstream's sparkling new shopping and dining conglomerate. I obliged by gazing with interest at the trendy storefronts we passed.

The cabby smiled in the rearview mirror. "Is nice, no?"

"I *love* it," I responded with the big smile. The place was pretty amazing. A gal like Kate could rent office space. She could shop in stores that competed with the offerings on Rodeo Drive, get a pedicure, a wax job, her hair done, or buy sexy lingerie. Afterwards, she could hit one of the many restaurants and bars, pick up a high roller, and finish off at the Westin Diplomat hotel, where, a sign informed, VIP casino members stayed for free!

The Russian dropped me off at the grandstand and before I went inside, my phone rang. It was Brian.

"Hey, what did you get? I asked.

"Not much. The preliminary results don't show any prohibited substances."

"I'm not surprised." But I was disappointed. "Is there anything at all?"

"Actually there is. The FBI seems to have an interest in this, because their lab helped us out. They found D-amino acid peptide in his blood. It's similar to the amino acid sequence of dermorphin."

I felt my stomach contract. *Frog juice.* "Damn, that's great work!"

"Don't get excited, Fia. It's not dermorphin, only similar to it, and no one has ever seen this stuff before. They have to obtain a sample of the drug for testing, and it could take months to find a conclusive way to test for it. And we have no way of knowing if this is the substance that caused a long shot like Primal to win and die."

"I'd bet my next paycheck it is."

"We'll keep working it at this end, Fia."

"And I'll work it from here." *Damned if I wouldn't.* "Thanks, Brian."

For a moment, I stood outside the grandstand, staring absently at the condos that rose skyward above the ocean only blocks away. As I thought about Primal's end, the salt breeze blew strands of red hair against my cheeks. I closed my eyes. Greed caused so much evil.

Someone had found or created a new drug. Someone who didn't care if horses, jockeys, and exercise riders were injured or died. And that bastard Serpentino was happy to use it.

I'd start with him.

# 22

When I entered the grandstand, my ears immediately filled with the stupefying sounds of ringing bells, electronic music, and the crashing noises associated with a video arcade. Bettors sat at machines lost to the time of day, unconcerned about peace or war, intent only on how many pineapples or stars lined up in a row on their screen. Welcome to casino living.

I hurried to the elevators and rode up to Christine Lee's where it was more civilized, at least on the surface.

Inside the plush lounge, Antonio Morales sat at the same table by the granite-topped bar. The glasses and bottles on the bar behind him still sparkled, and the bald bartender with the diamond earring acknowledged me with a friendly nod. Recessed lighting gleamed on Morales, highlighting the fine fabric of a moss-colored linen suit.

As I strolled toward him, he looked up, his face breaking into a smile. So fast as to be almost imperceptible, his eyes slid down my black top and my legs below the short skirt.

Standing, he said, "Kate, you look fabulous." He pulled out a chair, and signaled a waitress.

I sank into the soft leather, crossed my legs, and gave him the big watt smile. "Tony, I'm totally thrilled to become a part of your group. I've been studying the stable's stats, and they are so impressive! Is anyone else from BetBig joining us today? It would be fun to meet some other partners."

"Actually, John and Mary Smith will be joining us."

"Great," I said, beaming. John and Mary *Smith*? Maybe the Joneses would join us, too. Perhaps a silent partner or another incognito owner would materialize. Then again, maybe Smith was the couple's real name. Regardless, I'd be looking them up.

In a far corner of the room, a man was selling programs. "I'm going to get a *Form*," I said and headed for the newsstand, intercepting the waitress who approached our table. A brunette who was about my age.

Keeping my voice soft and rapid, I said, "Mr. Morales will probably order me a vodka tonic. Can you bring it virgin and keep the secret?" I gave her my comrades-in-crime smile, and she returned it with a nod and an amused gleam in her eyes.

I bought the *Form* and returned to the table where a moment later the waitress brought iced tonic for me and a scotch for Morales. I lifted my glass.

"Cheers, Tony. To a mutually beneficial partnership!"

"You *know* it," he said, tapping my glass with his.

I'd already read the entries for the day's racing and knew Bet-Big didn't have a horse running. Neither did Serpentino, but the opportunity to dig was what I wanted.

"So how much will it cost me to get in?"

He slid a tooled leather notebook across the table. "Here's the info."

I opened the embossed cover and found a number of sales photos. BetBig horses in the winner's circle with groups of grinning owners pumping their fists or giving a thumbs-up. Jockeys wearing black and silver silks beamed at the camera. Morning exercise pictures from different tracks showed sleek, hard–muscled Thoroughbreds flying past the camera wearing black and silver BetBig saddle towels, bandages, and bridles.

I flipped through and found the price tag. A 5 percent buy-in would cost between $7,000 and $20,000 depending on the horse. I thought about the $250,000 colt named Dixie Diamond that Morales had recently purchased for the syndicate. Just 5 percent of that horse would cost me $12,500.

I read the list of expenses for the trainer, veterinarians, black-smith, transportation, mortality insurance, and ongoing monthly business costs. Bottom line, I'd be paying about $30,000 a year plus the initial $12,500. Horse racing is a game for the rich, even with the load shared by many.

As if reading my thoughts, Morales said, "You gotta pay to play, Kate. But you've seen our stats. Our horses win! Think about it. If your horse wins a Breeders' Cup race, you earn fifty thousand in two minutes."

"Wow," I said before taking a generous swig of my tonic water.

He leaned forward, laying warm fingers on my hand. "People aren't in this game to get rich, Kate. You are buying into a lifestyle. It's about being an owner, sitting in that box on Derby Day, being in the winner's circle. Many of our owners have been interviewed on TV, and all of us have a lot of fun." He paused for a sip of scotch.

This guy should sell used cars. I withdrew my hand, took another gulp of tonic water, and wiped my hand on the napkin in my lap. Morales had been up to something the night before. His eyes looked tired, a little red, and puffy. And he could use a breath mint.

"It sounds like something I'd really enjoy," I said. "And the syndicate's stats are so good. I suspect BetBig owners *do* make a profit."

"Absolutely. Last year our stable had the highest win percentage of any."

A couple walked into the bar, and Morales's gaze swiveled to them. "But don't take it from me, talk to the Smiths who've just arrived. John! Mary!" He beamed as he rose from his chair.

Mary Smith had knowing eyes and masses of blond-streaked gray hair pulled into a chignon with a diamond clip. I suspected the masses were extensions. It was hard to tell her age. She'd had a lot of very good plastic surgery. John wore an expensive-looking suit that needed to be let out. His red nose and ample jowls suggested a love for drink and food.

After Morales introduced us, John chose the chair next to me and Mary sat on the other side of Morales, leaving him next to me. Without asking, Morales ordered Bombay Sapphire for Mary and Glenfiddich for John.

The waitress asked me if I wanted another, and when I nodded, she said, "The same?"

"Exactly," I said.

"So you're the new kid on the block." Mary's voice was tinged with condescension, her brows slightly raised.

"And we're delighted to have you," John rushed in. "Great outfit, BetBig. Yes indeed, a great outfit." He nodded as if to convince me. "We made so much money with that last horse. Won three in a row! Cashed a big bet on his first race." He shifted to Morales. "That's why you call it BetBig, right, Antonio? Get it? Big bet?" He hee-hawed, apparently finding his words amusing.

Mary's gaze rose to the ceiling. "We get it, John."

The waitress brought the new drinks. Mary reached for her gin and gulped down a quarter of her glass.

Oblivious, John continued enthusiastically. "And now we're getting a new one, aren't we, Antonio?" He grinned at Morales. His scotch had been served neat, and in one sip, half of it disappeared.

"The syndicate found a new horse," Morales said. "You

should get in on him while you can." He included me in his gaze. "This opportunity will sell out quickly. A well-bred, stunning colt named Dixie Diamond."

*Good old Dixie Diamond.* "I *love* his name." I leaned forward. "This is great, Tony! Are there others?" Before he could answer, I turned to John. "Tell me more about that horse that won three in a row. Is he—"

"He's retired," Mary said.

"What happened to him?"

"Does it matter?" she asked. "You want a new one. Have you ever owned a horse, Kate?"

"No. I've been a player at the window for years, but I've never owned." Now I was curious to find out what happened to that horse.

It was almost time for the first race, and the table grew quiet as everyone studied the race on paper. Though John's *Form* was already marked up with picks, his pudgy finger traced the past performances of several horses and he made a few more notes in the margin.

"I'm going to place my wagers," he said, and heaving himself up, he left for the betting counter. Morales trailed behind him.

When Mary finished studying her *Form* and looked up, I smiled at her.

"I don't know much about this business. I could use some advice."

She studied me. "What did you want to know?"

"I was wondering, if the horse John talked about was running so well, why did you guys retire him?"

"He'd earned all the money he was going to earn." She was still keeping information annoyingly close to the vest.

"So," I said, "was he really retired, or injured and unable to race?"

"You're not as wet behind the ears as you'd like Morales to believe, are you?"

I took a chance. "Not hardly."

She laughed. "Oh, I do believe you're my kind of gal. That horse had been used up by the trainer. You know about this guy, Serpentino?

When I nodded, she continued, "He's a man with a barnful of replaceable, juicy sponges. He wrings them dry and tosses them out. But"—her gaze lingered on my face—"John is making money now. He lost a ton before he hooked up with BetBig."

"This is the kind of stable I want to be involved with," I said quietly. "I need cash any way I can get it."

Mary and I smiled at each other. "Then, my dear, you've come to the right place."

"But how does Serpentino do it?" I asked.

"I don't know and I don't care. Just give me the money."

I felt like spitting on her, but held my smile, a smile that said she was my new best friend. These were the people who kept horse racing from being as popular as it should be. These were the people who ruined the game. I felt a new appreciation for the Thoroughbred Racing Protection Bureau and was suddenly very proud to be an agent.

I was so intent on my thoughts, I didn't see him coming. By the time I registered his presence, he was slipping into John's empty chair and giving me the beautiful smile that never reached his eyes.

"Calixto!" Mary's face flushed and she seemed to flutter slightly as she reached across the table to grasp his hand.

For a moment, I thought Mary would never let go. A flash of amusement sparked in Calixto's eyes when she finally relinquished her hold.

He'd changed his double C cuff links from gold to silver. A silver tie enhanced the sheen of his black silk jacket. I could almost feel the smooth starch of his crisp shirt. His gaze left Mary and settled on me. There was a reckless charm about him. Damn that full mouth. I pulled my eyes away and glanced at the tote board on the nearest monitor. He was just a handsome *crook*.

But Kate was pretty bent herself, so I crossed my legs and leaned toward him with my elbows on the table so he could take in the deep V in my black top. "Nice to see you again."

"So you already know Calixto?" Mary's smile was as knowing as her eyes.

"Yes," I replied.

"But not as well as you'd like to." Her smile became malicious.

I stared at her. Even Kate had her limits. "I think it's time for me to lay a bet."

I stood and walked toward the teller's counter. *Nice crowd you hang with, Fia.* I longed to leave the bar, Kate, and my new friends behind, but if I stayed, and the others drank enough, I might hear the bits and pieces I needed to get a line on what Serpentino was using. I needed to be a member of the team before the day ended.

At the window, I gave in to a sudden, quirky urge to lay a ten-dollar bet on Tumbling Dice. He was the longest shot in the first race, but I loved his name. When I got back to the table, Morales and John had returned. But Calixto remained in the seat next to mine. He stood and pulled out my chair. When I sat, his hand brushed my shoulder, sending a tingle of alarm to my core. I glanced up. The intensity in his dark eyes stilled everything inside me. I looked away.

Morales glanced at Calixto. "Kate's thinking of taking a share in Dixie Diamond."

"We all are," Mary said. Her gin had been replaced with a fresh one, the new glass half empty. "Are you joining us, Calixto?"

"Of course. I'll always get in bed with you, Mary dear," Calixto said.

Mary snorted. It sounded like a little pig squeal. I kept my face expressionless. Was Calixto simply a gigolo used to pull in the ladies? As he spoke to Mary, I watched his eyes. His shrewdness and pack leader abilities were obvious, but I sensed something deeper.

"And they're off!" cried the track announcer over the speakers. John's hand jerked as he clenched his tickets. He had quite a pile of them. Good thing BetBig made him money, because he had all the signs of a serious addict.

Everyone stared at the monitor, and I was surprised to see Tumbling Dice running third. I'd glanced at the program only long enough to know he usually lay far back and finished up with a weak close, rarely in the money. I checked the *Form* again. His trainer, Roger Copper, had a high win percentage. Good trainer? Or another Serpentino?

Tumbling Dice held third place around the final turn. At the top of the stretch, his jockey shook him up, the horse switched leads, and down the stretch he came. On the lead. He opened up and won by three.

I waved my ticket. "I had him. I had him!"

Morales leaned toward me. "Let me see that!" A strong whiff of scotch accompanied his words. When I showed him the ticket, he said, "Sixty to one, and Kate had him!" He threw an arm around me and squeezed. "You're hot today."

"I suspect she's always hot," Mary said.

Ignoring her, I eased out of Morales's hold, never losing my smile. "Tony," I said, touching his arm. "I'm ready to sign up for Dixie Diamond. But can I meet him first?"

His eyes lit with satisfaction. "He's coming in from Palm Meadows in two days. You can see him then and sign the papers. I'll send you an e-mail about his expenses and so forth."

Actually, I had no intention of seeing the horse. I certainly didn't have the money to buy in, and Gunny would have my hide if I didn't back out of this very soon. At least disentangling myself from BetBig would be easy; Kate knew how to disappear.

First, I needed to dig a little. I swallowed a gulp of tonic and leaned closer to Morales. Keeping my voice low, and slurring, I said, "Tony, tell me more about this Slerpanteeny." I giggled. "Does he put fairy dust on his horsies?"

Morales put his arm around my waist. "Serpentino has his ways. He's found—"

"Antonio." Calixto's voice, sharp with warning.

Morales released me and sat up straight. "Let's just say you won't be disappointed, Kate."

*Damn Calixto.* Mary was watching me, too. I didn't dare push harder. "I think I'd better powder my nose," I said. And rising from my chair with the exaggerated care of a drunk, I wobbled off to the ladies' room. As I headed across the room, my phone made its text waiting sound. When I checked it in the ladies' room, I was surprised to find a message from Gunny.

Gracie told me where U R. Get out of there now! Things you don't know. Call me.

What was this about? I was ready to go, anyway. There was nothing else to learn at Christine Lee's today. But when I stepped back into the lounge, Calixto was leaning against a pillar, waiting for me. His jaw was tight, his expression filled with displeasure. He grabbed my arm and pulled me into an alcove outside a service entrance.

"What are you up to, pretty lady? You ask so many questions." He pulled me so close, I could feel the warmth of his breath. "Tony will be surprised when I tell him you're pretending to be drunk, no? You must forgive me, but I tasted your drink."

His grip hurt my arm. His proximity was overwhelming, his eyes almost cruel. The tight anger in his facial muscles frightened me.

"Let go of me!"

He did, and so suddenly that I stumbled away from him.

"You," he said, "should stop your games before you get hurt. Don't try to play with the big boys."

"You're crazy," I said. When I twisted away, I heard him laugh.

I hurried back to our table feeling like I'd stumbled into a wasp's nest. I told Morales I wasn't feeling well, and got the hell out of Dodge.

# 23

When my cab dropped me off near the rental, I hurried into the pink stucco house, quickly shedding the persona of Kate. Frustrated, I threw everything that was Kate into a tote bag. The cover was blown, and I had learned nothing.

*Great work, Fia.*

Moments later, I sped my Mini toward Southwest Ranches and called Gunny as I drove up 75 toward the Griffin Road exit.

When he answered, his sharp tone told me my name on his caller ID had not inspired happiness. "What the *hell* are you doing, Fia? You want to lose this job, too?"

"No, sir, I do not."

"Can't you follow orders? *Never* circumvent my authority by asking permission from my assistant! Your wild Indian charge at Morales put Gracie in an awkward position. It put you in danger because—hold on a minute."

I heard what sounded like a lid being unscrewed followed by something like dice rattling in a cup. When he spoke again, I could hear him chewing. Was I causing heartburn?

"This office has a lot going on, Fia, things you don't know about. I don't need any of my agents going off the reservation like this. I'm coming down to Gulfstream tomorrow to sort things out."

That sounded ominous. "Believe me, sir, it won't happen again."

"If it does, it will be the last time."

He paused, and I tensed, waiting for the axe to fall. I had to work to keep my right foot from jiggling against the gas pedal. "Mr. Jamieson, I'm sorry—"

"And for God's sake," he said, "call me Gunny."

I hid the astonishment from my voice. "Sure, okay. Listen, I shouldn't have—"

"What time will you finish up with Rosario tomorrow?" I told him and he said, "Meet me at the rental house at noon. You got that?"

"Yes, sir."

"It's time I got you people down there organized."

*People?* "What people?" But he'd already hung up. Probably just as well. My questions would only irritate him. I eased my fingers out of their death grip on the steering wheel, wiggling them a little.

I couldn't figure out what he meant. Was he pulling Rosario into the operation? That didn't feel right. He kept referring to things I didn't know. So why didn't he just tell me?

When I slowed to pull off 75 into Southwest Ranches, I slid the windows down. Flowers from the neighborhood's carefully tended gardens perfumed the warm breeze that flowed into the car. I passed by a paddock where two cream-colored ponies grazed. Jilly's neighborhood watch flyer with Valera's ugly picture was posted on the fence. I smiled; there had been no more incidents of butchered horses in the area.

When I slowed to turn into Patrick's drive, I spotted an SUV easing around the corner up the street, angling on to Lead Pony

Lane and heading my way. *Zanin.* Like he'd been waiting for me. He followed me in.

I pulled up to the terrace, cut the engine, and Jilly burst out the front door. She stopped, and looked beyond me to where Zanin was parking his SUV. Her eyes brightened with excitement. She slid her hands into the pockets of her purple hoodie and shifted her weight from one foot to the other, waiting for Zanin to emerge.

He did, wearing a tight black tee shirt with cutoff sleeves, blue jeans, and work boots.

"Hey," I called to him. "You know, my phone works."

He walked quickly toward me. "I'm not using any phones until I pick up some disposables. They bugged my office."

"Someone bugged your *office*? Who?"

"Valera! It was him, wasn't it?" Jilly's pocketed hands wrapped protectively around her waist, accentuating her tiny frame.

The sun behind Zanin put his face in shadows, leaving his eyes beneath the thick brows unreadable. But his sigh was heavy.

"Yeah, it was probably Valera or one of his men. I must have really touched a nerve on the dude since I've been asking around to see if anyone knows what he's doing with that building. It's a good thing we keep antisurveillance stuff in the office. Betsy did a sweep yesterday and found a bug on the phone line where it connects to our building."

A chill brushed my spine. "You should back off, Zanin. You know how dangerous these people are. You aren't the police. You don't have the backup." Oh, God, I sounded just like my brother.

Zanin's teeth gleamed as he smiled. "That's why I have you."

"Cool!" Jilly said. "I can fight that piece of shit, too!"

"Jilly!"

"Well he *is,* Aunt Fia."

"He may be, but you are not *fighting* him." I glared at Zanin. "Can we take this inside and get something cold to drink before Jilly charges off to battle?"

"Sure. Sorry," he said. "Jilly's so fierce, I tend to forget she's still a kid."

"I'm not a *kid.*"

"Kitchen. Now," I said, walking to the front door and holding it open.

When Zanin walked past me, he touched my arm. "Florida agrees with you, McKee. You should stick around for a while."

I wasn't sure how to respond. His touch was nice, but it didn't stop my heart. He was a better man than Calixto. I liked him. But how much? "I'll be here for the season." He looked at me and I could almost hear him thinking, *Is that all you've got for me?* Then he followed Jilly into the kitchen.

She was already at the refrigerator pulling out bottles of Diet Coke. Zanin made himself at home, taking three glasses out of a cabinet and filling them with ice.

"Jilly," I said. "Would you like to come and help out at the track? Mr. Rosario said he'd be happy to have you. The pay won't be much but—"

"Really? Yes, *awesome!* Like, when?"

"Day after tomorrow. You'll have to get up early."

"No problem!" She darted out of the kitchen.

"Where are you going?" I called after her.

"I have to figure out what to wear!"

"But it's not until—" Her door slammed, and I gave up.

Zanin was shaking his head. "She's a pistol."

"That's what I'm afraid of," I said, pulling a chair out and sitting across from him. I took a long cool sip of soda.

"It's just as well Jilly left," he said. "I finally got some info this morning. Word is Valera has gone to Puerto Rico for a few days and taken some of his men with him. If there's ever a time to find out what he's up to with that new section and building on his property, this is it."

"How reliable is this information? You don't want to go in there and find the whole gang waiting for you."

"No, it's cool. I helped this guy out once. He's a distant relative to Valera, does side work for one of Valera's guys. But he hasn't forgotten what I did for him and he has no reason to set me up."

"Unless he gets *paid* to."

He shrugged, paused, and his expression grew serious. "I want to know if you'll be my backup, Fia."

"What?"

"You're the perfect person to do it. You told me you've worked undercover, you have a gun, and you know how to use it, right?"

"Zanin, wait a minute."

He leaned forward and his eyes opened wide. I hadn't been sure of the color before. Dark gray. It was the first time I'd been sure of anything about him.

"Hear me out, Fia. My friend, Juan, has a legit reason to be there tonight. He's working on an electrical problem in one of the barns. He'll signal me if it's okay to go in. I have that thermal imaging camera, some bolt cutters, lock picks, and stuff. But I need you to watch my back. You can play my dumb girlfriend again." He grinned. "You were really good at that, remember?"

I stared at him.

"Fia, you're blushing."

"Zanin, this isn't something to joke about. It's really dangerous."

"We'll be in and out fast. If we find evidence to bring a police bust, Valera won't be killing any people's horses, right?"

I rubbed my temples. "I don't know."

"Come on, Fia, you know what this bastard put Jilly through."

My foot started jiggling. I saw the gory scene, the blood. The memory fast-forwarded, and I heard Jilly's screams.

"I'll do it."

# 24

Once I'd agreed to go with him, Zanin left quickly, saying he'd pick me up at eight. With the sound of the Tahoe's tires receding down the drive, I scribbled a note to Patrick that I'd be out for most of the evening and left it on the kitchen counter.

After a shower, I crawled under the turquoise comforter, determined to take a nap. Sleep would be scarce during the night ahead.

When I woke up, it was seven thirty and dark outside the bedroom window. I pulled on a long-sleeved black tee and cargo pants, then slid a cap on my head. After lacing on steel-toed boots, I clipped the holster with my Walther to my belt. I stuffed two extra bullet clips, a folding Buck knife, and a pair of work gloves into the cargo pockets. After adding a long canvas vest to hide the gun, I stepped into the hallway.

I heard music coming from Jilly's room, and the sounds of Patrick unloading the dishwasher in the kitchen. I slipped quietly outside the house and walked to the end of the driveway to wait for Zanin on Lead Pony Lane.

He arrived on time, and I climbed into his Tahoe. The seat squeaked when I sat, and the hinge grated a little as I pulled the door closed. I had to arrange my boots around a crushed soda cup and an empty takeout chicken box lying on the floor mat. The car's scent was all Zanin. A little stale sweat on the uphol-stery with a dash of testosterone. His clean clothes added a fresh touch of laundry detergent to the mix.

We didn't speak, and as he gunned the SUV down the street, I glanced at his face. He'd shaved recently and I picked up a whiff of soap. His eyes looked tired, more recessed beneath his brow bone than usual.

I twisted and looked into the backseat. There were cans of bug spray, a machete, work gloves, a canvas backpack, and a piece of electronic equipment I didn't recognize.

"That thing that looks like a yellow box on a stick," I said. "Is that the thermal imaging camera?"

"Yeah. It's made by Fluke. High-end, excellent product. The stick's so you can hold it with one hand. It'd cost me eight thou-sand to buy that thing. I was lucky to find a guy who'd let me borrow it."

"Do you know how to *use* it?"

"Don't be a smart-ass, Fia." He stamped on the accelerator, and his eight-cylinder engine tossed me back against the vinyl seat.

I looked outside and saw the same endless stucco housing developments, shopping malls, and garden centers I passed days before on my way to find Jilly.

"So what's the plan?" I asked.

"Back to the C-Nine Basin. To 178th Street, close to where it intersects with Flamingo Road."

"But *not* by those feral pigs?" I didn't try to hide my distaste or fear.

"No. We're coming in from the other direction."

"Good."

"Juan will meet us. Let us know if it's still okay."

"Couldn't you just call him on your disposable?"

"He's paranoid. He won't use a phone when he's in the C-Nine."

We rode in silence for a while. It was nighttime and the traffic sparse compared to the afternoon I'd searched for Jilly. We zoomed under Interstate 75, and Pines Boulevard narrowed to two lanes. We hit the dead end and swung left onto Okeechobee Road. When we passed over Snake Creek Canal and entered the C-9 Basin, my boot started jiggling against the crushed paper cup and the empty chicken box.

Zanin glanced over. "We're going into Valera's on foot."

I nodded, and he concentrated on driving, turning off Okeechobee before 137th Street, taking a different route. In the gloom, with the trees closing in, I couldn't read the street sign, but moments later we angled onto 178th Street, and he cut his lights. He'd rigged the Tahoe so the dash remained dark. We didn't speak as Zanin followed the pale outline of sandy road. We bumped into a weedy field and rolled to a stop behind the dim outline of an abandoned barn.

He cut the engine, slid the windows down, and listened. I heard frogs, the soft call of a night bird, and the distant drone of a plane overhead. A figure emerged from the dark shadow of the barn, and I tensed.

"It's Juan," Zanin whispered.

"How do you know? It's black out here."

"I recognize the gold tooth."

I peered into the dark and sure enough, a fleck of gold glowed in the ambient light. It seemed to float on a dim white outline of teeth. Juan was smiling. This was good, right? I relaxed a hair.

"*Hola, amigo,*" Zanin said.

Juan approached Zanin's window, and their hands did one of those convoluted man-shakes.

When we climbed out of the SUV, I glanced up. Stars stenciled the dome overhead, and a quarter moon rose above the horizon.

Juan nodded at me and turned to Zanin. "Is good, man. Only three guys. They watch boxing match. Drink beer, smoke weed. No trouble tonight."

"Good. Thanks, Juan, I owe you one."

"You don't owe me nothing, man. *Eres como un hermano para mí.*"

Saying Zanin was like a brother. I hoped he meant it.

"*Buena suerte,*" he said to us. He slipped back into the shadows and disappeared.

After we doused ourselves with the bug spray, I pulled on my work gloves. Zanin put the Fluke inside the canvas bag, slung the pack over his shoulder, and grabbed the machete. I'd already seen the gun on his right hip and pressed a palm against my own holster, reassured by the feel of the hard metal inside.

Zanin touched my shoulder. "Let's do this."

I nodded. For good measure I shoved a can of bug spray into one of my vest's large zippered pockets, before following him into the tangle of brush and pines.

"Stay close behind me," he whispered, slicing the machete through a vine with large, smooth thorns that gleamed in the night light.

"Like glue," I said, remembering the large reptilian entity that had slid through the muck near the pigpen. "Is there much swamp on the way?"

"Fair amount. But avoidable if you know the path."

*Path?* I saw no path, only dark dirt, pine needles, fallen palm fronds, and the indistinct outlines of big, scratchy bushes. Every so often the arms of two plants locked thorns and blocked our way. Zanin's machete sliced them apart, leaving a strong wet scent like green blood.

Tree frogs and bullfrogs croaked a raucous chorus, providing the musical score for our trek through the jungle. As close as I shadowed Zanin, I was careful not to bump into him when he'd stop to get his bearings. Up small rises, down along the edge of banks with careful steps to avoid a fall into the murky water. After the third set of eyes glowed at me from the slough, I stopped flinching. My boots made sucking noises as we moved through wet spots, but I never took the dreaded drop-step into deep, stagnant water. Zanin knew what he was doing.

About the time I decided I'd been pulled into an endless, Stygian nightmare, dim light became discernible ahead. Moments later, we halted before a fence made of heavy strands of electrified wire. Beyond it lay a cleared field, and in the distance, what looked like the trees and netting I'd seen in Zanin's photographs. Beyond that, another open field and lights that glowed from a distant building. Valera's home?

Zanin dropped his canvas bag, rooted through it, and withdrew a heavy set of rubber gloves and rubber-handled wire cutters. He snipped the four strands of wire, and using the rubber gloves, twisted the wire back on itself, leaving us a narrow square to walk through.

We moved quietly across the recently cleared field, careful not to stumble on cut roots or jagged stumps of bushes and trees. I hoped our silhouettes didn't stand out like black billboards announcing our presence to any eyes that might be watching.

As we approached, it sounded like a thousand crickets were chirping inside the cage. Nearing the steel frame supporting the netting, I could see the fabric's weave was fine enough to contain insects.

Zanin paused. "Look up. See how the chain link and the netting go right across the top to the other side?"

"Yeah." As we drew closer, a dull orange glow became visible from inside. "Are those heat lamps?"

"Yeah," Zanin said, "I think so."

"The net makes it so dark, I can't see anything but trees and the lamps. Are they raising birds?" I peered into the dark until a reflection caught my eye.

"Zanin, look at the ground. Is that water?" I tried to keep my voice steady as a spider of doubt crept down my spine. "Valera's got something in there that needs trees and water. Do you think it's *snakes?*"

"I don't know, but the entrance has to be through the building."

"We're not going *in* there," I insisted. "Can't you look through the camera?"

"Yeah, but I want to get closer. Come on."

We followed the chain link to where it attached to the edge of the cinder-block building. Zanin pulled the Fluke out, cranked it up, and we both stared at the boxlike screen attached to the handle.

"Except for the heat lamps, it's just vague, muted colors," he said. "I'm gonna see if I can adjust the temperature lower. If anything's inside, it's not putting out enough heat."

I remembered Jilly asking Zanin how the camera could see something cold-blooded like snakes. *Nope, not going in there.*

Zanin's fingers adjusted a control on the camera, and he aimed it at the closest tree inside the fence. We stared at the screen.

A small image stared back. As my eyes adjusted, I made out a number of them sitting on twigs and branches of the tree. Some were moving. "Yuck," I said. "Frogs." Then it hit me. "Frog juice! He's making frog juice!"

"Why would he? You said they already test for that at the track." But he started shooting pictures with the Fluke.

"Maybe he's making it for people. We have to get in there,"

I said. "I need a couple of those babies to take with us. I want to see if they're the ones that make dermorphin."

He grabbed my arm to halt my forward surge. "Wait a minute, Fia. Let's make sure those frogs aren't food for something bigger that lives in there."

I shuddered. "Okay." I wondered if the creatures could be poisonous. Why hadn't I read more about them?

Zanin slowly panned the Fluke over the area closest to us, and we didn't see anything but frogs—no alligators, no pythons. We walked along the fence line to the far end, following its rectangular outline across the narrow end and back down the far side before returning to the cinder-block building. Nothing but frogs and the sound of crickets chirping on the ground inside the pen.

"I guess the frogs eat the crickets," I said, feeling my lips grimace.

Zanin looked at the time indicator on the camera screen. "We need to get in and *get out*," Zanin said.

"Works for me."

When he saw that a padlock secured the door to Valera's building, Zanin reached into his bag, pulled out his bolt cutters, and broke the lock. I tensed when he opened the door, fearing the sound of sirens and the flashing of lights. Chirping crickets and darkness continued to rule the night, but a funky smell stopped me in my tracks.

Pausing, we both switched on penlights. I pulled on my work gloves, gritted my teeth, and forged into the building behind Zanin. Shining the tiny lights inside the rectangular space revealed a concrete floor and a long metal worktable that held two plastic gallon jugs of nail polish remover. When we examined the shelves bolted to the walls, we discovered several cardboard boxes containing smooth wooden sticks like tongue depressors. There were about a half dozen cartons packed with two-inch-by-three-inch clear plastic boxes, like those used to store computer flash drives.

The only other items in the room were a box of shop rags and a large trash barrel half filled with discarded rags and sticks. My eyes stung from the reek of acetone coming off the old rags.

Zanin shrugged his shoulders. "What do you think?"

"The sticks," I said slowly, trying to work it out, "might be used to scrape the wax off the frogs. The tiny plastic boxes could be used to store the wax."

"And the acetone and rags for cleaning the stuff up?"

"Yeah," I said. "That sounds about right. Now let's grab some frogs."

A screen door in the far wall of the building led into the cage. After Zanin eased the door open, we stepped into the pen. Ambient light filtered through the netting and defined four long rectangles of water. I knelt to shine my penlight on one and felt my knee crunch a cricket. *Oh, yuck.* I looked at the water.

"Jesus, Zanin, look at these tadpoles. Valera's got to be raising these things."

"Then no question there's money in it for him. You want me to grab a frog?"

Glancing up, I said, "You've already got too much stuff to carry. I'll get them."

A cricket hopped onto my thigh and I knocked it off, stood up, and stared at the nearest tree. I saw the outline of a frog, and moved my hand toward it very slowly. It started walking away, but was slow. After gently working my gloved fingers around it, I dropped it into one of my vest pockets. It surprised me that these frogs weren't hoppers and were so easy to catch. I nabbed another one, eased him into the same pocket, and closed the zipper.

"Let's get out of here. It smells gross."

I could see a flash of white as Zanin smiled. "You know, they say smell is particulate."

"Thank you for that," I said, trying not to think about breathing funky particles into my lungs.

We went back through the screen door, moved through the

building, and out the front, walking fast across the stubby field. I heard a droning sound and glanced toward it. On the dim horizon of treetops a light grew stronger and larger.

"*Plane,*" Zanin said. He started running.

I ran, too, glancing over my shoulder, I could see the plane's lights were about to sweep over us. Was it Valera returning early with the rest of his thugs? Dipping a wing, the plane began a circular path over the field we ran through, probably preparing to land on the cleared field closer to Valera's house.

We couldn't run fast enough. The lights swept over us making us as vulnerable as fish in a barrel.

"*Damn it,*" Zanin said. "No way they didn't see us."

We sped forward. I glanced back and saw the lights in the distant house come on. A car engine started up. Headlights flared and bounced quickly across the far field, heading our way. Someone in the plane must have alerted the three men in the house.

We ran hard, stumbling on roots and small stumps, somehow regaining our feet without falling. The electric fence and swampy woods grew closer, but so did the roar of the vehicle's engine. I stubbed my boot toe hard on something and fell to one knee, stifling a shriek of pain as something sharp pierced me.

Zanin rushed back. "What's wrong?"

"My leg."

He shined a penlight. A thin tree stump had pierced my calf.

"Get me off this thing," I said.

He put out a hand. I pressed my palm against his and pushed myself up with a small scream. The sharp end of a stake protruded from the ground, painted with my blood. I tested my leg, carefully standing on it. Maybe only a flesh wound? It hurt, but my ankle still flexed and my calf held my weight.

"Fia, can you run?"

Instead of answering, I took off toward the swamp. My stride was off, but I moved pretty well and I could hear Zanin right behind me.

With a last look back, I saw the plane touch down in the far field. As it taxied forward, its headlights backlit what looked like a Jeep roaring into our field.

Moonlight reflected off the lines of electric fence outlining the small gap where we'd entered. Behind me, I could hear Zanin gasping for air as we ran toward it. I was probably in better cardiovascular shape than him from galloping, but my leg hurt.

The sound of the Jeep's engine grew louder. We were almost to the gap when shots rang out. Automatic fire from the careening Jeep went wide, not touching us.

We made it through the gap and into the woods. No way I'd find the path through Valera's jungle. I slowed to let Zanin pass me. Behind us, I heard the Jeep crunch to a stop. Whoever had the automatic weapon raked the woods with fire, hoping to nail us. Tree bark, twigs, and leaves erupted around me. My heart pounded like it was trying to beat its way out of my chest, but somehow, a bullet never found us.

Zanin didn't pause, and by the time the next burst of fire strafed the trees we'd shifted to the left and worked deeper into the tangled vegetation. I heard shouting, but the voices didn't move into the woods. Maybe they were as afraid of this place as I was.

Zanin moved as fast as he could to find the trail. I struggled behind, trying to keep up with my limping run. The pain intensified, and I felt my energy draining. I thought about my dad and tried to let the good memories comfort me. Suddenly I remembered an oldies tune he'd liked and could almost see him on his shedrow, hear him singing along with the radio, "Runnin' like a dog through the Everglades."

Then I remembered finding his body. I ran harder.

# 25

We burst from the twisted, swampy brush, ran through the weedy field, and piled into Zanin's Tahoe. He cranked the engine, and the SUV's tires spun, sliding across the grass and vegetation until they grabbed traction on the gravel and dirt of 178th Street.

"I've got a first aid kit," he said as he drove the SUV down the sandy road dimly lit by the quarter moon overhead. "As soon as we get far enough away, I wanna stop and look at your leg."

"It's not that bad," I said, but I could feel his gaze on me. Staring through the windshield, I forced myself into the present, pushing dark thoughts about my father's last moments into the past.

"We're stopping anyway."

I felt a stirring in my vest pocket and the pressure of little feet and legs pushing against my side. "Okay," I said. "We'll stop. The sooner the better. I think these frogs just woke up."

"Are we squeamish?" His smile was barely visible in the moonlight.

"You know, Zanin, they could be *poisonous*. I think running through the woods scared them, put them in a kind of possum mode. But now that I'm still, they are seriously on the move. They need to meet a box."

"We'll find something," he said.

About a mile farther, he flipped on the Tahoe's headlights and hit the gas pedal. Moments later, we swung onto Okeechobee Road, where he pulled into the lot of a boat rental and cut the engine. While he grabbed his first aid kit from the backseat, I unlaced my boots and pulled my bloodstained pants leg up to my knee. With the aid of a strong flashlight, we examined my calf.

"You're lucky," Zanin said. "It's a puncture, but not very deep, and it looks like it bled clean."

"I told you it wasn't bad," I said. "But the frogs are driving me crazy. I'm taking this vest off." I did, and laid it carefully on the seat next to me. It started moving toward Zanin. "You *see*?"

Ignoring the approaching vest, he grabbed a bottle of hydrogen peroxide from the kit. He unscrewed the lid and poured the disinfectant into the hole in my leg.

He might as well have hit me with a flamethrower. "Jeez!" I blinked back tears.

"Sorry. Had to clean it out."

He had gentle hands for a big guy and when he applied Neosporin, gauze, and Vetrap, I felt better. He put the first aid kit back, and made an impatient sound. The frogs had caused my vest to creep across the seat. It was nudging at his thigh.

He pushed it away. "What's *with* these things?"

"Girl frogs," I said.

"Don't go there, Fia. Do you mind putting them on the floor?"

I did, and rode back to the house with my feet safely propped on the dashboard.

Zanin stopped at the end of Patrick's driveway a little after midnight. He cut the engine and turned to me.

"Fia, thank you for coming with me. I'm sorry about your leg."

"My leg? We were dodging *bullets* out there, Zanin. We could be dead meat in the hog pen. My leg is nothing."

"I know, I know," he said rubbing a hand against his eyes. "I'm sorry."

"Well," I said, softening, "we got what might be great evidence. If we're lucky, we can use it to bring this guy down." I pulled my feet off the dash and folded my legs on the seat.

Zanin stared at me. "Can we maybe get together sometime when it's not about Valera and dead horses?"

I hadn't realized how much I'd hoped to put this moment off, but I had to answer. "For right now, I have to say no." I could feel him withdrawing. "Hear me out, Zanin. I'm going to trust you with something." Meeting his gaze, I held it. "I'm still working in law enforcement. Undercover. I can't tell you the details, but right now my life is so crazy, I just can't . . ."

"Whoa, you're a piece of work, Fia."

I stiffened.

"No, I mean that in a good way." He rested his fingers on my left leg. "As long as it's just for 'right now' like you said, I can wait."

"Zanin, I may be pulled out of this area and sent somewhere else. My life isn't my own."

"Let's just let it play out. That's all I'm asking. No promises, no strings."

"Okay," I said.

Quicker than I had time to think about, he slipped an arm around my waist, pulled me across the seat, and kissed me. He smelled good, all male. His kiss was strong and hungry. I was too startled to respond until his hands started to wander. Gently, I pushed him away. "Easy, big guy."

We were both short of breath, and the heat in his eyes said he wanted to kiss me again. "Zanin, I've got to call it a night."

He was smiling. "Fine by me, babe. I've got something to take home and dream about now."

I wasn't going to touch that comment and felt a sudden twinge of guilt as I remembered my surge of desire for Calixto. I wasn't ready to deal with so many mixed emotions. I grabbed my vest and scooted out of the Tahoe like a thief.

After slipping through the front door into the living room, I walked softly across Rebecca's turquoise carpet, and tiptoed down the hall to my room. Though 4:00 A.M. was only a few hours away, I was too wired by everything that had happened to sleep. Besides, I had to do something with the frogs.

Someone, probably Rebecca, had stored shoes on the top shelf of the guest bedroom closet. I rolled my desk chair inside, climbed up, and snagged a shoe box. I pulled it down, opened the lid, and found a pair of turquoise sandals with four-inch orange heels.

They screamed Rebecca. I set them on the white carpet and took another look. They wouldn't even look good on Kate. I grabbed scissors off the desk, punched holes in the box, and found a small glass dish in the kitchen. After adding water, I returned to the bedroom and put the dish in the box. I pulled on my work gloves and unzipped the vest pocket a little. A frog nose pushed through the hole. *Oh, yuck.*

I gritted my teeth, pulled the first toad out, and plopped him in the box. Quickly, I pushed the lid in place. My work gloves were discolored with a waxy fluid and a bit of frog poop.

Gingerly, I got hold of the second frog, held it under the desk lamp, and studied it. Iridescent blue with purple stripes. The legs were long and thin. Small drops of the sticky liquid seemed to be secreting from glands above the creature's eyes. Was it dermorphin?

Using my phone, I took pictures of the frog before putting him in the box. A closer look at his box mate revealed the same exotic coloring. After putting a book on the lid to secure the toads, I booted up my computer and looked up dermorphin. Pictures appeared of various but similar-looking waxy monkey tree frogs from South America. Each one produced the peptide found in dermorphin.

Although I knew nothing about chains of "amino acid monomers linked by peptide bonds," I did know my frogs had a different body shape. Their legs were longer and their snouts more pointed. Their blue and purple markings were quite different from the green frogs pictured as dermorphin-producing South American tree frogs. I scrolled through tree frog images until my eyes felt like they'd crossed but never saw examples like my Bluesters, a name I promptly adopted when it floated through my head.

Where had Valera found these things? Deep in South America? They appeared to be unknown. I'd check with the TRPB technicians first, but it sounded like we'd need a herpetologist to make an ID. *If they could.*

By now my head was heavy and my eyes half closed, but I had one more thing to do. I got a juice glass from the kitchen and slipped outside my bedroom's sliding door. Chirping sounds rose from the grass around the pool. I took a deep breath and went hunting.

A few minutes later I had two crickets in the glass, my hand covering the top. The insects bumped my palm with their hard shells and pricked my skin with their sharp, sticky feet. And they emitted an unpleasant odor like the funky stink in Valera's frog cage. *Totally disgusting.*

Had I really signed up for this job?

I managed to get the crickets in the box with the Bluesters. After securing the lid, I put the container in the bathroom and washed my face and hands. On my way out, I glanced back at the box.

"You guys do whatever it is you have to do, but please, don't talk about it in the morning."

I shut the door, fell on the bed, and was out like a light.

# 26

The next morning, Rosario and I watched Last Call for Love as she stood in her V, gazing proudly up and down the shedrow like she was the queen and the other horses her subjects.

"I think she's happy," I said.

"Between your room-with-a-view and Julio hand-grazing her in the evening, she's calmer, anyway."

"Put on a little weight, too," I said.

Rosario nodded. "But she needs to earn her keep. You ready to try Her Majesty on the track?"

"Absolutely. I'd better warm her up first, right?"

He nodded, and after I tacked her up and turned her loose in the round pen, she bucked, reared, and tore around like a cyclone for five minutes. Afterwards, Julio held her, and Rosario gave me a leg up.

"Here goes nothing," I said. I squeezed her with my legs and she walked forward. On her own, she took the path that led to the track, marched out to the sandy surface, and broke into a trot when I asked.

Rosario had mounted his pony and followed at a slight distance. I glanced back at him.

"Go on with her," he called. "See if she'll gallop a mile."

I nodded, shortened the reins, shifted my weight forward, and smooched at her. She surged ahead, and without the pony dragging on her mouth, she was a lovely ride—smooth, light on her feet, quick as a cat.

"Easy, girl. We're not racing today." But she wouldn't settle to anything slower than a two-minute lick, so rather than fighting her I let her have her two-minute mile before pulling her up.

When I rode toward Rosario, he was grinning. His grin widened when he realized how easy Last Call was breathing, as if she'd been out for a stroll.

"If we can work her five-eighths out of the gate next week, I'm putting her in for six furlongs. Her owner's tired of waiting."

Running her after one work, even if the race was a sprint, seemed too soon to me. But I knew an impatient owner was a royal pain who could send their horse to another trainer faster than an oncoming migraine.

"Sure," I said, stroking Last Call's neck.

When we arrived at the barn, Wendy Warner's vet truck rolled by, heading toward Serpentino's shedrow. Last Call had been my final ride of the day, so after handing the filly over to Julio, I walked to the barn's far side.

Wendy stood by her white truck, where she'd opened one of the side boxes. She took out a glass vial and a handful of syringes and put them in her vest pocket. As I got closer, she glanced up.

"Hey, Fia. What happened to you?" Her smile reached her pretty eyes. "You look like the cat dragged you in last night."

"I think he did, early this morning."

"I know how that goes. What can I do for you?"

"I have a friend who's looking for a trainer," I lied. "Rosario's full up, and I noticed you do some work for Roger Copper. Is he okay?"

She stilled for a moment. "Roger Copper? Why the interest?"

"He had a win with a long shot the other day. Has a good win percentage. Maybe he's someone my friend should look at?"

Wendy smiled. "He's okay. But your friend could do better. Here." She pulled a small memo pad and pen out of her truck. She scribbled down some names. "These guys are competent, fairly priced. They'd be good to look at."

"Better than Copper?"

She frowned. "Sure. Look, I gotta get this Lasix to some of Serpentino's horses that are running today." She gestured at his shedrow. "Good to see you, Fia."

"Yeah. Thanks." I watched her retreating back. Asking her about Copper had touched a nerve. She was hiding something. As I turned to leave, I felt someone's eyes on me. I scanned Serpentino's shedrow and saw the young groom, Angel, watching me from where he stood outside a stall.

"Hi, Miss Fia," he said. "How is your pretty filly?" He stepped forward and the sunlight caught his gold horsehead earring and lightened the shadows around his eyes.

"Good," I said. "She galloped on the track today."

He nodded and started to say more, but disappeared into the stall when Serpentino came out of his office.

The trainer gazed at me, tilted his long neck in my direction. "Can I help you?"

"Uh, no, Mr. Serpentino. Just saying hi to Doc Warner. You have a nice day." I faked a smile, then retreated almost as fast as Angel. Once I rounded the corner of the barn, a glance at my watch shifted my focus to my upcoming meeting with Gunny and whoever it was he needed to "organize."

By the time I reached the pink stucco house with the orange-tiled roof, my late night caught up with me. My head ached, my eyes were tired, and I needed sleep, food, and a shower. Except Gunny's last text had indicated the meeting would start momentarily, and the rental car parked in the drive suggested he was already inside waiting. *Damn.*

I breathed in, lifted my chin, and strode into the house. Gunny sat on one of four rattan chairs at the rental's glass-topped dining table. There was no one else in the room or in the small kitchen.

"Mr. Ja—Gunny," I said. "I hope I'm not late?"

"You're fine, Fia. We're waiting for one more person."

I bit my lip and didn't ask who. Instead, I said, "Be right back."

I zipped into the bathroom and ran cold water over my face, drying it with a towel. My hair had grown long enough to get tousled, so I fluffed it up and finger combed it back. I needed to bleach my roots. My skin looked pale, my eyes dark and hollow.

I heard the front door open, and a male voice. Stepping outside the bathroom, I stopped like someone had driven nails in my feet.

"Fia," Gunny said, "I believe you've met Agent Coyune?"

A pang of fear rushed through me. The last time I'd seen Calixto, he'd threatened me. Now he stood by the rental's entrance next to Gunny, wearing white jeans and a cotton tee, his long dark hair slicked back into a short ponytail. *What the hell is this?*

"I don't understand," I said, feeling a prick of anger. "This man is an *agent?* For who?"

"Same as you," Calixto said, walking to the table and pulling out a chair. "I work for the TRPB."

I stared as the reality I'd constructed broke and shifted into pieces. Calixto was one of *us?* Suddenly I was furious. I took a step closer to where he sat, appearing relaxed, his long legs stretched under the glass-topped table.

"Why didn't you *tell* me?" My glare lifted to Gunny who was still standing. "Why didn't *you* tell me?"

"Sit down, Fia," Gunny said. "You busted into Coyune's undercover operation. *Twice.* Calixto wanted to let it ride, and I agreed with him. But you showed up *again*. You could have blown your cover."

"Or mine," Calixto said.

"No way would I have done that." I glared at Calixto. "And thank you so much for convincing me I'd blown *Kate's* cover."

Calixto grinned at Gunny. "*Una pequeña leona.*"

Now he was making fun of me, calling me a little lioness. Not knowing how to take his comment, I sat, fixing my eyes on Gunny. "You should have trusted me."

"Couldn't take the chance. You're the new kid on the block, Fia. I can't risk a good agent like Calixto with someone who hasn't been here long enough to earn the agency's full trust. I *told* you not to go back in there without getting *my* permission."

I had no comeback for that. Sitting there silent, beneath his unforgiving stare, my hands on the cold glass of the table, I felt humiliated.

"Thing is, Gunny, she's good."

Startled, I stared at Calixto.

He continued speaking to Gunny about me in the third person as if I wasn't there. "She had me totally fooled. She's a pro, level-headed. Besides, she's in it now. I could use her."

"Excuse me," I said. "Do I have any say in this?"

Gunny lifted a hand to quiet me and turned to Calixto. "You want her in there with Morales?"

"Yeah," he said slowly, nodding. "She does this sexy bimbo act and Morales falls for it like a landslide." A smile curved his mouth. He flicked his gaze to me. "I didn't realize at first just how much he likes your 'Kate' persona. When you disappeared yesterday, he was upset. The thing is, I thought I should get you out of there before you got hurt. Now I've had time to reconsider. I think we should *use* his attraction to you. I'm sure you know how to work him to our advantage, yes?"

I shrugged, gave him my best dead-eye cop look, waiting to see what Gunny would say.

"All right, Calixto," Gunny said. "What's your plan?"

"Morales thinks Kate O'Brien is going to buy a share of his colt, Dixie Diamond. Let her do that to get closer to Morales."

"So," I said to Calixto, "you've been following the drugging end from your position as a partner?"

"Yes."

"And you want me to get closer to Morales, see if he'll spill info to me?" When Calixto nodded, I said, "I may wear a tiny skirt, but I have my limits. Just how 'close' do you expect me to get?"

"Nobody," Gunny said, finally pulling out a chair and sitting down, "expects or wants you to demean yourself in any way." He gave Calixto a hard look. "Right?"

"Of course," Calixto said, "but she could turn Morales inside out if she wanted to." He leaned forward, putting his elbows on the table. A whiff of his cologne drifted to my face. He grinned at me and, for the first time, the smile went right to his eyes, warming their dark golden-brown color. The skin on his forearms held the same tawny glow, but was many shades lighter. I did not like the way this guy affected me. I worked hard to keep my gaze from straying to his mouth.

Calixto sat back and glanced at Gunny. "She's moved herself into a great position. She's two people working it from *both* ends."

Gunny nodded. "Gracie told me that was your plan, Fia. The backstretch *and* the clubhouse."

"Exactly," Calixto said. "So we agree keeping her out of the loop at this point is a bad idea, yes?"

Gunny nodded.

I felt like a puppet and wanted to smack them both.

Gunny reached for a pen that was lying on the table. He twirled it slowly, briefly staring into space. "So, we know Morales and Serpentino have a drug."

"Probably Roger Copper, too," I said.

Calixto gave me a sharp look that changed into another smile.

"I told you she's good," he said to Gunny, before turning back to me. "The thing is, we don't know who the supplier is. Now I wish I hadn't stopped you from asking Morales more, but at the time—"

"You thought I was about to shoot everyone in the foot," I said.

A smile toyed with the corners of Gunny's mouth and his eyes gleamed. "Okay, let's talk about this mystery drug. Did both of you get the necropsy report on Primal?"

We nodded.

"Similar to dermorphin, but not dermorphin," Calixto said.

In the distance the drone of a jet grew louder and louder until it roared over the rental as if about to land on the roof.

"I have something to tell you, guys," I said, as soon as the engine roar faded enough that I could be heard.

They looked at me, curious.

"It's about some frogs I . . . acquired. I think they produce the drug that killed Primal."

# 27

My statement about frogs caused them to stare at me while the jet's din faded to stillness. Their silence filled the room.

"Let me show you," I said, and pulled the Bluester photo up on my phone before laying it on the table and sliding it toward Gunny.

He grabbed it and stared at the image. "Where did you get this?"

"Which?" I asked, finally enjoying myself. "The photo or the frog?"

"The *frog,* Fia. Do you have it in your possession?"

"Yes, at home."

Calixto leaned forward to examine the picture. "I've never seen one this color. Why do you think this particular frog is the producer?"

"Because of the man who raised him."

"Okay, Fia," Gunny said. "You'd better explain."

"It's a long story."

"And I want to hear it," Gunny said. "*Now.*"

So I told them, starting with the death of Cody. I told them about Zanin, Valera, and some of the details about my two trips into the C-9 Basin. "I think Valera is raising these frogs to produce an untraceable form of dermorphin. I think he might be Serpentino's supplier."

Gunny's eyes on me were hard and unreadable. Nerve-wracking.

"I didn't report this to you," I continued, "because it started out as a family matter totally unrelated to the drug problem at Gulfstream."

"Okay," he said. "I'll buy that. So what would be your next step, Fia?"

Across the table, Calixto watched me with interest. I could almost hear the thoughts whirling in his head. I just couldn't decipher them.

"You're full of surprises, *pequeña leona*. Please tell us. What is your next move?"

"We should test the wax secreted by these frogs," I said. "See if it matches the peptides the lab found in Primal's blood."

"One thing that's odd," Gunny said. "The quantity of frogs you saw indicates they're harvesting the wax directly from the amphibians. Why not just synthesize the drug? Substances like this are usually synthesized and produced in abundance. Scraping wax from live frogs seems an absurdly poor method of obtaining their product."

"These people are thugs, not chemists," I said. "You haven't seen them."

Calixto's focus appeared to turn inward, something I figured he did when he was thinking. He seemed to stare at me, but not to see me. Slowly, I felt the intensity of his gaze return.

"I think you're right. But if they want to make money," he said, "they'll catch on quickly."

Gunny nodded. "Probably so. And after you test your wax for a match, Fia, what then?"

I gave my isn't-it-obvious shoulder shrug and spread my palms. "Catch Valera or his men delivering the drug to Serpentino. Shut the bastard down."

"No," Calixto said. "We need to go one step farther. We need proof that Serpentino is dosing horses before they run."

"There are more trainers involved than Serpentino," Gunny said. "You mentioned Roger Copper. I want them *all*. I want a sting operation that cleans house."

Calixto nodded, and I felt a sudden charge of energy that we were working as a team.

Calixto smiled at me, stretched his arms over his head, then placed his manicured hands back on the table. Did he really live on Fisher Island? Was he rich, or had the information I'd gotten about him been falsified by the TRPB?

I squelched my curiosity, and as we remained silent a moment, I remembered something. "There's this vet, Wendy Warner. I've known her a long time, and I think she's a straight shooter, but she's working for both Serpentino and Roger Copper. I don't think she's that happy about it, but she told me she 'had to take what she could get.' Maybe she can provide some useful information."

"Careful," Gunny said. "You don't know whose side she's on. Don't tip your hand,"

I watched Calixto lean forward, unable to ignore the muscles in his forearms and the sharp planes of his face.

He glanced at Gunny. "I think the lady is smarter than that. You should see her in action."

This was the second time he'd complimented me. Somehow, it made me wary. Did he want something?

I shook myself mentally and continued. "I'm just looking at options. There's also a young Mexican groom named Angel. He's working for Serpentino. He's lonely, afraid of Serpentino. Might turn out to be useful."

I sounded so uncaring and cold. Truth be told, I wanted to

help this kid, not *use* him. But I was a cop first, and the need to bring down Valera and Serpentino burned too bright in my veins.

The pen in Gunny's fingers twirled faster and faster, until he abruptly set it on the table. "All right. Calixto, you work the owners' end. See what you can find out from Serpentino. Maybe show an interest in this Copper fellow. If he smells money from you as a possible new owner, he may loosen up."

His gaze switched to me. "Fia, your Kate is going to work Morales. He might say something to you he wouldn't to Calixto."

Except that usually involved pillow talk, and I wasn't going there with Morales. But I didn't mind making him *think* I would go there.

"And I still feel, Fia," Gunny continued, "you're most valuable on the backside, watching Serpentino. See who comes and goes at his shedrow."

"I can do that."

"Okay, then," Gunny said, pushing back from the table. "We know what we're doing?"

Calixto and I nodded.

Before I stood to leave, a little warning bell rang in my head. With the dramatic shift in my relationship to Calixto, I'd have to remember that only *Kate* knew him. Fia had never met the guy, and couldn't afford to let his name slip out.

My fear of messing up released a tiny adrenaline surge that I liked. I'd always been a bit of a thrill junkie, and in my line of work that wasn't such a bad thing.

# 28

The next morning when I shuffled into the kitchen seeking my first shot of caffeine, Jilly was already up and raring to go. She'd fixed coffee, and two bowls of yogurt with nuts and fruit on top were set on the kitchen table. She'd just taken a large bite, and since her mouth was full, she waved her spoon at me.

"Morning," I said, hustling over to the coffeepot, and grabbing the clean cup she'd set out. I filled it to the top, breathing in the aromatic steam. After stirring in a dab of cream and some sugar, I took the first sip and closed my eyes in ecstasy.

"Think you'll live?" Jilly asked.

"Yeah, thanks. What *is* this?"

"Hazelnut cream mixed with Colombian."

I took another long sip, and felt the caffeine rushing into my system. But looking at Jilly, I decided the way her blue eyes radiated energy, there wasn't enough coffee in Broward County to raise me to her level.

"So, how long," she asked, "does it take to get there? I mean, we have to be there at, like, six, right?"

I nodded and finished my coffee before pulling the breakfast bowl closer. I dug in, liking the sharp tang of yogurt liberally laced with sweet honey.

"So, I'm gonna, like, walk horses around the—what do you call it, *shedrow*?"

When I nodded, she continued.

"To cool 'em out after they gallop, right?

"Mmm."

"And I always stay on the right-hand side of all the horses, and when I'm walking around, I stay close to the inside wall of this shedrow thingy, and if I'm gonna stop with my horse, I say, 'Whoa back, 'right?"

The kid was making my head spin, but I was pleased she'd listened to the advice I'd doled out the night before.

"Right," I said. "Finish your breakfast, you'll need it."

After we scraped up the last of the yogurt, I made a to-go cup of coffee, we piled into the Mini, and headed for Gulfstream Park.

Four hours later, Jilly stood outside Last Call's V, stroking the filly's white blaze. "Wow. She's *beautiful*."

"Yeah, but pretty is as pretty does," I said, "and this lady has some issues."

Last Call pushed into her V as far as she could and pressed her face into Jilly's shoulder. Jilly blinked once, and burst into tears. "God, I miss Cody so much!"

I didn't know what to say, so I put an arm around Jilly and for a few moments, we seemed to have a group hug. Jilly got a grip, I stepped back, but Last Call never stopped pressing her face into Jilly's stroking palm. She closed her big eyes almost blissfully.

Most of the Not for Loves I'd seen had those big, intelligent eyes and were good horses. But this filly was a puzzle. I hoped my efforts had unlocked her ability, or Rosario would banish her from his barn. I didn't want to think about the dim future awaiting a flighty horse that didn't want to run.

"So, I did pretty good this morning, huh?" Jilly had recovered, and her smile was impish.

"You did," I said, pleased with the natural ability that had quickly surfaced when she'd led her first horse round the shedrow at six thirty that morning. The horses seemed to relax in her hands, she was a quick study, and most important, Rosario had appeared pleasantly surprised by the fifteen-year-old.

"The kid's all right," he'd said.

But since Julio was approaching us with Last Call's tack, I shifted my attention back to the present.

"Track closes at ten," I said to Jilly. "We don't have much time to get her out since she needs the round pen first."

Turning Last Call loose to release her evil spirits was working so well, Rosario and I weren't ready to abandon the pen just yet.

"I want to watch," Jilly said.

I didn't want her near Serpentino, but what could happen if she stayed close to me outside the pen?

She did, and Last Call put on quite a show, rearing and bucking, flying in a tight circle around the pen, her black tail flaring behind. When movement caused me to glance beyond the fence, I saw Angel, his gold earring gleaming beneath his jet-black hair. As he approached the pen, his eyes were not on Last Call. They were on Jilly.

"*Hola*," he said, giving her a tentative smile.

"Hi," she said, pivoting away from me and taking two steps toward Angel.

I couldn't see her face, but Angel's hopeful smile lit up like a breaking dawn. *Oh, boy.*

Time to go. I clicked the shank's snap in my hand, and Last Call came to a stop, waiting for me to approach her and lead her from the pen.

By the time I walked her through the gate, Jilly and Angel were giggling, talking fast, and using hand gestures as they tried to work through the language barrier. Jilly turned toward me, her hair a black cloud framing huge blue eyes, the color echoed by the sapphires in her ears. She was so *alive*.

"*Hola,* Angel," I said. "Come on, Jilly. You can help me take her to the track."

"Can Angel come, too?"

"*No es posible,*" Angel said quickly, suddenly downcast, looking toward Serpentino's office. "I better to go. *Pero le vere otra vez?*" Asking if he would see her again.

"*Sí,*" Jilly said with a huge grin that caused Angel to blush.

As we walked the horse away, I asked Jilly if she spoke Spanish.

"Some, I take it at school. His English is kind of limited, so this is a great opportunity for me to practice."

*Of course it was.*

"He's *so* cute. Did you see his earring? It's so cool!"

Unsure about any of this, I did what all grown-ups do. I nodded and smiled, while inside I could almost hear Patrick yelling at me, "How could you let this happen?"

But I was being ridiculous. Jilly would only be here during the Christmas break. What could go wrong?

When we reached our shedrow, Rosario gave me a leg up on Last Call while Jilly held her. Looking down, I saw how pumped and well-defined the filly's muscles were. Her neck was crested, her coat damp from exertion.

A cooling breeze drifted past, carrying the scents of grain, molasses, and hay. Tiny bits of straw particles floated along with it. Restless, Last Call shifted her legs and raised her head high.

"Better lead her toward the track, Jilly. Down that path there, past the big palm. If she gives you any trouble, let her go."

"Okay," Jilly said, and walked forward. To my relief, Last Call went right with her. By the time we passed the palm and stepped onto the bridle path leading to the track, the filly was practically dragging Jilly.

"Let her go!" I called. Jilly did, and Last Call rushed forward.

She was anxious to go, but I kept a snug hold on her, which caused her legs to move rapidly up and down without much forward motion—like sewing machine needles.

When I let her loose on the backstretch, she stretched out as smooth as glass, performing an excellent two-minute lick until I set her down the last eighth. She ignited forward, and the wind rushed my face so hard it snatched my breath away. The sound of air pumping in and out of her massive lungs was music to my ears. *This filly had talent.*

After I stood in the stirrups, got her settled, and walked to the gap opening to the bridle path, I found Jilly waiting for us. Last Call was pumped, breathing a little hard, but still dancing and eager to go.

"She was *flying* at the end!" Jilly said, rising up on her toes.

"Oh, she can run," I said.

As Last Call's long legs churned me forward through the deep sand, Jilly struggled to keep up with us.

"So," Jilly gasped, "is she, like, a stakes horse?"

"Not even close. She won a few cheap claimers. But her current owner saw her zip from last to first and win one. Her late speed figure in that race was off the charts. So the guy had his previous trainer claim her. Next time she ran, she was nowhere. So the owner switched her to Rosario."

"But what happened in that last race?" Jilly asked.

"Who knows? Like I said, she has issues. It's all about figuring them out."

By now we had reached the end of the bridle path and passed the big palm tree. When our barn came into view and I stared ahead, a sudden jolt of tension in my hands and legs caused Last Call to surge forward, leaving Jilly behind.

Shyra Darnell stood on our shedrow. She was wearing a Coastal Transport jacket and talking to our other exercise rider, Meg Goffman. I wasn't surprised that Rosario's exercise rider from Maryland knew a former Pimlico groom. The racing world is that small. But still. Maybe I should mention her presence at Gulfstream to Gunny.

She glanced up and saw me riding toward her. Her immediate grimace was followed by a resigned shrug, as if maybe I wasn't her favorite person, but there was no reason to bolt. I wasn't a cop anymore, just another backstretch worker.

I rode the filly into her stall, and since Jilly trailed behind, Meg stepped inside and held the reins while I dismounted. Shyra moved into the doorway. Her hand held a folder of papers.

"Hey, Shyra," I said.

She nodded and gave me a cold stare.

As if sensing the tension between us, Meg threw me a bright smile. "Shyra's got a van meeting her at Serpentino's in a few minutes. He's got three horses coming in, right, Shyra?"

She nodded.

*Probably new candidates for frog juice.* I pulled the bridle and saddle from Last Call as Julio came inside and slid her halter on.

Stepping past Shyra onto the shedrow, I heard the sound of a truck engine and saw Wendy Warner's white truck rolling past the edge of our barn toward Serpentino's.

"I gotta meet the vet," Shyra said, taking a step toward the end of our shedrow. She waved the folder. "Doc Warner needs these papers."

As if on cue, I heard the deep whine of a diesel engine in first gear. A Coastal van eased toward us on the road between the barns.

Jilly watched its approach for a moment and moved into the filly's stall, knowing Julio expected her to cool out Last Call. I put my tack away and walked toward Serpentino's side. I wanted to see Wendy Warner again, get a sense of what she knew about Serpentino.

As for Shyra, I wanted, but knew I wouldn't get, additional information about the man I had killed. Still, it was a puzzle I itched to solve.

When I rounded the corner onto Serpentino's shedrow, the two women stood close together, speaking in low tones. Suddenly, Wendy's voice rose.

"This isn't good. You should have told me about this sooner. I—" She stopped abruptly when she saw me.

"Fia, hi." Wendy's quick smile faltered.

I kept my expression neutral. "I didn't know you knew Shyra. Figures since we've all spent time at Pimlico." I smiled at Shyra. "Like old home week. Wendy used to work with my dad when he was a trainer."

Shyra stood still. I watched her eyes go almost as dead as they did the night the man tried to strangle her. A moment passed before she regained focus. I could see thoughts starting to spin inside her head. Not good thoughts, apparently, since the blood left her face, leaving her skin a brownish gray.

Shyra's voice was so low I could barely hear her. She said, "You're Mason McKee's daughter?"

"Sure," Wendy said, stepping closer to Shyra, momentarily blocking my view of the other woman's face. "You probably just didn't recognize Fia. She used to have long brown hair and she wasn't so thin." She glanced at me. "Right?"

"Yeah, that's probably what it is." *Why would knowing I was Mason McKee's daughter make Shyra act like she'd seen a ghost?*

"So, Shyra," Wendy said. "Those papers you got there are for me, right?"

"Yeah." Shyra's expression and voice were lifeless enough to cast in a zombie movie.

"So let me have them," Wendy said, briskly reaching for Shyra's folder. "I'll check 'em out, and you should probably meet the van, right?"

The vet was working so hard to get Shyra away, she actually gave the taller woman a little push toward the van easing to a halt nearby.

Still in zombie mode, Shyra wandered toward the rig, where the driver was already out, dropping the side ramp.

Beside me, Wendy made a show of flipping through the papers in the folder. "Did you need anything, Fia?"

"Not really. I just came over to say hi."

"Oh, you're sweet," she said. "But I gotta get these horses straightened out. They've been having trouble with shippers coming in without the right vaccinations."

"Sure," I said. "I'll catch you later." I sketched a wave at her and left.

I'd just rattled a skeleton and wondered what else might be lurking in Wendy's closet. I planned to let the TRPB computers run a background check on Ms. Warner. She was hiding something.

# 29

That evening, I sat at the orange-topped kitchen table with Patrick and Jilly, eyeing an order of hot pizza that had just been delivered. As I pulled my first slice from the box, Jilly was bubbling with enthusiasm, talking about her day at the track.

"Racehorses are *so* beautiful! And I got to walk five of them. And Rosario was really nice and—"

"Are you keeping an eye on her, Fia?" Patrick said, giving me a sharp look. "I don't want her getting hurt by some hyper horse."

"*Dad!*" Jilly rolled her eyes. "*Everyone* was looking out for me. And the horses are so cool. They have, like, their own personalities. There was this one horse that had a chicken sitting on his back in the stall and—"

"A *chicken*?" Patrick appeared doubtful.

"Actually, a lot of people keep chickens at the track," I said, blowing on my hot slice.

Jilly sent Patrick a dirty look. "You always tell me not to interrupt. But *you* just did. Anyway, this first horse thinks it's totally cool to have this chicken on his back. But when I take Last Call down the shedrow, this little rooster comes out from under the railing and the filly freaks. She leaps straight up in the air!"

Patrick set his drink down abruptly. "That's just the kind of thing I'm worried about."

"She'll be fine," I said.

"I *am* fine," Jilly said, standing up and making a little pirouette while holding her arms out. "See?"

I almost felt sorry for Patrick. "Eat your pizza, Jilly. You have to get up early."

"Yeah, yeah," she said. But she sat and forked up a bite of salad.

Watching her, it occurred to me Patrick had done a great job with her since Rebecca walked out. I felt myself smiling at him. Maybe spending time with him wasn't such a bad thing.

We finished dinner, I helped with the kitchen cleanup, and when I reached my room, my cell rang. *Zanin*.

"Hey," I said.

"You and your family okay?" he asked.

"Yeah. What's going on?"

"We've got more dead horses."

"Oh, no." Had I really thought it wouldn't happen again? "Where?"

"About ten miles north of Southwest Ranches, and this time a girl got hurt."

"Is she—"

"She's okay. But they knocked her lights out. Then they killed her horse. I know you don't have a horse there anymore, but I was worried about you. And Jilly."

"We're fine," I said. "And I've got my gun."

"Yes, I remember it well. Just wanted to give you a heads-up and check on you before I disappear."

"What do you mean? Where are you going?"

"Undercover. You won't be able to reach me for a few days. Fia, be careful. Okay?"

"Yeah, I will. Zanin . . . thanks."

"Sure, babe." He hung up.

I hated thinking about another kid with a butchered horse. I didn't like thinking about Zanin putting himself in harm's way either. There wasn't anything I could do about it at the moment, so I booted up the laptop and connected to the TRPB's search site. I typed in "Wendy Warner, D.V.M."

A recent news article appeared about her donating time to a Maryland horse rescue operation near Baltimore. I didn't find much else except an old two-line mention in the business section announcing her partnership with Dr. Chambers.

Telling myself not to feel guilty, I looked into her bank records, which I could do through my secure link to the TRPB server. I was surprised to discover a measly $115.00 in her checking account and only $345.00 in the companion savings account. She had to have more money somewhere, didn't she?

Without being at my Fair Hill desk and directly connected to the TRPB server, I had limited access to search further. I sent a query e-mail to Brian, hoping to hear back from him the next morning. I was startled minutes later to receive a reply.

"You got lucky tonight, Fia, I'm working late. Interesting history here. Read attached."

I did, and could feel my mouth drop open. It appeared Wendy had a little gambling problem with the stock market. She had a brokerage account with Merrill Lynch and had bought stocks on margin that had not served her well. She owed Merrill Lynch almost $40,000.

I scrolled back in time, and was able to follow the account to its inception almost ten years earlier. She'd been with Merrill Lynch when I first met her, back when she'd worked for my dad.

I studied the history of her stock trades and fortunes over the decade. Before the time we'd met her, she'd had almost $225,000 in the account, with a lot of money in financials like

E★Trade, Countrywide Financial, and Citigroup. Then, *bam*, they went down as much as 84 percent overnight and she sold them at a huge loss. She'd scrambled to buy other stocks, bad decisions that plummeted her further and further away from the financial security she'd once enjoyed.

The year she'd started working as Dad's vet, she'd been down to $8,000. In June of that year there was a $25,000 deposit made into the account. *I'd like to know where that came from.* She'd put the entire $25,000 into the clothing store, Chico's.

I didn't know much about the stock market, but I knew better than to put all my eggs in one basket. And this basket had been a shooting star. The per share price had risen from $17 in 2004 to $49 by November of 2006. Two years later, with the 2008 crash, it was worth $2.55. *Ouch.*

In January of 2009, Wendy had acquired another cash infusion. I stared at the date, my scalp tingling with recognition. She'd deposited $50,000 a week after someone knifed my dad to death and I had found his partially frozen body behind a Dumpster at Pimlico.

The past crashed into the present, and I shivered. It had been so cold the day I found him, and my first reaction had been a crazy, desperate need to get his body to a warmer place, as if by doing so, I could bring him back to life.

I shoved my chair away from the desk and turned my back on the computer. Fast steps to the sliding door. Stumbling into the night air, I wrapped my arms around my rib cage and looked up at the sky, soothed by the vast canopy of quiet stars.

I stood for a while, breathing, letting myself settle. The sound of chirping crickets drew me back to the present. I should feed the Bluesters. I needed to go inside and finish my study of Wendy's finances. This had to be a bizarre coincidence, right?

Jilly and I had stopped at a pet store on the way home and picked up a small terrarium for the Bluesters. Even though they'd

be going to the lab the next day, I hadn't wanted to leave them
in Rebecca's shoe box another night. I went back to my room,
grabbed my cricket glass, and returned to the pool. I caught four
bugs and dumped them into the Bluesters' glass house.

I watched the brightly colored amphibians for a moment and
shook my head. "That's a good look for you, Blue. That cricket
in the mouth thing."

I couldn't believe I was becoming fond of two frogs, but that
slow methodical way they walked was kind of cute. Except just
then, Blue Two went after a cricket. I turned away. One could
only take so much carnage.

Having managed to bolt a door on the past, I went back to
my chair and studied the screen. Wendy had enjoyed better luck
with her $50,000. It appeared she'd put the money in high-
yielding oil well trusts, transferring the dividends into her checking account on a regular basis for most of the past eight years.

Then two of the oil trusts had bellied up, losing most of their
value overnight. Had the wells run dry? She'd invested what was
left in more stocks, followed by more bad luck, followed by buying on margin, borrowing from Merrill Lynch until she'd screwed
herself to a wall of debt.

But three days earlier she'd deposited $10,000 against the
debt. So close to the day Primal died. The very day Roger
Copper's horse, Tumbling Dice, won at incredibly long odds.
I couldn't believe this was a coincidence. No way.

*Wendy, you fool, what have you gotten yourself into?*

The next morning, we spun through training at Gulfstream. I
brought Jilly home, grabbed the Bluesters' terrarium, and headed
for a local testing lab affiliated with the Florida Racing Labora-
tory, part of the University of Florida's College of Veterinary
Medicine up in Gainsville.

Gunny told me he'd prefer the university lab, but it was hours
to the north and his contact from the steward's office at Gulf-

stream had suggested a lab in the outskirts of Miami. Said that
the lab's chemist, Dr. Steve Craigson, was excellent.

I followed my GPS instructions as the Bluesters hung out in
their terrarium on the Mini's passenger seat. Exiting off 95 onto
Dolphin Expressway, I soon turned onto a side street that led to
an office park. I found TestTube lab sandwiched between a plumbing showroom and a countertop fabricator. Scraggly fan plants
and bushes struggled to survive in the sandy spaces between the
buildings.

Outside the Mini, the warmth rose in soft waves from the
lot's asphalt surface as the heat continued to build in the mid-
afternoon sun. I carried the terrarium through a glass door, hearing a bell announce my entrance somewhere in the back.

I set the Bluesters on the green counter. A guy about my
age with bright red spiky hair and glasses appeared from behind a
partition.

He stared at the Bluesters. "Help you?"

"I have an appointment with Dr. Craigson."

The guy pursed his lips and frowned. "He's not here."

"Do you expect him?"

The guy took his glasses off and rubbed his eyes. "I couldn't
say. He hasn't been here today. It's kind of weird, because he didn't
come in yesterday, either."

"So, he's *missing*?"

"Now that's what I'm wondering. His wife called this morning looking for him."

Great, a missing chemist. "Craigson was supposed to test
these frogs for dermorphin. Is there anyone else that can test the
wax they secrete?"

He slid his glasses on and straightened. "I can do it. I'm Craigson's assistant. Licensed chemist." He pointed to one of the framed
certificates on the wall.

"You're Michael Brewer?"

"Yep."

"Let me make a call," I said, before gesturing at the frogs. "Okay if I leave them here a minute?"

"Fine by me."

I stepped outside, called Gunny, and explained about the chemist.

"This Brewer guy have carrot red hair?"

I said yes, and Gunny told me to go ahead and use Brewer. "He's all right, but . . ."

There was a pause. I was pretty sure I heard him opening a bottle of acid tabs. When he continued, he was munching on something.

"Gulfstream's stewards like this guy Craigson," he said. "They use him a lot. My guy at Gulfstream says this is very unusual behavior for Craigson. His wife's filed a missing persons report."

"Huh. Would you like me to ask Brewer if his boss has acted odd recently?"

"Might as well. Let me know if you learn anything."

"Sure, Gunny." I disconnected and went back inside.

Brewer showed me where to leave the frogs. "You can pick them up tomorrow," he told me.

"Um, can you feed them? I have some crickets in the car."

"I can do you one better. Craigson keeps a Phyllomedusa sauvagei."

"A what?"

"A tree frog. He spent so much time studying dermorphin, he wound up keeping a frog for a pet."

"Sounds like an interesting guy," I said. "So, what do you think is going on with him?"

"No idea."

"Has he acted preoccupied or has something been worrying him recently?"

"Nope." Brewer shrugged, dismissing the subject. "Anyway, Craigson's got a bottle of frog food. Nasty-looking stuff, but I'll give some to your guys."

"Thanks," I said.

Feeling better about the fate of my Bluesters, I headed back to 95. I wasn't as optimistic about the fate of Craigson. Why would he suddenly disappear?

# 30

A few days later, I watched as Julio led Last Call for Love from her stall. She plunged out like she knew we planned to work her from the gate, making enough noise that the gelding next door snorted in alarm. In the distance, another horse whinnied anxiously. Bits of straw and dust swirled around Last Call's legs, settling to stillness as she shifted into her statue pose.

Jilly held her bridle, and Julio tossed me into the saddle. The filly didn't feel like a statue, more like a small bomb with a lit fuse. Jilly led us off the shedrow, and Rosario came out of his office with a stopwatch, following us out to the track. Beyond the mile oval, palm trees rose in the morning sun against the backdrop of condos that lined the beach of the Atlantic Ocean.

Once we hit the sand of the track, I warmed up the filly. Minutes later, an assistant starter led us into the three hole of the starting gate. Rosario had arranged with another trainer to work two of his horses with Last Call, and they were led into the slots on either side of us. I prayed Last Call wouldn't freeze in the gate.

The starter watched the traffic on the track, and when a gap in the merry-go-round of horses appeared, he hit the electronic switch.

The bell clanged, the metal gates burst open, and Last Call exploded on to the track. She outbroke the other two, leaving them on her flanks as we blasted down the backstretch. My internal clock advised me not to urge her. She was fully detonated.

I sensed the horses on either side dropping behind. Glancing back, I saw we'd opened up by three lengths. The rhythm of her pumping lungs and pounding hooves played my favorite kind of rock and roll. We busted through the turn, down the stretch, and at the wire we were four lengths ahead of the other horses.

When I rode back to Rosario, he gave me a thumbs-up and said, "One minute flat for the five furlongs. Not bad."

Jilly stood next to him. "*Not bad?* She was *awesome*. She left those other horses in her dust!"

Last Call was pumped, her walk fast, and Jilly and Rosario couldn't keep up. I called back to Jilly, "Don't get too excited, I'm sure at least one horse worked the distance in fifty-nine or less." I didn't want her thinking Last Call was the next Zenyatta because she would be sorely disappointed. This was a game where high hopes often led to crushing lows.

After training, Jilly and I went to the lab to pick up the Bluesters and the results of the chemist's test. When we climbed out of the Mini, Jilly and I were confronted by a dazzling new display of chrome and stainless-steel kitchen sink faucets in the window of the plumbing supply next to the lab. There were enough levers, dials, and nozzles to seduce a rocket scientist.

Jilly stared at the glittering array. "Wow. These are really cool!"

I squinted at the price tags. "Not unless they come with a maid and a built-in bar."

The glass door to the lab opened and Brewer stuck his head out. "Hey. Wondered when you'd show up. Got some interesting results on your frogs."

We followed him inside. He told me he'd be right back, disappearing into the recesses of the lab. He returned carrying a file folder and the Bluesters in their glass terrarium. He set everything on the green counter and pushed the folder toward me.

"Take a look."

I picked up the folder, but before opening it, I glanced at my frogs. I'd felt bad about leaving them with Brewer, which was ridiculous. I didn't need to get attached to a pair of frogs. Still, the way they marched determinedly around the terrarium floor made me smile.

Jilly peered at it over my shoulder as I opened the folder and read. "The amino acid sequence of dermorphin is H–Tyr–D–Ala–Phe–Gly–Tyr–Pro–Ser–NH2." This fascinating revelation was followed by more scientific jargon with phrases about "receptors" and "peptides." I looked at Brewer.

"You're going to have to explain this to me in English. I have no idea what it means, okay?"

"Sure," he said, taking the folder back. "First, I was unable to identify the species. I can't find anything that accurately fits their physical description."

"Like, psychedelic?" Jilly giggled.

"I suppose you could put it that way," Brewer said, with a slightly sour expression. "There is another blue frog, but not with purple stripes. I assume these frogs are a rare subspecies, probably from South America. Now, interestingly, there is a subspecies that was once found in Africa—"

"So what did the test show?" I asked.

"I'm getting to that," Brewer said, his body posture stiffening.

"Sorry," I said. "It's just that we're short on time."

"We are?" Jilly asked.

I threw her a look. She began studying the frogs in their terrarium.

"Fine," Brewer said. "The DNA sequence in the secretion of these particular blue and purple frogs is different from that of dermorphin's. While the sequence doesn't match, it does contain a powerful opiate similar to dermorphin, only stronger."

"Stronger?"

"Yes," Brewer said.

*And in the hands of the worst kind of people.* "Do you think it would affect the performance of a racehorse?"

Brewer's response was terse. "Ms. McKee, I'm neither a vet nor an animal behaviorist."

"But if you had to guess?"

"Chemists don't guess."

*Oh, for God's sake.* "Fine," I said, leaning forward to take the folder back. Then, remembering I'd been warned repeatedly about my smart tongue during my Baltimore PD days, I said, "Thanks for this and for turning it around so fast."

He nodded curtly. I started to walk out but paused halfway to the door and turned back. "Has there been any word from Doctor Craigson?"

"No." Brewer's annoyed expression slowly dissolved. "It's really weird. I'm afraid something has happened to him."

"I'm sorry," I said. "Will you let me know if you hear from him?"

"Of course."

I headed back to the glass door and Jilly followed me out carrying the terrarium.

The next morning, Julio found heat in Last Call's left front tendon, proving the accuracy of my warning about the highs and lows of horse racing. The groom held Last Call's halter as Jilly and I watched Rosario kneel by the filly's leg and run his fingers down the skin on the back of her cannon bone.

Anxiety twisted Jilly's face. "What's wrong with her?"

"Working on a bow," Rosario said.

"You mean, like, a bowed tendon?'

Rosario nodded.

"How bad is it?" she asked.

"It depends," he said. "She's not lame on it, and if we can get the heat out before it swells too much . . ."

"But she won't be able to run!" Jilly's face crumpled with disappointment.

"That still depends," Rosario said.

I didn't like the sound of that. Racing a horse with heat like this was begging for a ballooned-out tendon and a possible breakdown on the track.

"Rosario," I said, "don't you think—"

"I've got to call the owner." Rosario stood up abruptly. "Julio, get an ice boot on that leg."

Julio hurried off to the supply room, and Rosario headed for his office, pulling out his cell phone as he walked. Jilly ducked into the horse's stall and wrapped her arms around the filly's neck. Last Call angled her head toward the girl and pressed her nose into Jilly's side. *Like Cody.*

When Jilly looked back at me, there were tears in her eyes. "Do you think the owner might sell her? She's so sweet. I could nurse her at home and—"

"I don't know. Just play it by ear, okay?"

Jilly scowled at me and turned away, burying her face in Last Call's mane.

I remembered my own impatience with adults. Always with the annoying phrases like "it depends," and "we'll see." Getting a straight answer was like pulling teeth out of a chicken. I tried to think of something else to say, and couldn't.

Julio returned with the neoprene boots Rosario kept in his supply room freezer. Made to fit a horse's front leg to the knee, it had numerous pockets for crushed ice on the inside. Jilly watched while I helped Julio wrap the boot around Last Call's leg and secure it in place with the attached Velcro straps. I hoped the ice would be enough to suck the heat out of the tendon.

When we were finished, and I stepped outside the stall,

Serpentino's truck was leaving the barn area. Late in the morning, he was probably done for the day, and moments later, Angel appeared at the end of our shedrow. I knew who he wanted so I pointed at the stall behind me.

He approached, his eyes widening as he saw the filly's leg. "*Qué pasa?*"

Jilly leaned against the stall gate and grasped the woven metal with her hands. As she explained about the tendon in careful Spanish, Angel brushed the palm of his hand across the tops of her fingers where they curled through the wire gate.

"*Lo siento,*" he said.

Feeling like an intruder, I left the two of them to commiserate. But as I walked away, an idea poked into my head. If Jilly hung out with Angel, she would be in a great position to learn things about Serpentino's barn. As a teenage buddy to Angel, she'd be practically invisible. I gave myself a mental head slap. Why was I thinking like this again? *Stop being a cop, Fia. Family first.*

As I walked past the large poinsettia Rosario had placed on a bench near his office, I paused to touch the soft blooms. Christmas was only a few days away. So much had happened, especially to Jilly. I should pick up something for her. Patrick, too.

This was my first experience with a tropical Christmas, and the lights and decorations I'd seen in Hallandale Beach and Southwest Ranches seemed out of place surrounded by warm breezes, fan plants, and palm trees. The sudden vibration of my phone interrupted my musing. I glanced at the ID. *Gunny.*

I answered, and he wasted no time. "We sent the TestTube lab results to a professor of pharmacology at Oklahoma State University. He helped bust the demorphin ring at Remington Park. He's very interested in your frogs. Wants them shipped ASAP."

"*Shipped?* Won't that kill them?"

"Says he wants them alive. Call him. He'll tell you how to get them there. I'll text his number."

"Okay."

"He thinks what you've found has disastrous potential. We need to stop it before it spreads to other tracks."

*Duh.* "I'm on it," I said. As I disconnected, Rosario came out of his office. Beyond him, Jilly and Angel had left Last Call and were walking toward me.

Turning to Rosario, I asked, "What did the owner say about Last Call?"

"Run her for a tag, get her claimed."

"You're kidding," I said, hoping Jilly hadn't heard him. *Too late for that.*

She rushed at Rosario, her eyes blazing with righteous anger. "You're going to *run* her. Sell her in a *claiming* race? Why would you *do* that?"

"Jilly." I scooted forward and grasped her arm before she reached the trainer. Lowering my voice, I said, "I don't like it, either, but it's what the owner wants. Rosario has no choice."

When she started to yank away from me, I said, "I don't want you to get fired."

That stopped her long enough for Angel to catch up. "*Es verdad?*" he asked.

"*Sí,*" she replied quickly. "*Carrera de reclamo.*"

Someone had been studying her Spanish. She must really like this boy. The thought filled me with alarm, which was silly, right?

"How much?" she asked Rosario. "How much is she running for?"

"Five thousand," he said, "if we can find one that cheap on the overnights."

"I'll buy her!" Strong emotion tautened Jilly until she reminded me of an arrow about to be released from a bow.

Rosario's lips compressed. "The owner wants to run her, get her claimed, and hopefully win some purse money at the same time." Seeing Jilly's expression, he said, "I know, it sounds heartless, but that's how racing is sometimes."

"Then I'll claim her!"

"Jilly," I said, "you have to be a licensed owner with five thousand in cash in your owner's account. And you have to name a licensed trainer that will take over the filly's training." I could see her mind racing and headed her off. "And a minor can't obtain an owner's license."

"Dad will do it."

*Good luck with that.* Yet it was so wrong. The filly was quirky, not crazy. She was sweet, responded to kindness, and probably would make a wonderful riding horse for Jilly.

"I'll try to help you," I said.

Jilly threw her arms around me. "Thank you, Aunt Fia!"

Angel, who'd been following the exchange like he was watching a tennis match, broke into a smile. "*Muy bueno.* She make good horse for you."

Jilly whirled and headed back to Last Call's stall, and Angel followed. Rosario stared at me and shook his head.

"What are you going to tell Jilly if that filly breaks down when she runs? The girl's heart would be broken and your brother would be out five thousand. You won't get any thanks for that."

He was right. "I have to believe that won't happen," I said.

Rosario sighed. "Sometimes I hate this business. I'd like to see the filly go to your niece." He paused, his fingers fidgeting with his goatee. "Tell you what. Doctor McDougall owes me a favor. I'll see if I can get him to ultrasound the tendon. At least you'll know if the fibers are torn or not."

"Thanks, Rosario."

In the end, it didn't matter.


"Absolutely not!" Patrick said, that evening.

"But, *Dad,*" Jilly pleaded as she stood next to me in the living room.

Patrick, exasperation building on his face, sat on Rebecca's orange and cream print couch holding the *Miami Herald.* "I am *not* buying you a racehorse. They are too high-strung. And this one, for God's sake, has an *injury*."

He glared at me. "Fia, what were you thinking. Are you crazy?"

Refusing to get sucked into the argument, I kept my voice calm. "She's a nice filly, Patrick. Really beautiful, and she likes Jilly."

"I don't care." Patrick said.

"But, Dad," Jilly wailed, "she could go to the killers if we don't claim her."

"Not my problem. I offered to get you a nice riding horse. You weren't interested."

"I don't want a riding horse. I want Last Call for Love!"

Patrick slapped the newspaper onto the couch cushions. "No!"

"I hate you!" Jilly screamed. She dashed away from us through the living room. The front door slammed behind her.

# 31

An hour after Jilly stormed from the house, Patrick and I were more worried about her than we cared to admit. When she finally texted me to say she was at a neighbor's, I sagged with relief.

"I'm coming home," she wrote, "but tell Dad I am not speaking to him."

*No wonder I'd avoided this family stuff for so long.*

I returned to my room surprised to receive an encrypted message from Calixto, as well as an e-mail from Morales. Calixto's was a heads-up that I would be hearing from Morales about the two-year-old colt, Dixie Diamond.

"If you don't have a checking account in Kate O'Brien's name," he'd written, "open one. The TRPB will wire money for your share of the colt. Send account information to Brian ASAP."

I hadn't thought it would go this far, that cash would be available for a share purchase. After my meeting with Calixto and Gunny, I should have expected it. I wasn't sure how I felt about receiving orders from Calixto, a reminder that I was the junior agent.

I sent him a confirmation, then opened the e-mail from Morales.

"Kate," he'd written, "Dixie Diamond shipped in this morning and is available for inspection at Michael Serpentino's barn. He's recently had several excellent works at Palm Meadows and should run very soon. Are you available to look at him tomorrow morning at eleven?"

He explained how I could find his trainer's barn, which left me wondering at the duplicity of my life. "I shouldn't have any problem finding Mr. Serpentino's," I replied. *Huge understatement.*

I told him I'd see him the next morning and signed off. Now I just had to figure out how to change into Kate when I was supposed to be taking Jilly home from the track. Leaving my desk, I stepped into the hall outside my bedroom, and listened. I could hear music coming from Jilly's room and was relieved she was home.

I returned to my bedroom, checking my disguise bag to make sure I had everything I needed for the next day. After digging in my dresser drawer, I removed a tiny recording device and added it to the bag. Then I grabbed tubes of bleach and dye from a bathroom cabinet and colored my dark roots to electric blond. Using sharp scissors, I chopped my hair back to super short.

With the early training schedule and a new performance as Kate planned for the next day, it was time for bed.

In the morning, Rosario's vet performed an ultrasound of Last Call's tendon. As Jilly listened anxiously, the vet gave his findings to Rosario.

"I'm not seeing an actual tear, but with the heat she's got, the fibers in her flexor tendon have definitely been stressed. If the owner wants to get her claimed, I wouldn't advise another work. Put her in the first race you can."

The vet's warning about avoiding a work gave Jilly another dose of racing's harsher side. If the filly worked again, she could go lame or worse. The owner would be stuck with the horse and the day-rate charges until she healed, and Rosario would be left with a horse in his barn that couldn't run.

I'd already explained to Jilly that nothing she could say would change anything beyond Rosario asking her to leave. I shot her a warning glance when she started to speak. She closed her mouth. But her face was as easy to read as a billboard, with the words "furious" in bright red ink, about twelve feet tall.

"Jilly," I said, "why don't you start hosing down the shed-row so Julio can rake it?"

She gave me a dirty look, but uncoiled the hose, turned on the hydrant, and began painting the dry shedrow sand with a fine mist of water. As mad as she was, she loved the other horses and understood that keeping the dust down was an important part of protecting the horses' pulmonary functions. A horse that can't breathe easily is a horse that can't run.

"Listen," I called to her above the noise of the spraying water, "I've got an errand to run. I'll take you home in an hour or less, okay?"

"Whatever."

I glanced at my watch. It was almost ten thirty and Kate had to be on the other side of the barn by eleven. Walking fast, I reached the Mini and drove to the TRPB's rental house on Second Street.

Among the bagged items reserved for Kate was a pair of short red and black cowgirl boots, which I pulled on after struggling into a tight, stretchy animal-print top and designer jeans I'd found on eBay. The animal print had shades of red and green that worked well with my wig. I popped in the green contact lenses as fast as I could, applied makeup, including the painted-on lips, and left the rental.

A cab ride, and a walk through the backstretch later, I stepped onto Serpentino's shedrow, where Morales and Calixto stood together outside a stall.

By the time I reached them, Morales was on his phone, so I nodded at Calixto and peered in the stall at Dixie Diamond. The horse's dark gray coat was spectacularly dappled, the darkest spots gleaming like polished black diamonds. A moment later, Morales ended his phone call, I almost spoke to him, but Jilly came out of Serpentino's tack room with Angel. *Damn,* she had sharp ears. She'd recognize my voice.

I put my hand on my throat and whispered to Morales, "Sorry. Laryngitis."

"Poor baby," Morales said, giving my upper arm a brief pat. "Let me do the talking."

As Calixto watched our exchange, I thought I detected a twitch of amusement at the corners of his mouth.

When Jilly glanced at us, her eyes moved over Morales and me, quickly dismissing us. Her gaze came to a screeching halt at Calixto. The perfectly proportioned face, the hard body in a white polo, slacks, and woven leather shoes. If she'd had a paper fan, she would have waved herself with it.

Serpentino stepped out of his office and nodded at Morales. "Tony, let's give your friends a look at this colt. Angel, could you bring Dixie Diamond out, please?"

"*Sí, Señor Serpentino.*" The groom grabbed a lead shank, ducked into the colt's stall, and led him out.

Serpentino waved at the area beyond the shedrow. "Take him out on the grass."

Angel did, and we followed the horse off the shedrow, Jilly tagging behind. While Angel held Dixie, we walked around him, making our own assessments. He was a nice individual, with a fairly elegant head, attractive lines, good muscle, and straight legs.

In rapid Spanish, Calixto asked Angel if he would walk, then jog the horse. The colt displayed nice action. But a walk at the barn is light-years away from a drive down the stretch. There was no way to know what we had with this horse, but I smiled and gave Morales a thumbs-up.

"So you like him?" he asked.

"Yes," I whispered. "I'm in."

"I thought you'd like him," Morales said, looking at me intently. "Beautiful horse, beautiful woman. We should seal the deal with a drink."

I let my shoulders sag, feigning disappointment. "I need to go home, get rid of this." I pressed my fingers to my throat and grimaced slightly.

A trace of annoyance crossed his features, but shrugging, he said he understood. He pulled some folded papers from his wallet. "The horse will run very soon. This is the contract you'll need to sign and the invoice for your payment. The syndicate needs both by the twenty-sixth."

I smiled again and nodded, taking the papers and sliding them into my leather purse.

Serpentino told Angel to put the horse away, and when the groom was done, Jilly said, "Angel, let's get a burrito."

He grinned happily, and the two of them headed toward the road leading to the track kitchen. I was relieved when they were gone.

After stepping away from Calixto and me, Morales walked a few feet away with Serpentino. Keeping their backs to us, they had a hurried conversation. Calixto had remained standing next to me and for a moment, I breathed in his scent.

In a low voice he said, "I like you better with blue eyes."

I ignored his comment and walked quietly toward Morales, who had turned so I could see his profile. He appeared to be scowling at Serpentino. I only caught one sentence.

"I *told* you," Morales said, "I'll have more for you tomorrow." When he saw me, he clammed up, quickly smiling instead. Face composed into just-a-friendly-guy, he waved a magnanimous hand at Serpentino.

"My apologies. You two haven't been introduced. Kate, this is our trainer, Michael Serpentino."

I was glad when the trainer looked at me without a trace of recognition. But when he shook my hand his dry grasp was powerful and controlling, like being squeezed in the coil of a python. I had to force myself not to snatch my hand away. Instead I smiled. Damn, I was sick of smiling at these people.

# 32

That evening, to avoid a stressful meal with Patrick, I took Jilly out for Chinese. I was tired of the two of them and watching my lame attempts at conversation bounce off their wall of silence.

The long day had left me starving, and as soon as the waitress delivered them, I dipped a hot, crispy egg roll into a dish of tangy duck sauce, and took a bite. *Instant foodgasm.*

Across the table, Jilly poured a cup of dark tea from a red porcelain teapot. "After work," she said, setting the pot down, "Mr. Serpentino lets us use his computer to visit those English-Spanish translation sites."

"That's nice." I thought about how tense and angry Morales and Serpentino had appeared earlier. What had Morales been talking about when he'd told Serpentino he'd provide "more"?

"I'm helping Angel with his English," Jilly said after swallowing a bite of egg roll.

"Mmm." I had to remember to drop the check and BetBig contract in a FedEx box to be overnighted to Morales.

"So afterwards," Jilly continued, "these people showed up to look at Serpentino's new colt."

I stopped chewing. "Really?"

"Yeah. They were, like, a syndicate or something. But this one guy was *wicked* hot. You should have seen him. I mean he was *gorgeous*!"

"What were the other people like?"

Jilly looked at me like I was stupid. "I don't know. Just people. But this *guy* had the most beautiful eyes. I mean, he should, like, wear dark glasses so he doesn't start a stampede or something."

"Huh. I think it's nice you're helping Angel with the language," I said, changing the subject. "Do you like him?"

"Yeah," she said, her mouth breaking into a smile.

"So where's he from?"

"Mexico."

*Like Morales.*

"Why all the questions?"

I shrugged. "Just curious." Good to know Angel wasn't related to Serpentino.

Jilly put both hands on the table and leaned toward me. "Aunt Fia, why can't *you* claim Last Call for Love?"

*No beating around the bush with Jilly.*

"I don't have five thousand lying around. And even if I did, what would you do if your dad refused to stable the horse? You'd have to board, and that's expensive."

I could see the frustration crowding into her face. "Listen," I said, trying to head of an explosion, "if she runs poorly, whoever claims her may want to cut their losses and sell her for less. Whatever happens, we'll make another run at your dad. Just give it a few days, okay?"

She closed her eyes and exhaled. "Okay."

"Tomorrow's Christmas Eve, Jilly. You might want to start talking to your dad again."

"I *hate* Christmas," she said.

The holiday arrived, the dawn gray and bleak, the skies soon filling with rain and wind. Jilly and I got most of the morning off as the track was closed on Christmas, and the horses walked the shedrow. At the McKee residence, Patrick and Jilly were once again speaking to each other as the rain dripped down the outside of the living-room windows.

The highlight of the day was Jilly's squeal when she opened the necklace of horse charms I gave her. Patrick did not appear to hate his tie, and I was absolutely *thrilled* to receive a flannel nightgown and a pair of socks. Obviously, Patrick had done the shopping, allowing another glimmer of insight into Rebecca's abandonment of her husband. Still, I'd never forgive her for leaving Jilly.

That afternoon, Rebecca phoned to speak to Jilly. Her call made Jilly's and Patrick's expressions so tense, their faces looked ready to crack. Jilly took the phone to her room and didn't come out for a long time. Eventually, the snoop in me won out, and I eased open an extension. *Dial tone.* When Jilly did return, her eyes were slightly red and swollen.

"You okay?" I asked.

"Fine."

Maybe Jilly had asked her mother to buy the horse. I didn't pursue it. When I was her age, I hadn't wanted to talk about my mother, either.

We survived Christmas, and two days later, I received a new e-mail from Morales.

"Thanks for contract and payment," he'd written. "Dixie Diamond running in maiden special weight tomorrow. Sixth race. See you at our usual table!"

For her first race as an owner with BetBig, Kate needed something new to wear, so late that afternoon I went to the Aventura Mall and hit the sales racks, finding a black silk romper with lots of gold zippers and buttons. The damn thing was hot enough to burn my skin. Morales would love it.

---

Just before I stepped off the Gulfstream Park elevator that had ferried me up to Christine Lee's, I pulled down the zipper on the front of the romper enough to expose some serious cleavage. Trying not to totter on my new four-inch heels, I entered the plush lounge to see Morales wearing a fedora and sitting at the usual table by the granite-topped counter.

Behind him, the glasses and bottles on the bar still gleamed, and the bartender with the diamond stud in his ear gave me a little two-finger salute. Morales, busy with the *Form,* hadn't seen me yet, so I flagged a waitress and asked her to bring me a tonic water.

I hoped not to waste another afternoon gathering useless information. It had happened too often. But as I walked toward Morales, a sudden tingle of recognition stung me. The rakish fedora he was wearing. *I'd seen him in it before.* But where? Staring at his hat-rimmed profile brought a memory back to me. *Pimlico.* But when? I'd have to figure it out later.

Now I strolled brazenly toward him, my romper shorts so skimpy I had to resist a constant urge to tug them down to cover my upper thighs.

He looked up, breaking into a smile, his face flushing slightly as his eyes slid over my cleavage and legs.

"So," I said, sliding into the chair next to him, and crossing my legs, "do you think we'll win today?"

"I feel like I already have," he said, his eyes filled with heat. "I have a feeling we'll both get lucky today." He took a swallow of scotch, and inhaled a breath as if trying to get a grip on his libido. "Glad you got your voice back, Kate. You must be feeling good, because you look fantastic."

"We aim to please," I said with a slow smile, deciding it was time to push this guy for information. It would be easier to do if I kept him thinking with the wrong head. My virgin drink arrived and I lifted my glass to him. Keeping my voice low and slow, I said, "Here's to getting lucky."

Another flush stained his cheeks, but he remained silent.

I smiled, leaned forward, and stretched my hand toward his racing program. "May I?"

"Whatever you want, Kate."

A brief look at the page showed Dixie Diamond's morning line odds were long. Probably because he was a first-time starter, and several other maidens in his race had already run once or twice, showing good form.

"So, Tony, what should we bet on Dixie? Serpentino is a magician at bringing in the long shots. Should I bet a bundle?"

"Yes," Morales said, "but here's how we'll do it. I'll buy you a five hundred win bet on Dixie, and if he comes in, you come with me to the Diplomat for a drink."

Good thing I had a practiced poker face, because I wanted to throw my drink at his. I knew he kept a penthouse suite at the Westin Diplomat and why he wanted to take me there. I flashed a smile and took a slug of tonic water.

Morales grinned like a Cheshire cat stuffed with canary flesh. He seemed so certain he would win his bet with me. Serpentino must be using his best drug on Dixie.

I leaned forward again and slid my hand over his. "Tell me, Tony, how does Serpentino do it?"

He grasped my hand with his, rubbing the pad of his thumb over my palm. "I'll tell you after we win."

Like Calixto, his hands were well-manicured. But unlike Calixto's hands, his were delicate, almost effeminate. I didn't like this latest scene in Kate's ongoing act, but I forced a wicked smile. Looking up, I was relieved to see John and Mary Smith approaching our table. Her knowing eyes took in our joined hands and my outfit. Morales sat straighter, disengaging his hand from mine.

After the usual exchange of greetings, Mary said, "Where is Calixto today?"

I'd been wondering that myself, as my last communication with him had indicated he'd be at the race.

Morales said, "He couldn't make it today."

"We don't need *him*," I said. But where *was* he?

"Speak for yourself." Mary's mouth turned down in disappointment. Her mass of blond-streaked gray extensions were pulled into the same chignon with a different clip. This one appeared to be adorned with sapphires, and her blue dress matched it perfectly. But her perfume was musky and cloying.

John frowned at his wife. "Kate's right, we can have an equally enjoyable time without Mr. Coyune."

Mary rolled her eyes, muttered something under her breath, but perked up when she saw the waitress coming with a tray of drinks. She immediately downed a large slug, and John, not to be outdone, emptied almost half his glass.

I glanced at his strawberry nose and heavy jowls. When I'd run his background, I'd discovered he was formerly John Swolinsky, from New York, and had been the worst kind of slum landlord. He'd been arrested several times for criminal negligence, but the cases fell apart. I suspected he'd either threatened his accusers into dropping the charges or paid them off.

*Classy company you keep, Kate.* But since he'd never been named in a case involving the racetrack, he wasn't an issue for the TRPB

The afternoon rolled toward the sixth race with a venture to the buffet table, gambling on the first few races, and another round of drinks, courtesy of Morales. As soon as he left to make another bet, I whisked my glass filled with straight vodka to the bar, where I exchanged it for tonic water.

The bartender handed me a new glass and gave me a wink. "You're a clever lady," he said, "and a pleasure to watch in action."

I put my finger to my lips, and he said, "What happens at my bar, stays at my bar."

When Morales returned to our table, I was reading the *Daily Racing Form* and making pencil notations. He sat in the empty seat next to me and placed a Gulfstream win bet on the *Form* before me. I picked it up. Five hundred to win on the four horse in the sixth race, Dixie Diamond.

"If Dixie comes in," I said, "I hope I don't have to go to the IRS window to get my money."

"Oh, he'll win, but with the current odds it shouldn't be more than eight or nine thousand. Then you can come to *my* window."

"Can't wait," I said. We grinned at each other, and I felt dirty. Then I thought about Primal dropping at my feet, and a cleansing, angry resolve washed through me.

When his race came up, Dixie Diamond was so wired, he broke through the front of the starting gate while they were loading. The gate crew guy that loaded him managed to hang on to the horse, and with help from another starter, pushed him back into his slot and closed the door. A moment later, the field sprang from the gate and Dixie Diamond rushed to an early lead, led all the way, opened up in late stretch, and won by three.

"Holy shit!" I said, not needing to fake my reaction. The odds had dropped from twenty-to-one to fifteen-to-one, probably because the smart money knew Serpentino's horse would win. But my ticket would still pay $7,500, more cash than I'd ever held in my hand.

I beamed at Morales. "I should have brought a suitcase!"

"I'll buy you one," he said, staring at my barely concealed breasts, "and I'll stuff it for you with cash, perfume, and sexy lingerie."

The man was coming on to me like a freight train. I needed to get him totally inebriated and derailed. "We need another drink for the win," I said. *And a triple for the road.*

John and Mary were whooping it up across the table. I could only imagine how much they'd bet as both of them emptied their glasses and made a beeline for the IRS window—where the government took their share automatically out of your winnings if you won ten thousand or more.

"I'm buying the next round," I announced, leaving the table to flag down our waitress. I placed an order for everyone, specifying a double for Morales and tonic for me. I headed for the window, unsure if my small purse would hold that much money, especially with my gun lying in the bottom. Stuffing cash in my romper was a nonstarter. Fortunately, they wrote me a check that fit nicely in my wallet.

Mary and Morales returned proudly waving their big checks, but John came back with a bulging plastic bank bag like small businesses use to make their deposits. Maybe slum landlords prefer to deal in cash. He dumped the bag on the table with a loud *thwack* and ordered another round of drinks.

Our two drink orders arrived simultaneously, and the air around the table soon reeked of liquor. I hoped the fumes wouldn't give me a buzz. I also hoped Morales didn't plan on driving us to the hotel.

Finished with the thrill of his win, he looked at me with hungry eyes. Leaning close, he whispered, "Let's get out of here."

"There's a horse I want to bet in the eighth," I said with a slight pout. "And you should finish your drink, sweetheart." I traced a finger across his mouth. "You'll *need* it."

A slight shiver ran through him. "Sure. You collect your winnings after the eighth, and then I want to collect mine."

I raised my glass to him and drank a third of the liquid inside. He did the same, then watched me as I studied the eighth race in my program. "I like this one," I said pointing to the seven horse."

"*Bet* this one," Morales said, placing an unsteady finger on the nine horse.

The entry was trained by Roger Copper. My radar clicked into high gear.

"Copper's got tricks up his sleeve like Serpentino, doesn't he?"

"You're a smart girl," Morales said, his face close to mine. His breath stunk from dissolute living and too much scotch. "Bet him."

Mary watched us intently, so I flashed her my best I'm-totally-plastered smile and deciding what she couldn't hear wouldn't hurt me, I whispered to Morales, "Come on. You *promised* to tell me about their tricks."

"After we get to the Diplomat," he said, "I plan to teach you all kinds of tricks."

"We should drink to that," I said, tossing down the rest of my tonic water and trying not to gag.

His lips curled in a lascivious grin, then he sucked down the rest of his scotch.

My forced smile was the most difficult I'd ever pulled off. This guy was so disgusting. Still, I had to get him talking. But would it happen without letting him *touch* me?

# 33

I sprawled as if drunk in the backseat of a Lincoln Town Car as the driver maneuvered through late-afternoon traffic on the way to the Diplomat hotel. Morales sat next to me, holding a gold pillbox and working cocaine powder into a little paper cylinder. When he'd finished loading the white powder, he offered me the drug.

"Thanks, but I think I'll just thick to the vodka." I giggled as if my mispronunciation was hysterical.

"You're cute," he said, and sucked the powder into one nostril. He closed his eyes and rocked his head back, like he'd had a mini-explosion in his brain. His jolting movement knocked his fedora off. I stared at the hat where it sat on the seat next to him, and suddenly, the memory came to me.

I *had* seen him at Pimlico, sitting outside in an owner's box on Preakness Day, wearing the same brown fedora. The day my dad ran a horse in one of the Preakness undercard races. He'd been sitting with a woman . . . *Wendy Warner.* My thoughts raced like a herd of wild horses.

As the car rolled over a bridge crossing the Intracoastal Waterway, I turned away from Morales, glad I'd switched on the tiny recorder in my purse before I'd climbed into the limo. I looked out the Lincoln's passenger window as if fascinated by the speedboat cruising below the bridge, keeping my face averted until I had my thoughts under control.

Dad had seemed unhappy that day, unhappy about Wendy sitting with Morales. I hadn't really understood his discomfort before. I did now. My mother and Dad had been separated by that time, and now I was certain my suspicions from those days were correct. Dad and Wendy had been more than friends. They'd been lovers.

Sitting in the back of the limo, I struggled to grasp the significance of Morales being in the picture so long ago. He and Wendy back then; Wendy working with Serpentino now. My head whirled with questions, straining for answers.

Sooner than I wanted, the Lincoln reached the hotel's entrance. We went inside, and Morales stumbled across the cream-and-black-tiled floor of the lobby. He walked me to the elevator bank, and I was blasted skyward, building an almost painful pressure in my ears. The car didn't stop until we reached the thirty-third floor.

Morales led me down a long hall, unlocked a set of double doors, and waved me through a mirrored entry foyer. Finding myself in a large corner suite with dizzying views of the Atlantic Ocean, I walked to one of the huge plate-glass windows and gazed out. Toy tankers and cruise ships floated on the distant horizon. Far below, green palms swayed in the ocean breezes above a long expanse of sandy white beach.

"Wow!" I didn't have to pretend to be awestruck.

"The bank keeps the suite for me," he said. "I live here."

The world was so upside-down. I thought about my salary and mentally shook my head. No wonder some cops went on the take.

Without another word, Morales slipped behind me. Snaking his arms around me, he cupped my breasts, squeezing them with his soft hands. He pressed himself against my back. Grasping his hands and parting my lips as if aroused, I turned to face him. I traced a finger across his lips, trying to ignore the animal that appeared to be waking up inside his trousers.

"I don't want to rush this, Tony, I want to enjoy it. One more drink to celebrate my arrival?"

"Of course," he said. "Whatever you want." He was not annoyed by my delay. He was that sure he'd get what he wanted.

He walked unevenly across plush white carpeting, past a large column, through expensive, conversational groupings of furniture. There were fresh flowers, potted palms, and displays of coral and pottery. Stepping onto a terrace of marble, he stumbled to a black enamel bar against a far wall. I looked around for a lamp base or appropriately sized knickknack in case I needed to hit him. As a last resort, my gun was in my purse, but pulling it would blow my cover.

Taking a deep breath, I walked to the bar, noting the pair of candlesticks that stood at one end. I leaned forward and put my elbows on the countertop as Morales poured drinks. At this point, I could have used some vodka.

"Tony," I said with a pout. "You *promised* to tell me about Serpentino and Copper. What is their secret?"

He finished making the new drinks and raised his glass of scotch to me. His expression changed. The lust faded, replaced with a furtive, excited look, the kind people get when about to reveal a delicious secret. His anticipation was so great, he forgot to hand me my vodka.

"Are you familiar with the drug demorphin, Kate?"

"No," I lied. "What is it?"

He launched into a slurred explanation about frog juice, all but rubbing his hands in glee as he told me. "But we have some-

thing better! An unknown frog. We call its secretion 'blue juice.'
And whereas dermorphin can be anywhere from forty to one
hundred times stronger than morphine, this stuff is always at least
ninety times stronger than morphine! And it imparts an extraordinary sense of well-being to the animal."

"You're saying it makes them high as a kite?"

"Yes, but much faster than a kite!" His laugh was almost
girlish.

I prayed my voice recorder was working. "That's awesome,"
I said. "Is that how Primal won?"

"Yes, but he was weak and the drug was too strong for him."
He waved a hand, dismissing the death of Primal. "But you saw
with a strong colt like Dixie, it's not a problem. And best of all,
there's no test for blue juice. We will make so much *money* off
this drug!"

I had the bastard now. It was time to go.

"Tony, you're incredible," I gushed.

He reached for me, but I sidestepped. "I need to take a powder." I leaned forward, grabbed my vodka, wobbled unsteadily,
and headed for the bathroom. I hoped there was another exit from
the suite.

As I stepped into the suite's marble plumbing extravaganza,
the doorbell rang in the entry foyer. I closed the bathroom door
with an audible click, poured half my drink down the sink, and
eased the door open a crack. Morales was disappearing into the
foyer, so I slipped outside with my drink and followed.

"I've told you not to come here," Morales hissed. "I have
a *guest*."

"Tony, your phone's been off all day."

*Wendy's voice?*

"That's my business," he said, his tone dismissive.

"But I'm really worried. They pulled an awful lot of blood
from Dixie Diamond in the test barn. I'm afraid the lab—"

"I told you they won't find anything."

"I don't want to go to jail, Tony." Her voice was almost a wail. "Please, I am begging you to let me out of this!"

"Keep your voice down. Get a grip, for God's sake. The drug isn't even illegal yet."

Was my recorder getting this? I crept closer until I saw them reflected in the foyer's mirror. Wendy's face was pale and twisted with fear. But if I could see them . . . I backed up until their figures disappeared.

"Find another vet, *please*."

"Shut up," Morales whispered angrily. "Unless you want to do serious jail time as an accessory to murder, just shut up!"

"You *bastard*." Her voice broke and it sounded like she was crying.

"Get it together, you old bitch, and do your job."

I heard the suite door open and slam close. I ran back to the bathroom and after easing the door shut, I locked it.

Moments later, Morales was just outside. "Kate, are you coming out?"

I made a loud retching noise. "Oh, Tony, I'm *so* sick. Oh." I followed with more sounds of vomiting. I flushed the toilet. "I can't leave the bathroom," I moaned. "I'm too sick."

"Oh, for God's sake." He didn't sound happy. "I'll be in the living room."

I would sit chilly and wait for that opening. Before too long, the sound of snoring drifted to the bathroom. Cracking the door open, I peeked out. Morales was sprawled on one of the sofas, out cold.

Quickly and quietly, I padded around the suite, my four-inch heels grasped in one hand. One of the two bedrooms had been made into an office. A long carved table acted as a desk, but Morales had been careful, and I found nothing among his papers and files related to racetrack drugging. The materials proved to be take-home work from the Mexican bank that employed him.

I opened drawers and found pencils, pens, and notepads without notes. I lifted his blotter. Nothing underneath. Then I picked up the hotel phone and a small piece of paper fluttered to the desk with handwriting I was sure belonged to Morales. A phone number and the name Valera. *Bingo!*

I put the note in my purse and fled from the suite. I caught an elevator and on the way back down, shoved the high heels onto my feet and pulled the romper's zipper up as high as it would go. Then I clacked across the tiled lobby, and exited the chilly, air-conditioned hotel.

Outside, the salty ocean air enveloped me with warmth. I drew in a long breath, and for a wild moment, I wanted to laugh. I stifled the urge.

A cab drove up to the entrance and I climbed in. Giving the address of the TRPB rental, Kate made her permanent exit from South Florida.

# 34

As soon as I got to the rental, I stripped and took a hot shower, relieved to shampoo my hair where the wig had left it sweaty and plastered to my scalp. If only I could erase the memories of Morales's soft hands as easily as the streaming water rinsed the soap from my hair and skin. I couldn't wipe out the desperate look on Wendy's face, either.

Wouldn't the FBI step into the arena if this blue juice showed up out of state? Couldn't they give Wendy immunity if she turned on Morales and the rest of them? Yes, I nodded to myself as I cranked off the water. That's how this should play out.

As soon as I was dressed, I called Gunny and dove right in.

"I've got Morales on tape talking about the new improved dermorphin."

"Fia . . . that's *excellent*." I'd never heard him sound excited before. He also sounded relieved. After a beat, he said, "And you're all right?"

"I'm fine, but I'm done playing Kate. Morales's sexual expectations are already out of control." I stared at the red wig I'd tossed on the bed.

"You're right. That job is over. Now tell me what happened."

"I will," I replied, "but first, where was Calixto today?"

So briefly that I wasn't sure it even happened, Gunny hesitated. "He got called away on another job."

"More important than *this?*"

"*Equally* important, Fia. He's . . ."

"He's what?" I asked.

"Let it go. Besides, after what you accomplished today, we don't need him trailing Morales so closely."

After what I'd risked earlier, I did not like being left out of the loop. Didn't Gunny trust me yet? I gritted my teeth. "Won't Morales wonder where Calixto disappeared to?"

"Calixto can stay in touch by texting."

I dropped it and asked him about Wendy receiving immunity.

"It doesn't work like that, Fia. You know the TRPB has no power to make arrests. We are mainly an information gathering agency. We will take this to the Florida Division of Pari-Mutuel Wagering. Then it's in their hands."

So the information I'd worked so hard to obtain would be left to the decisions and actions of political appointees? People who ran the gambling machine for horse racing, dog racing, and Indian gaming? I hated this. How corrupt were these people likely to be?

"But what about the FBI, or the DEA?" I asked.

"What Morales said to Doctor Warner was right," Gunny replied. "The drug isn't illegal yet. It has to be added to the Association of Racing Commissioners International's list and to the Florida Division of Pari-Mutuel Wagering's list of prohibited substances. And it takes time. Bills have to be passed at the state level. There's a lot of expensive testing that will have to be done."

His words made me squeeze my eyes shut in frustration. "But horses are *dying*."

"We do what we can, Fia."

His resigned tone made me furious. "Racing needs a single authority with consistent rules," I said. "Why couldn't the TRPB be that authority?"

"I hear you, Fia, but there are too many fiefdoms, too many people determined to control money they can use to feather their own nests. People are working on change, but the money and politics stretch across dozens of states and hundreds of jurisdictions . . . it's an uphill battle."

I felt deflated. It was time to go home and drink the vodka I'd avoided all day.

Forty-five minutes later, I stood in Patrick's kitchen, tossing back Stolichnaya on ice. The drink helped so much, I decided to make a second one. Feeling slightly more optimistic, I wrote up a report for Gunny about the events with Morales, and sent it as an encrypted e-mail. After making a copy of the tape recording, I forwarded it as well.

I wondered how the Bluesters were doing. The pathologist at the University of Oklahoma would probably think I was crazy checking on their welfare, but I planned to call his office the next day.

I lay in bed that night with too many scenes playing in my head. Cody's body in the barn, Primal's death, Wendy's frightened face in the mirror, and Morales's disgusting hands and hot, polluted breath. I tried to quiet my mind, and think how to proceed.

The evidence I'd found linking Morales to Valera, and his voice on tape talking about "blue juice" was huge. If I could find a way to help Wendy escape Morales's tangled net, maybe she would talk. And what was with him threatening to blackmail her for a connection to murder? I wanted to sit down and brainstorm again with Gunny and Calixto. Where was Calixto, anyway?

Sometime in the middle of the night, I finally fell asleep.

At the track the next morning, Rosario took me aside and spoke quietly.

"The secretary put a five-thousand claimer going six furlongs on the overnight." If there were such a thing as a guilty-looking rabbit, Rosario's face would be the perfect illustration. "I entered Last Call in the race, Fia. She's running tomorrow."

"Oh." I stared at the ground. *Jilly will freak.* I looked along the shedrow, and saw her walking toward us. She was leading Last Call who'd galloped a few minutes earlier. Jilly stroked the horse's neck as they walked toward us.

This wouldn't be pretty. "I'll tell her," I said, "after she puts the filly away."

He nodded, no doubt relieved not to be the messenger bearing bad news. He disappeared into his office. When Jilly finished with Last Call, I just wanted to get it over with and told her.

Her eyes heated with anger. "I can't believe you people are doing this!"

"It's not Rosario's choice, Jilly. It's what the owner wants."

"Then the owner's an idiot!"

"That may be true, but it doesn't change anything. Anyway, Last Call might not get claimed."

The flicker of hope in Jilly's eyes made me feel treacherous. Had I just set her up for more disappointment?

Jilly glared at me. "If nobody takes her, the next time, I swear I'll claim her myself. But tomorrow . . . there's no *way*." Her last words were almost a wail.

"I'm sorry. I wish I could change this."

"Yeah, well, whatever." Jilly pivoted away from me and stalked off toward Angel's side of the barn.

I sank onto a nearby hay bale, hating that I'd let Jilly down, feeling like I had no control over anything. Pulling my phone, I placed a call to Zanin, hoping he was safely back from his under-cover job.

"Hey, Fia," He sounded so happy to hear from me, I almost felt guilty.

"Good to hear your voice," I said. "I get worried when you go undercover. Is it over?"

"Yeah. It was a farm where they were starving the animals. I documented it. Film and audio. The SPCA raided the place yes-terday and removed the livestock. Dogs, too."

"People are really sick," I said. "Those horses that were killed before Christmas? I never heard any more about that. You got anything new?"

"I know it was Valera or his people. Those assholes butch-ered three horses in three locations and left no evidence. Nothing to track them with." He made a little noise of frustration. "Fia, when can I see you?"

I didn't want to lead this man on, but I did want to see him. "Um, how about tomorrow? Could you come over in the eve-ning?" I asked.

"To your *brother's* house? I was thinking about taking you out somewhere."

"The truth is, we could use your support." I told him about the probable claim and the effect it would have on Jilly. "If that happens, it would be really nice to have you around. She'll prob-ably be at Patrick's throat and you could—"

"Defuse the situation?"

"Exactly," I said. "But there's something else. Remember when I told you I'm still in law enforcement?"

"Yes."

"Some things have happened that might tie in with Valera. We may be able to nail the son of a bitch."

"Music to my ears. Tell me."

"I'd rather not on the phone."

"Fine. I'd rather hear it in person, anyway. Tomorrow evening, babe."

I remained on the hay bale for a while, looking along the line of stalls as the horses tugged on their hay nets, grinding the grass with their molars. Luceta's nose and lips worked at the bottom of her net. She snatched at the tufts so vigorously bits of hay fell from the top, decorating her ears and forelock like mistletoe.

Nothing could soothe me like the sounds and scents of a barn full of contented horses. I let the relaxation and sense of peace restore me before rising to round up Jilly and head home.

# 35

That night a cold front blasted down the East Coast from Canada, and the day of Last Call's race dawned chilly. A stiff wind blew dark clouds over Hallandale Beach until a dismal lid covered the racetrack and colored it gray.

After I gave Last Call an easy jog, it was painful to watch Jilly's face as she cooled out the filly for what would probably be the last time. We had decided to stay at the track until the race went off at two, and I used the time to call the pathologist in Oklahoma and inquire about the well-being of my Bluesters.

"They're fine," he said when I reached him. "Quite extraordinary, really. I still haven't been able to identify the species. But I did reach a colleague in Paraguay. He looked at the photos, and he's never seen anything like them before, but he's making inquiries."

"What happens to the frogs?" I asked.

"Do you need them back?"

*Need* them? Hardly. "Um, yes," I said. "They're evidence."

"We'll get them to you when their tests are finished."

"They need to be alive," I said.

"No problem."

I thanked him and disconnected. I was such a sucker for animals.

That afternoon, as post time drew close, I thought about the Not for Love filly my dad had trained before he died. I'd been smacked so hard by his murder, I didn't know what had happened to the horse. Probably Dad's whole string had been picked up by new trainers. While grieving for my life that had changed forever, I'd set about divorcing myself from the backstretch. I'd been so lost back then.

Dwelling on the senseless murder had stoked the rage that still burned inside, and left the acid question "why" unanswered. That year, I'd enrolled in the criminal justice program at Towson University in Maryland, and after obtaining my degree, I'd applied to the Baltimore PD.

My thoughts were interrupted when a horse rattled a feed bucket, and a loudspeaker clicked on, calling horses for the first race. With a sigh, I made an effort to let go of the past. Maybe Gunny was right, and we should do what we could. It was better than nothing.

When post time drew near, Jilly and I walked up to the grandstand and stood along the rail waiting for Julio and the other grooms to lead the horses over from the backstretch. Ten horses were entered, and Last Call's odds were eight-to-one.

Eager, beer-swilling fans milled around us, munching on fries and hot dogs. As they chattered happily in the warm sun that had broken through the clouds, Jilly and I stared glumly at the long stretch of empty sand before us.

Rosario was watching from a box seat with Last Call's owner. Knowing it was useless, I glanced through the crowd to see if I could spot a trainer who might have put in a claim. I couldn't, and all too soon the horses appeared.

During the post parade, Last Call's coat gleamed, and she held her head high, surveying her competitors with interest. Jilly's teeth chewed so hard on her lower lip, I almost expected to see drops of blood. Moments later, the field was sent to the gate to fight to the finish.

When the race went off, Last Call's jockey sat chilly, like he'd been instructed. The filly surged into third place as the field raced up the backstretch, and the horses maintained that order to the top of the stretch where Last Call's jockey put his whip into action, striking her twice. Her tail lashed like an angry cat. She stopped running.

"What's wrong," Jilly cried. "Is it her tendon?"

"She doesn't like the whip," I said. Rosario had instructed the jockey not to use the whip, but apparently the rider thought he knew better.

The guy hit her twice more before he decided to follow instructions. Once he started hand riding the filly, she came back like a bullet, regaining ground, and finishing second.

"Damn, she would have won if he hadn't hit her," I said.

I was excited to see our filly run so well, and I felt like celebrating. Until I remembered. With Jilly on my heels, I hurried to where Last Call's number was posted on the rail, the spot where her jockey would dismount, and Julio would remove her bridle before leading her home. She galloped back looking pleased with herself, her nostrils blowing, her neck arched. Jilly's face glowed with pride as she watched.

Two men approached as our jockey dismounted. One was a track official, the other a groom I didn't know. The official spoke to Julio, who nodded with resignation. The other groom put his halter on Last Call and led her away.

"No," Jilly said softly. "*No.*"

But she stood still, remaining quiet, apparently realizing that histrionics would serve no purpose. I was proud of her. She was growing up.

"Julio," I said, "who does that groom work for?"

"Copper."

"Who is Copper?" Jilly asked quickly.

"He's a good trainer," I lied. No point in making it worse.

The groom had led Last Call about fifty feet away when she stopped, turned her head back to stare at Jilly, and whinnied anxiously. My view blurred as my eyes filled with tears. Next to me, Jilly started sobbing. The new groom jerked Last Call's head forward and got her walking again. Then she was gone.

As soon as I could, I drove Jilly home, but not without an argument. She'd wanted to go to Copper's barn to see Last Call and I'd refused. Rosario had patiently explained that having run second, Last Call would be in the test barn, and Jilly would not be allowed in there.

"Besides," Rosario had said, "she belongs to a new owner now, has a new trainer, and he won't want you in his barn."

As I drove north, Jilly's sorrow hardened into anger and she refused to speak. I tried to think what words would have soothed me at her age and came up empty. Arriving home, Jilly ran to her room. She closed her door and I heard the lock click. Shrugging, I decided I needed some alone time myself and went to my room.

I'd just turned on my laptop when my cell rang. The caller's number was not familiar to me. The voice was.

"Fia, I'm in trouble," Wendy said. "I don't know who to call." Her voice faltered. She sounded so desperate. "You used to be a cop, so I thought . . . oh, maybe this is a mistake."

"Wendy, wait. Let me help. What's wrong?"

"I . . . I'm scared."

"Are you in danger? If you are, you should go to the police."

"No! No police. If I could just *talk* to you. I need to think this through with someone. Someone I can trust."

"Okay. Where are you?"

"I'm still at Gulfstream. I have to stay until after the last race. I could meet you somewhere."

I didn't want to wait. "I'll come to you. I'm leaving now."

"Oh, God, thank you, Fia."

Her voice broke and I could hear her crying. How does a person dig a hole so deep? Could I help her climb out? I scribbled a note for Patrick and Jilly, shoved my gun, handcuffs, and digital recorder into my purse, and fired up the Mini. Moments later, I zoomed out of Southwest Ranches.

When I sped through Gulfstream's stable gate into the backstretch, I called Wendy's number. It rang about six times and went to voice mail. She might be scoping a horse, and unable to answer. I left her a message, then started searching for her white truck along the dirt lanes crisscrossing the backstretch.

When I found her truck, I wasn't pleased to see it parked outside Serpentino's barn. Why *his* barn? He hadn't had a horse running, and his truck wasn't there. I drove around to Rosario's side, cut my engine, and slid my gun and handcuffs into my vest pockets. I climbed out of the Mini and walked around the end of Rosario's barn to Serpentino's shedrow.

It was after five thirty, and Serpentino's help had already come and gone. The horses were finishing their feed, rattling their buckets as they licked out the last bits of grain. Their hay nets were full. The aisle had been watered and raked, leaving the sandy dirt smooth and clean, which is why the two sets of footprints were as obvious as road signs.

My gaze followed their path. They led to Serpentino's office. Instead of being locked, his door was ajar. I didn't like it and pulled my gun. I crept closer, staying near the barn wall. Reaching the door, I strained to listen. I heard scuffling noises and a muffled sound of fear followed by two soft cracks.

A man with long shaggy hair and yellow-tinted goggles burst from the office so close to me I could smell the gunpowder on him. He had a semiautomatic with a suppressor shoved in the waistband under his open shirt. Shock froze his expression when he saw me. He grabbed for his gun.

But mine was already against his temple. "Forget it, asshole," I said. "Hands behind your back. Do it!" He did, and I cuffed him. Then I snatched his gun, shoving it into my waistband. "Turn around," I said. "Back inside. *Move* it!" Why did I feel like I knew this guy?

My thoughts slammed to a halt when I saw Wendy lying face down on the floor. Blood was pumping out of an exit wound on her back. She was still alive.

"On your knees," I shouted at her assailant. "All the way. Face down!"

I twisted back to Wendy. The son of a bitch had tied her hands and as I gently turned her over, I found duct tape covering her mouth. Her eyes fluttered open and she tried to speak. I knelt next to her and pulled the tape back.

"Fia," she whispered, "I'm sorry. Mason wasn't supposed to die."

*What?* Why was she talking about Dad?

"Wendy, don't try to talk."

She shook her head. "Please, forgive me, Fia. I didn't *know*." Her voice sounded so weak.

"Wendy, do you know who killed my father?

The man on the floor started to rise.

"I still have my gun on you, fuckhead. Get down." He sank to the floorboards. Wendy tried to speak. I leaned closer to her.

"I'm sorry, Fia, I never thought . . ." Her breath caught and she closed her eyes.

I clutched at her shoulders. "Wendy, if you know who killed Dad, *tell* me." I put my ear to her lips.

"The man . . . the man who—" she coughed and blood trickled from her mouth. A sigh escaped her before a glaze shut off the light in her eyes.

*Goddamn it.* I stared at the man who'd shot her. Something . . . his scent when he'd tried to rush past me. Recognition clicked into place. I reached over, grabbed his hair and wrenched it. The shaggy wig came off in my hands.

*Fucking Morales.* If I'd disliked him before, I hated him now. I had played him for a fool, busted him for murder, and I wanted him to *know* it.

But as my glance shifted to Wendy's crumpled body, my sense of satisfaction disintegrated. Unleashing my anger wouldn't bring her back. There was a chance I hadn't blown my cover with Morales, and this case was far from over.

Still, I couldn't resist nudging him with my boot. "The county prosecutor," I said, "will love how your wig adds *premeditated* to his charges. Can you say *murder one*, asshole?"

Morales remained silent, his gaze fixed on the floor. I took a deep mental breath and pulled my cell to call track security. I told them there'd been a shooting and to get an ambulance.

"Call the Broward County Police," I said. "We need someone from homicide. A woman's been murdered."

# 36

Since Broward County's Hallandale Beach PD is located just across South Federal Highway from Gulfstream's main entrance, the cops arrived almost as fast as the racetrack security guards. It didn't take long for the county police to stuff Morales and me into separate squad cars and hustle us over to headquarters.

As we pulled away from Serpentino's barn, I looked back to where crime scene lights already spilled from the stall where Wendy lay dead. I was still consumed by a desire to help her, and felt like I was abandoning her. How I wished she'd told me what she knew about Dad's murder. Too late for any of that. I could only chill. Wait for that next opening.

They put me in an interview room on the second floor in the homicide division. I sat there a long time while two detectives came and went, alternately questioning me, and making calls to the Baltimore PD and the TRPB to verify my story.

One of the homicide detectives, a woman named Bailey, entered the room not long before they finally released me.

"You got any idea," she asked, "what this Morales guy is so afraid of?"

"Afraid?"

The detective had short, spiky red hair, with a personality to match. "I'm asking you," she said, "if you know why he's so afraid to talk?"

"He doesn't want to go to jail?" *Fia, queen of the smart answer.*

Bailey rolled her eyes. "Come on. Help me out here. It's more than fear of prosecution and jail time. He's afraid of something else."

And suddenly I knew. "That would be Luis Valera," I said, and told her what I knew about the man and his operation.

"Okay," Bailey said, "we'll try and see if Valera's name gets a response out of him." But when Bailey finally released me, she told me that Valera's name had resulted in Morales lawyering up and refusing to say another word.

Around eight thirty that evening, a beat officer drove me back to my Mini, where I checked my cell and found a text from Gunny asking me to phone him. I could only imagine the calls he'd gotten from the Hallandale Beach PD. As soon as the Mini was rolling out of the backstretch, I pressed his speed dial.

He wouldn't let me talk about Wendy until I assured him I was okay. After that, I plowed in. "Morales was the blue juice man. He's the one who gave it to Wendy, then she'd provide it to trainers like Serpentino and Roger Copper."

"That solves part of our puzzle," Gunny said, "but the police will be more interested in proving their homicide case than helping us or the Florida Division of Pari-Mutuel Wagering."

"True." I paused a beat. "I'm not sure where we go from here. Morales isn't talking and Wendy's . . . dead."

I had to brake for an older woman who'd slowed her car to a standstill in the lane in front of me. I'd seen a lot of old-timers driving like lost turtles in South Florida. As I drove around her, she was squinting through thick glasses, sticking her neck forward to peer through her windshield like she wasn't sure where to go. *She could get in line behind me.*

"Gunny," I said, "Valera will have to find a way to sell this drug."

"He will." He paused and I was pretty sure I heard him going for his antacid tabs. "Fia, do you think Morales recognized you as Kate?"

I thought a moment. As Kate, my voice had been breathless and flirtatious. Today, Morales had heard a tough, angry Baltimore cop, and I didn't look or act like Kate.

"No."

"Okay then, you stay on top of Serpentino. Like you said, Valera and the others are greedy. They'll have to make a move. We'll need to be ready."

By the time I parked in front of Patrick's house, I was beat. Too much thinking, too much action. So many memories of Dad and the past had been raked up throughout the long day and now they simmered on a mental back burner. As I stared through the dark yard at the warm light spilling from Patrick's windows, his house suddenly felt like my home. My thoughts distilled into a sharp realization—Patrick and Jilly were not only family, they were precious, and not to be lost.

I hurried across the terrace, and when I opened the front door, I was startled to see Zanin sitting on the orange and cream couch with Patrick. They were drinking beer and watching a football game on Patrick's big-screen TV.

With all that had happened, I'd forgotten I'd asked Zanin over. At the moment, he seemed totally absorbed by the game. Patrick appeared more involved with trying to ignore Jilly who stared at him from a cross-legged position on the carpet. She looked like she was trying to kill him with stony eyes and silence. She did not greet me.

"Don't everybody jump at once," I said.

Jilly scowled.

Zanin held up a hand in greeting, or maybe it was a just-a-minute gesture. "Thirty seconds left in the game," he said.

"Jilly's not speaking to me," Patrick said.

I should go back to the track. Maybe the horses would be glad to see me. I went into the kitchen, washed my hands, and made a stiff vodka with lots of ice and a juicy squeeze of lime. Returning to the living room, I sat in a turquoise chair and put my feet up on the matching leather ottoman. At least Rebecca's stuff was comfortable.

I sipped my vodka until a roar from the TV accompanied by those obnoxious horns indicated the game was over. Zanin slumped with disappointment. His team must have bombed.

Zanin rose, stretched, then walked across the room. He pushed my feet to one side of the ottoman before sitting on the other edge.

He glanced at Jilly who was still glaring at her father. "So, Jilly, I guess you're pretty upset about that horse being claimed today."

"What do you care?" She impaled Zanin with a nasty look.

Zanin shrugged. "I'm sorry you lost her, Jilly. It always hurts to lose a friend. But at least she's not being starved to death or mistreated like some animals I've seen lately."

"You don't get it. I love that horse. If Dad had only—"

"Jilly," Patrick said, his voice sharp, "you told me you didn't want a horse until we caught whoever's killing them around here. Zanin told me three more horses were killed just last week, before Christmas."

"So what? It's not like you knew that when you refused to claim her. *Did* you?"

"No," Patrick said. "But I told you I didn't want you owning a hot-blooded racehorse, and I still don't!"

"Screw you," she shouted, storming away from us and disappearing down the hall.

"Jesus, Patrick," I said, "you didn't have to run her out of the room."

Patrick rose abruptly from the couch, stalked across the carpet, and went out the sliding door to the pool terrace. Before he
closed the door, I heard an engine idling out on Lead Pony Lane.
Then a car door slammed. Probably someone dropping off a
neighbor.

"That went well," I said to Zanin before dropping my head
into my hands and massaging my sore temples with my palms.
"It's been a really bad day, Zanin."

"I could tell that when you walked in. It looked like something was going on beyond the Jilly thing. What's up?"

I gazed at his face a moment. Sitting close to this man who
was straightforward and kind was a nice change. No hidden
agenda, just a good guy who wanted to save animals. I made a
decision. I wouldn't be working Gulfstream as Kate anymore, and
Zanin knew as much about Valera as any of us. I told him.

He stared at me like I was as odd a specimen as the Bluesters.
"Damn, Fia, you could have been shot by this Morales guy."

"Well, I wasn't." I closed my eyes a beat. "If only I could have
stopped what he did to Wendy."

His eyes narrowed. "I can't believe you've been working
double undercover. This whole Kate act, the danger you put
yourself in. Are you going to be safe from this Serpentino guy at
the track?"

"Sure. He still thinks I'm an exercise rider."

"But the woman, Wendy. She knew you used to be a cop.
Don't you think she might have told someone?"

"I think she was too afraid to say anything, and even if she
did, I've been open about quitting the department and going back
to my racetrack roots."

Zanin lay a calloused hand on my arm. "Just tell me you
have no reason to go back to Flamingo Road."

"No way," I said, "that place gives me the creeps. We'll have
to wait for Valera to come out of the basin with his blue juice. Once
we catch him in the act, we can get the cops to raid the place."

Zanin rubbed at his forehead, his expression doubtful. "That may be harder than you think. You know they hate going into the basin, and a drug that's used on horses ain't gonna be high on their priority list. Nothing to do with animals ever is."

I sighed. "I can't think about this anymore. My brain is fried."

He nodded and squeezed my arm gently. "Let me know if I can help you, Fia."

As Zanin spoke, Patrick came in through the sliding door. "You two look cozy," he said. "I'm going to check on Jilly, see if she'll at least say good night to me. Then I'm turning in."

Zanin stood to leave, and the three of us made good-bye noises. Patrick headed down the hall, and as I walked Zanin to the front door, Patrick thundered back into the living room.

"Jilly's gone!"

"Are you *sure*?" I asked.

"She's not in her room, I didn't see her outside, and her backpack's gone."

I remembered the car I'd heard on Lead Pony Lane. "Is there anyone that might have picked her up?"

"At ten o'clock at *night*?" Patrick's voice was shrill. He called Jilly's cell. It went directly to voice mail. He left an angry message telling her to call him immediately.

*That would help.*

"Did she leave a note?" Zanin asked.

Patrick rushed back to Jilly's room while Zanin and I searched the kitchen. We didn't find a note. But when I checked my room, I saw Jilly's handwriting on a yellow sticky pad on my desk.

Angel called. My filly bowed and Copper is getting rid
of her. We are going to rescue her.

As worried as I was about her, if I could have somehow reached out far enough I would have smacked her.

# 37

The three of us read Jilly's note and Patrick's face flushed with anger. "Damn it, Zanin, this is your fault. You've infected her with all this 'save the animals' bullshit."

Zanin stared at Patrick without answering.

"That's not fair," I said. "Zanin's got nothing to do with her being so headstrong."

"Well, if anyone knows about headstrong, it's *you*, Fia."

"Are you two going to fight, or look for Jilly?" Zanin asked.

"You're right," Patrick said, visibly deflating. "I'm sorry."

Zanin held up the keys to his Tahoe. "I'll drive you both to the track."

"There may be no point," I said. "The horse may be gone already. Let me try to reach Copper."

I switched my phone to speaker and called the stable gate where the duty guard gave me a cell number for Copper. When he answered his phone, I explained the situation and asked if Last Call was still in his barn.

"Oh, that one. Dumbest claim I ever made. Tendon big as a

grapefruit by the time we got her to the barn." He paused, as if contemplating his bad luck. "I already shipped her out. And those kids have no business going into my barn, anyway."

"You know how kids are," I said, hoping to defuse him. "They're crazy enough to try and find her. Can you tell me where you sent her?"

A cold silence. Then, "That's my business."

"Mr. Copper," I said, "they're just kids, and it's late at night. Please, if you know anything . . ."

"If they're out joy-riding and getting into trouble, that's your problem."

*Nice, Copper, really nice.* "If they go missing, the police may be coming to *you* with questions. Why not just tell me what you know?"

Copper hung up.

"What a prick," Zanin said.

Patrick's shoulders sagged, as if he were already defeated.

I called the stable gate duty guard back and asked if he had an address for Angel.

"Serpentino's groom? He lives here, in the groom's quarters."

"Does he have a car?"

"Let me see," the guard said. "Yeah, he has one listed. You want the tag number?"

"Please." I wrote it down, thanked him, and hung up.

"Between us, we've got three cars and three cell phones," I said. "Let's map out some areas to search. We can split up. I'm going to the track."

Patrick frowned. "But that guy said the horse isn't there."

"But Angel might be in his room."

"With *Jilly*? Forget it, Fia, I'm coming with you."

"Okay, okay," I said with a sigh. I hoped he didn't mind participating in a little breaking and entering, because I planned to search Copper's office.

A few minutes later, as we parked outside the stable gate, Patrick tried Jilly's cell again, but the call routed to voice mail. We approached the guard and explained our predicament. He placed a call to his supervisor, then gave us Angel's room number.

We hurried up a set of stairs on the side of the groom's concrete building to the third floor. Hustling down a motel-like walkway, we searched the room numbers until we found Angel's.

A light from inside filtered through makeshift curtains along with the sound of salsa music. I knocked on the door, and the groom with the thick mustache who worked for Serpentino opened it. I should have realized Angel would have a roommate. The last time I'd seen this guy he'd been pushing a wheelbarrow and smirking at me when his boss had told me not to mess with his help. Peering over the guy's shoulder into the tiny room, I didn't see Angel.

"*Hola,*" I said. "We're looking for Angel."

"He's not here."

"Do you know where I can find him?"

"No."

Gritting my teeth, I said, "Does Angel have a cell phone?"

"No. He pay to use kitchen phone." With a smug look and a classic Latin shrug, he said, "I can't help you."

Next to me, Patrick seemed to expand. "Listen, jerk, he's got my daughter with him, and I'm not leaving here until you tell us where he is!"

*Go, Patrick.*

Like a typical bully, when seriously confronted, the groom scuttled back, dropping his gaze to the floor. *Not smirking now.*

He darted a worried glance at Patrick. "Angel didn't say where he was going. I haven't seen him since this afternoon. I don' want no trouble."

"You think he's telling the truth?" Patrick asked me.

"Yeah." It wasn't like we could beat more information out of him. "Let's go."

We raced down the stairs and back to the car. After rolling

through the gate into the deserted backstretch, we headed for Copper's barn. We climbed from the Mini and walked to his shedrow.

At eleven at night, the only occupants were the horses, a scrappy stable cat, and a few chickens roosting above our heads in the rafters. Like most stable offices, Copper's was safely shut with a padlock.

Reaching into my tote bag, I pulled out the Phillips screwdriver I'd tossed inside before leaving the house. No way I could unlock the heavy padlock, but it would be easy to loosen the screws that fastened the hasp into the door frame. I started twisting the first one.

"Fia! What are you doing?"

"You want to find Jilly or not?" I kept turning the Phillips.

"Yes, but you can't break into this guy's office."

"Watch me." A few minutes later, the screws loosened their grip on the frame. I tugged them out of their holes, leaving the hasp and the lock swinging uselessly against the door. On either side of us, Copper's horses had their heads out, watching me curiously. I turned the doorknob and walked in.

"You coming or not?" I asked.

Outside on the dirt aisle, Patrick glanced nervously up and down the shedrow. "I'll stay out here and keep watch."

"Okay." I shut the door so the overhead light wouldn't flood into the dark outside. I flicked a switch, and blinked from the sudden illumination.

Like a thousand stable offices I'd seen before—a desk, some chairs, a bulletin board, supplies, papers, and charts. The room smelled like liniment and trash that needed to be emptied. Glancing in the can, I saw pizza boxes, a half-eaten chili dog, and a number of empty beer cans. Grimacing, I poked through the mess looking for discarded papers, following my theory that one man's trash is an investigator's treasure. Not today.

I riffled through the papers on his desk with the same result.

I went through his desk drawers finding more beer, a box of condoms, bills, condition books, and a *Playboy* magazine. I held it by the spine and shook it just in case anything might fall out. Fortunately, nothing did.

Copper had a filing cabinet against the opposite wall, so I yanked out drawers, and pawed through files. Ten minutes later, I still had nothing, and it occurred to me the one person who might have told us Last Call's fate was Wendy. She'd been Copper's vet. *Damn everything.*

I switched off the light and stepped onto the shedrow.

Patrick emerged from the shadows. "Did you find anything?"

"No. Let's call Zanin. Maybe he's had some luck. Then we should hit the streets and look for those kids."

"For God's sake, Fia, they could be *anywhere*. We'll never find them."

I worried he was right. "We won't find them standing here," I said.

Patrick gave an impatient shrug. I moved past him, and climbed into the Mini. When I cranked the engine, he scrambled into the passenger seat.

Zanin had said he planned to search the area farms he often spied on, the type where an injured racehorse might be sent. As we drove out the stable gate, my call to him went straight to voice mail.

When I pulled onto Hallandale Beach Boulevard, the late traffic had thinned to a trickle, making it easier to see license plates, and the features of passengers under the bright streetlights.

"What can Jilly be thinking?" Patrick asked. "They don't have a horse trailer. They don't have any money."

"I guess Jilly just wants to find the horse and talk to whoever has her. She's probably afraid they'll sell her to the killers."

Patrick's expression was tight with anxiety. "I wish I'd claimed the horse for her. I don't like her out with this boy. You said he's seventeen? You don't think—"

"She'll be all right."

With the windows down, I could smell the sea, exhaust, and a trace of the fragrant flowers growing in the gardens on side streets. The air flowing into the car was cool, and above us, a breeze was rattling the palm fronds. It occurred to me how much I hated the twenty-four-hour rule on searching for missing persons. It would have been nice to have the police searching for Angel's tag number.

"You know," Patrick said, "my daughter is just like you. And the way history repeats itself with her makes me crazy."

"What do you mean?"

"Mom ran out on us. Rebecca ran out on Jilly. You love horses more than anything and so does Jilly. But you were close to Dad, and I can't bridge that gap with Jilly."

"We had the horses, Patrick."

Patrick leaned forward in his seat, the streetlight above playing across his face, revealing a familiar anger in his eyes.

"For Christ's sake, Fia, it was way more than that. Dad let you do *whatever* you wanted. You could do no wrong. You two were thick as thieves."

"Nice analogy, Patrick. And you were Mom's little darling. So there it is."

"Come on, Fia. You know Dad never had time for anyone but you. How can you blame Mom for leaving?"

The bitterness I'd carried from Patrick's close relationship with my mother lashed out like a venomous snake, shocking even me.

"So it's *my* fault Mother ran out on us like your stupid wife did?"

I'd had myself convinced I hated the arrogant woman who'd left us for a wealthy man and left Dad with a broken heart. My anger had provided an unbending shield against her. Suddenly, the truth broke through and I realized her abandonment had shattered my heart, too.

The silence in the car was colder than steel and just as impenetrable. I exhaled a long breath. *And if my heart was broken by my mother, what had Dad done to Patrick's?*

"I'm sorry, Patrick, I shouldn't have said that about Mom. Or Rebecca."

He didn't answer, just stared ahead, his jaw tight as a vise.

The street suddenly plunged downhill before dead-ending South Ocean Boulevard, where the big water tower says WELCOME TO HALLANDALE BEACH. Beyond it was the ocean. After turning left, we passed by the Diplomat hotel. I looked at every person I could see inside the passing cars and on the sidewalks. I stared at countless license plates and decided searching for Jilly was as useless as my argument with Patrick.

He still maintained his icy silence, staring at the road ahead. Looking at his profile, I could see faces from our past, the features he'd inherited from our parents. It occurred to me he'd married Rebecca because she was so much like our mother. And me? I was probably still looking for Dad.

Patrick sighed, then gazed out the passenger window at a group of three people on the sidewalk. He rolled his shoulders, turned, and stared at me.

"They didn't make it easy for us, did they, Fia?"

It took me a second to catch up. "No, they didn't. Not even a little bit."

"You know they played us against each other?"

And it was still happening. I hated to think Dad had been involved in that kind of game, but deep inside, I suspected Patrick was right.

"They weren't perfect," I said. "Maybe we should stop letting them run our lives."

His smile was weak, but it was there. "We can try. After we find Jilly."

"Works for me," I said. The sudden ring of my cell startled both of us.

It was Zanin. "No sign of Jilly yet, but I think I found your filly."

Something in his tone caused a frisson of dread to course through. "Where?" I asked, but I knew the answer before he spoke.

"I'm sorry, Fia. She's at Luis Valera's place."

# 38

Zanin's words left me clenching my cell phone so hard, I was surprised it didn't break. "*Valera* has her? Oh, shit."

"*What?*" Fear sharpened Patrick's voice. "Valera has Jilly?"

"No, Patrick, no. He has the horse."

Patrick sagged with relief, and Zanin asked, "Is that your brother?"

"Yes." I pulled the car over to a side street, stopped, and put the phone on speaker.

"What are you going to do?" I asked Zanin. "You can't go in there with a trailer and get her out. And she's probably too lame to lead out. Besides, you might be killed if you tried."

"I have an idea," Zanin said.

"Well, that's good," I said, "because I'm fresh out. What is it?"

"I'm thinking I could—"

"Zanin," Patrick said. "Forget about the horse. What about Jilly? Do you know anything?"

The regret in Zanin's voice was palpable. "I'm sorry, Patrick, I don't. But at least she's not at that place."

I wanted to know Zanin's idea and said so.

"We'll need money," he said. "Patrick, can you cough up some cash?"

A guilty expression crossed Patrick's face, like maybe he was remembering how he'd refused to buy Last Call. Then a fire lit his eyes. "To keep the bastard that butchered Cody from doing it again? You bet."

"Good," Zanin said. "Fia, you remember my friend Juan, who's related to Valera?"

"Yes." I'd never forget how the man had scared me when he emerged from the dark outside Zanin's Tahoe.

"If we give him some cash," Zanin said, "he can buy Last Call from Valera."

"Is Juan in the habit of buying horses?" I asked. "Won't Valera be suspicious?"

"I'll help him make up a good story."

"How much money will you need?" Patrick asked.

"Around a thousand for the horse, that's meat market price, and a couple hundred for Juan."

"Not a problem," Patrick said. "We passed my bank on Hallandale. I've got more than one ATM account there. I can pull that much out tonight."

My brain was spinning like paper bills in a money counter. "You know I met those Hallandale Beach detectives today, right? Since I'm going to be a material witness in their murder trial, maybe I can talk to them, get them to loosen up on that twenty-four-hour rule and start a lookout for Angel's tag number."

"Yes!" Patrick said. "Maybe that'll work. At least we can talk to them."

I pulled my car from the side street and headed back to Hallandale. "Zanin, how about we get the money and meet you somewhere in between, like where Pines Boulevard dead-ends at Okeechobee?"

We agreed, disconnected the call, and Patrick and I sped to his bank where he withdrew two thousand in cash. On the way to the meet with Zanin, I called the Hallandale Beach PD, and was told that Detective Bailey would be on duty at eight the next morning. I left a message on Bailey's voice mail about Jilly's disappearance, explaining that it connected to Morales's murder through the players in the drug scam at Gulfstream. Not confident I'd receive the results I wanted from a phone message, I planned to visit her the next day.

At midnight, we pulled into a landscaping business on Pines Boulevard. The night had cooled, and moisture from condensation beaded and wiggled down the windshield as we waited for Zanin's arrival. Moments later he drove into the lot, and Patrick gave him the bank envelope filled with cash. The skin around Zanin's deep-set eyes wrinkled with exhaustion, but his expression showed determination.

"You're the best," I said to him. "Thank you." He nodded and climbed back into his Tahoe.

Back on the road, Patrick and I hit a mental wall. He placed more fruitless calls to Jilly, and my endeavor to think up clever ways to find her came up empty. It was time to go home. We had to sleep.

Unfortunately, I spent most of the night staring at the ceiling over my bed.

At six the next morning I called Rosario and told him I wasn't coming in, that Jilly had run off with Angel, and I would be searching for them.

"Angel?" Rosario asked. "You mean the kid that works for Serpentino?"

"Yeah, him."

"How about I walk around right now?" he asked. "See what I can find out?"

"Would you? Thanks, Rosario."

But when he called back a few minutes later, he said the kid wasn't there, Serpentino was pissed off, and nobody knew anything.

*Lot of that going around.* I thanked him, then punched in Jilly's number, feeling resigned when the call routed straight to voice mail. *Damn.*

I headed into the kitchen, made a pot of coffee, and fixed some breakfast. I wasn't hungry, but I made myself eat.

When I heard the sound of tires on the gravel drive, I darted to the kitchen window. Outside, a banged up truck, pulling a dilapidated horse trailer, was rolling by, heading for the barn behind the house. Juan was driving, and Zanin sat in the passenger seat. As the trailer bumped past, I saw the familiar glossy bay hindquarters and black tail that belonged to Last Call for Love. *If only Jilly was here.*

Patrick erupted into the kitchen, still in pajamas, his hair sticking out in different directions. "Who's out there?"

"The horse, Patrick. It's just Zanin bringing the horse in."

He sank into a kitchen chair and I poured him a cup of coffee. "There's no news," I said.

Patrick's lips formed a grim line. "When I get my hands on this Angel kid . . ." He shook his head in frustration.

"I'm going to go out and help them with Last Call." I left him staring at his coffee cup like he wasn't sure what it was or what he was supposed to do with it.

Outside the living room's sliding-glass door, I passed the pool, where oblivious to human events, the sweeper robot gurgled and bumped against the blue tile, blowing perky little bubbles into the chlorinated water.

At the barn, Zanin and Juan had already dropped the trailer

ramp and were encouraging Last Call to back out. She did, and when she stood four square, I stared at her left front leg, startled to see the tendon was not "the size of a grapefruit" like Copper had told me.

There was a bubble there, but not as big as I'd seen on horses like the famous Maryland runner, Captain Bodgit, who with a noticeable bowed tendon, had won the Florida Derby and been a strong finisher in the Kentucky Derby and Preakness.

"Walk her a few steps," I asked Zanin. He did, and like Bodgit, Last Call showed no overt sign of lameness.

"Her injury isn't that bad," I said. "Why would Copper sell her for horse meat?"

Juan spread his hands and produced an excellent Latin shrug. "No sell for meat. *Para jugo azul.*"

"What?"

"Copper," Zanin said, "didn't sell her for cash, he traded her for blue juice."

"How does Juan know that?" I asked.

"Juan has his ways," Zanin said.

Juan grinned at me, raising his brows a little. "*Es verdad.* People talk, Juan listen."

This guy Copper was a piece of work; he'd condemned a horse that still had a future for a drug that would win money and probably kill more horses.

"Any news on Jilly?" Zanin asked.

I shook my head, took the lead shank from him, and led Last Call to Cody's stall. When Jilly had hoped to claim her filly, she had cleaned the stall, scraping it to the dirt and bedding it down in fresh straw. Now I finished up by filling the water bucket, and loading the hayrack with sweet-smelling timothy.

I let the filly stretch her legs a moment, then led her back into the center aisle, where Zanin helped me cold-hose her leg and slather poultice on the inflamed tendon. When finished, we put her in her stall, and as I was giving her a light portion of grain, Patrick entered the barn.

He stared at the filly. "I see why Jilly wanted her," he said. "She really is pretty."

*Too little too late.* "Yes," I said, and pulling my cell, I called the Hallandale Beach Police Department.

Late that morning, a male officer from homicide led Patrick and me down a corridor on the second floor of the Hallandale Beach PD. We passed a doorway I hadn't seen the day before, where uniformed officers worked at desks lined with computers, phones, and stacks of files. Cool air spilled from overhead vents, and the odor of stale coffee laced unpleasantly with a pungent scent of cleaning fluid.

We passed by the interrogation room where they'd grilled me after Wendy's death, and the memory released a feeling of unease that chased me down the hall. Moments later, we were led into an office where Detective Bailey was ensconced behind a large desk. After dismissing the homicide cop, she pointed at two uncomfortable-looking chairs facing her desk.

"Why don't you both have a seat?" she asked.

We did, and a broken spring immediately poked my thigh. My chair and Patrick's were both set to their lowest position, forcing us to look up at the woman.

"Detective Bailey," Patrick said, apparently unfazed by office politics, "thank you for seeing us."

Bailey gave us a tight smile. "I take it your daughter's still missing?"

"Yes," Patrick said.

I leaned forward. "Like I said on the phone, Jilly's only fifteen. The boy she's with is seventeen, and they've been missing since—"

"I got all that in your message," Bailey said. "Tell me more about how this girl's disappearance relates to the Warner murder."

I knew how this worked. Give her something and maybe she'd give me something.

"All right," I said. "I told you yesterday about the work the TRPB is doing. That we're tracing the source of illegal drugs allowing horses to win races at long odds?"

Bailey's red spikes sliced the air as she nodded. "Go on."

I explained again how we believed Serpentino and Copper were involved, that the boy with Jilly worked for Serpentino.

"This is where it gets tricky," I said. "The horse they went looking for was claimed by Copper. He traded the horse with Luis Valera for the dermorphin Valera produces on his farm."

Bailey stood abruptly. Her high-heeled pumps clacked on the tile floor as she rounded her desk and stood facing us. "The horse went to *Valera*? How do you know your niece isn't *there?*"

When I explained what Zanin told us, she said, "I hope this Zanin person is right. The death of two kids is not something I want to investigate."

Patrick paled and his skin looked clammy. Somebody needed to give this Bailey woman a lesson in tact. I gave her my best dead-eyed cop look.

"So, will you put out an alert on Angel's tag number?"

She nodded. "I'll see what I can do."

I thanked her, and put a hand on Patrick's shoulder. "Come on," I said, "let's go talk to Angel's roommate. Somebody at the track may know something."

Except, nobody did, and after driving around for hours, vainly looking for Angel's car, Patrick and I went home. He had a house closing the next day and had to run into his office for last-minute paperwork. After he left, I called Zanin and told him about our visit with Bailey.

"I wish I had new information for you," he said, "but I don't." He let out a long frustrated sigh. I knew exactly how he felt.

I spent the afternoon looking for new information on the remaining players in the blue juice scam. The overnight from Gulfstream indicated Copper had two horses running the next day and, no doubt, at least one of them would be running on blue juice. I knew it was too soon, but felt so much like a racehorse who's been blocked and stopped, I called Gunny anyway, hoping for progress in the development of a drug test.

"The pathologist," Gunny said, "up at the University of Oklahoma is working on it. After what officials went through at Remington Park, they didn't want this new one showing up out there. But it still takes time, Fia."

"I know," I said, staring through the window to the blue pool outside. After ending the call, I left my bedroom and went to check on the filly.

Her stall opened onto a half acre of paddock, only she couldn't have access because the enclosure had enough space for her to work up a gallop and aggravate the tendon. I thought a moment and smiled. Finally, something I could actually do.

I drove the Mini to the closest farm supply, bought a fence charger, plastic posts, and wire. When I got back, I pushed the pointed ends of the posts into the ground, strung the wire, and hooked up the charger. Now the paddock had a small rectangle sectioned off outside the rear door of Last Call's stall. I led her out on a shank, showed her the wire, then set her loose. One zap when her nose touched the wire was enough. She snorted and shied away from the fence, but didn't retreat to her stall. Instead, she walked about and grazed a little.

I took the opportunity to clean her stall, and felt calm descend over me as I left it spotless, changed her water, and freshened her supply of hay. Finished, I stood in her opened doorway and breathed in the scent of horse, dust, grass, and the ever present salt air. A pony at the farm next door trotted to the edge of its paddock, raised its head over the fence, and whinnied at Last Call. She stared at the pony and whinnied back.

Being with the horse relaxed me a little, and I dragged myself back to my room. After cranking the phone volume to max in case a call came in, I collapsed on my bed and, undisturbed, slept for hours.

Patrick woke me at seven that evening. He'd made me a drink, and loaded the kitchen table with takeout pizza and salad. We didn't say much while we ate, both of us listening for the phone call that didn't come.

It was dark when I went outside after dinner to spray another stream of cold water on Last Call's leg. A breeze had come up and blew through the barn, scuttling bits of hay along the concrete, and rattling the stall doors. Outside the rear barn door, I could see shadows moving as plants and trees swayed in the night air.

When finished with the hose, I rubbed the anti-inflammatory Surpass into Last Call's tendon. Thinking I should clean her feet, I grabbed a metal hoof pick and scraped dirt, straw, and manure from her hooves. I slid the pick into a pocket, put Last Call in her stall, and leaned on the door to watch her.

I thought I heard something outside and strained to listen. The breeze rushed more fiercely through the barn, no doubt the culprit.

My phone vibrated inside my vest pocket, and when I grabbed it, I didn't recognize the incoming number.

When I answered, the person's voice was so low, I could hardly hear.

"Fia, it's Shyra Darnell."

"*Shyra?*"

"Your niece is here. She's in trouble."

A sick chill crawled up my spine. "*Where?* Where is she?"

"Luis Valera has her. He'll kill me if he knows I've called you."

"Is she all right?"

"For now, but you have to get her out. They have terrible plans for her."

My thoughts flitted about like a bird in a cage. How the hell would I get her out? Valera's place was huge.

"Shyra, where, exactly, does he have her?"

"In the house." Her breath sucked in. "Someone's coming." The line went dead.

# 39

Clutching my cell, I called her name. "Shyra, are you there?" I stared at the phone, my only lead to Jilly had evaporated in my hand. I didn't push redial. If she'd been telling the truth, my call could get her killed.

But was Jilly really there? Or was this a setup to lure me out to Valera's? After all, I was the only witness to Wendy's murder, and knew the connections between Valera, Morales, and Serpentino. It was time to call Detective Bailey.

As I searched the call log for her number, something creaked, and the wind rattled fiercely through the barn. Last Call's head jerked up, and she blew softly, ears pricked, staring beyond me into the barn's center aisle. I turned to follow her gaze.

A tall man, gripping a shotgun ran toward me from the rear of the barn. A tiny black and ivory skull dangled on a leather thong encircling his neck. *Shit.* The Santeria I called Skull Man, the one who'd slammed his rifle butt into Zanin's head that day in the C-9 Basin.

*My gun?* In the house.

Had Valera sent him? His lips pulled back, revealing the distorted, toothless smile I remembered.

He raised the shotgun, pointed it at my chest. "Drop the phone, lady."

My pulse thundered in my ears as I frantically thumbed in Bailey's number. From behind, something hard struck my head and the phone dropped to the floor. I sank to my knees. Swiveling, glancing up, I saw the other Santeria, the one who'd had symbols painted on his chest. The one who laughed like a hyena.

He held a machete. His open vest revealed freshly painted marks on his skin, like war paint. Was he going to butcher me here in the barn like Cody? I lurched to my feet and whirled to make a run for Last Call's stall. I would sprint out the back, through the electric fence, and escape.

As my hand grasped the handle on her stall door, something hard struck my head. Back on my knees, my vision blurred, and my senses swam beneath a surface that grew dark. As I shook my head, trying to clear the dizziness, someone grabbed my arms, twisting them behind my back, tying them with what felt like cord. Grasping hands spun me around, and as I stared at the toothless smile of Skull Man, he plastered duct tape over my mouth.

"Valera say we kill you," he said. "But first, he say we have a little fun, yes?"

This time, I saw the butt of his shotgun rushing at my head. The crazy laugh of a hyena faded as my world narrowed to a tiny black circle and shut down.

I became aware of a swaying sensation, of a hard plastic surface against my back. *Wake up, Fia. Open your eyes.* I did, and saw treetops and stars rolling above me. I heard an engine whining and felt a relentless pounding in my head. Pain gripped my skull like a vise. I tried to sit up, but nausea and some sort of restraint stopped me. *Breathe. Think.*

I must be in the back of a pickup truck. Moving my head

very slowly, I surveyed my situation. My hands were tied behind my back, my ankles trussed. They'd tied my restraints to rings on the truck wall, firmly strapping me into the truck's bed liner. Any hopes I'd had of throwing myself out of the vehicle died.

The head pain was so intense, it took a while before I felt a hard, sharp object digging into my butt.

*Hoof pick.*

Squirming, and fighting nausea, I shoved the fingers of one hand into my rear jean's pocket, grasped the pick, and pulled it out. By twisting and bending my wrist, I was able to force the pick's pointed end into a knot. I picked and pulled and picked and pulled until I wanted to weep with frustration. My wrist screamed to be free from its unnatural, twisted position. I kept going.

As I worked, I felt the truck slow, and heard the whine of tires on pavement change to the crunch of rubber on gravel. Above me, the trees closed in, and I knew we were getting closer to Valera's. Was I such a threat to him he would have me killed? Maybe Shyra hadn't been trying to set me up. Maybe she'd only tried to save my niece. Maybe she'd been about to warn me the men were coming when the call went dead. But then again, she could have been trying to trick me in case Valera's men were unable to find me.

*Don't worry about that.* Instead, I pried and tugged until I found a rhythm, working harder and faster as I felt the knot loosen. Suddenly it gave and my hands were free. I raised my head, angling it toward the truck's back window. The two Santerias were up there and pulsating music leaked through the metal.

The truck slowed more, hit a rutted road, and I started working on my ankles. How much time did I have? Should I flip myself out of the truck? No, I needed my feet. I kept picking and prying at the ankle knot.

But then the truck stopped, the driver cut the engine, and I knew I'd made the wrong decision. I heard the men clambering from the cab as I ripped and tore at the knot binding my feet. It broke free as the two men dropped the truck's tailgate. My heart stopped when I smelled the stench of pig, saw the pen, and those huge, feral hogs staring at me through the electrified fence.

The hyena's laugh, when he saw my freed hands and ankles, was high-pitched, insane. He was soaring on something. Skull Man scowled and cuffed his buddy's head, rapidly spitting out angry Spanish words. Something about *estúpido* and *nudo*. Skull Man was apparently chastising his partner for tying stupid knots.

Did it not occur to them I'd used a tool? Palming the pick and sliding my hand behind me, I slipped it into my rear pocket. Behind the pen's gate, more pigs stampeded forward, squealing and drooling, their long curved tusks gleaming in the ambient light.

Skull Man stared at me intently and climbed into the truck bed. His eyes were bloodshot. He grabbed my wrist, yanked me out of the truck, and shoved me onto the ground. The impact jarred my head, and I moaned. Nausea rose in my throat. I remained on my hands and knees waiting for it to subside.

When I was able to glance up, the hyena stood over me with his machete. He held the blade high above me as Skull Man lowered himself to the ground and sat cross-legged next to me.

"Your niece is very pretty," he said, giving me his distorted smile and the stink of sour breath. "I think Valera keep her for himself, no?"

I gave him my dead-eyed cop stare.

Above me, the hyena cackled again. For some reason, I remembered the root word of hyena was Greek and meant "female pig." So appropriate. I smiled.

A vicious look twisted Skull Man's face. "You think this is funny, *puta?*" He reached inside his jacket and pulled out a hypodermic syringe. Bluish fluid floated inside. "We have gift for you from Luis. You are, how you say, his *experimento*. He want to know how blue juice work on *las personas*."

No way he was injecting that shit in me! Still on my hands

and knees, I scuttled backward, lurched to my feet, and tried to run. The side of the machete blade smacked my temple and I fell, sinking close to the edge of darkness.

As my senses cleared, hands grasped my wrists. I struggled, but the hyena twisted one arm behind my back. Skull Man grabbed the other, thrust the needle into the vein inside my elbow, and shot the plunger. He dropped my arm and drew back, as if afraid I might explode or turn into a demon. The hyena released my arm and scuttled a few steps away. They both watched me.

Sudden nausea overwhelmed my stomach, and I vomited my dinner. The sickness seemed to last forever, until I was dry heaving with chills. Then the lovely blackness took over.

I came to, gasping for breath, certain my lungs were filled with Freon. No room for air. I stopped trying. Let the darkness come back.

I heard my father's voice. *Breathe, Fia, breathe.* When I did, my head cleared, and the nausea receded, then faded completely away. Hyperacuity surged into my senses and I felt a wave of tremendous energy and strength pour into me.

The two men stared at me curiously, Skull Man aiming his shotgun at me, the other one holding his machete in both hands. Glancing at the shotgun, I recognized it as an old Winchester pump-action. Oddly, a sense of well-being flooded me and I smiled at them.

Skull Man smiled back, then glanced at his buddy. "First, we have fun with her, no? See how good this juice is. Then we give her to the pigs."

Hands grasped me again, yanking off my canvas vest. The machete cut my tank top and the men ripped it off.

My hand closed on the hoof pick, and as the hyena was about to slice away my bra, I shoved the pick's pointed end into his eye, twisting the tool, before jerking back. He screamed, a wounded animal. I shoved him away, and he crumpled to the ground. I turned to find the barrel of Skull Man's Winchester inches from my face. He clutched the weapon with both hands. On the ground, the other Santeria moaned and crawled away into the undergrowth. Skull Man's eyes widened as he stared at my bloody hoof pick.

"Drop that, or I shoot you now."

I shrugged and let the pick fall from my fingers. *I felt so good.* My head no longer hurt and I had a crazy sense of being one with the universe. Careful to stay out of my reach, Skull Man pointed the Winchester at the pigpen. "Over there."

"No *problema*," I said.

The smile I gave him seemed to frighten him and he jabbed the shotgun barrel closer. "Now!"

I walked to the gate. The pigs squealed, crowding and grunting, tearing at the ground with their cloven hooves.

"You see how hungry they are?" Skull Man asked. "When I shoot your legs, I throw you over the gate. You will live a little while." He smiled, enjoying himself, waiting and watching. He wanted to see terror in my eyes. "You beg me now, maybe I kill you before you go in pen, yes?"

"Nah," I said, and stepping in close, I grabbed the long barrel of his Winchester and tore it from his grasp. *I was so strong!* I flipped the shotgun, smashed his head with the butt, then picked him up. He seemed to weigh nothing. How could this be? *Who cares?* Using the gate as a fulcrum, I flipped him over it and he dropped inside.

His screams were horrible. The grunting and squealing of the pigs even worse. I looked once, saw a hog with a hand in its mouth, and pulled my gaze away. I snatched up the Winchester and the machete before running to the truck, realizing too late the keys must have been in Skull Man's pocket.

*Who needs a truck?* I started running down Flamingo Road.

# 40

The road curved around a bend and into a straightaway where low-hanging branches and impenetrable vegetation threatened to strangle the gravel lane. My senses were so acute, I smelled swamp to my left, and heard creatures slithering in the water. Mosquitoes whined in my ears and some sort of night bird called from the slough.

After I passed an abandoned hut on my right, a barbed-wire fence stretched beside the road into the distance. I made out vague shapes of livestock in the field, and a horse snorted in alarm. A goat bleated, and a small herd of the animals trotted after me on their side of the fence, their scent strong and gamey.

Jilly was somewhere ahead. And Valera. And more thugs. I ran harder. The goats lost interest and fell behind. A new field spread open on my left, and the swamp smell abated. Far away, I saw the same building lights I had seen once before. Valera's home. I passed the indistinct shape of the frog shack and its pen covered with netting.

I slowed to a walk, hugging the edge of the road, holding

the machete up to keep branches from scraping at my face. Glancing down, my abdomen's white skin seemed to glow in the ambient light. I searched the road for water and found a puddle squishy with mud. Dropping to my knees, I rolled in the soft brown slime, smearing it over as much skin as I could. After rubbing a handful onto my face and into my hair, I rose from the muck and walked swiftly forward, searching for the entrance to Valera's property.

His driveway cut between two palms. One had a sign that warned to me to keep out: PROHIBIDA LA ENTRADA. Something was fastened to the other palm. Squinting, I drew closer. A horse's tongue was nailed to the trunk. I could feel my lips twist in disgust. I'd heard of this Santeria ritual. Did Valera use it as a curse against his enemies, or as a repulsive symbol to guard his home? It sure as hell wasn't stopping me.

I rushed past it, zeroing in on the lighted windows of a sprawling one-story house. Built in sections, some of the structure's walls were concrete, some just wooden planks nailed haphazardly together. In the dim light it appeared that different types of shingles covered the roof and I could imagine the occupants looting construction sites for the bits and pieces that made up Valera's house.

Creeping clockwise, I began circling the building. It was shaped like a T. The front door was centered in the top bar, and a long tail of add-ons had been constructed behind. As I moved, I stared through the few windows not blocked by ratty curtains or blankets.

I passed a kitchen with a sink full of dirty dishes and a grimy stove. A whiff of salsa and rancid meat grease assailed my nose. I passed a high window that was probably a bathroom, and peered into a small room with two unmade beds at the tail end of the T.

No sign of Jilly. A dim light seeped from the window of the bedroom and I used it to examine my Winchester. The shotgun was an old 12-gauge pump-action. I could smell gun oil and when I checked the action, it was smooth. The magazine held six shells. I felt like kissing the weapon.

I strained to perceive sounds, scents, or the sensation of human presence. Nothing.

Quickly, I circled past the tail end of the house and moved up the far side. So much of the interior was hidden by blankets and burlap bags tacked over windows, I gathered no additional information.

But when I reached the front corner of the house, I froze.

Through a lighted window, I saw two men sitting on a battered couch drinking beer and watching TV. A third man, built like a fireplug with a severely battered nose, sat in a recliner holding a bottle of beer. I blinked, stared. The lid of the man's left eye sagged badly. Above his right eye, the brow rose high and formed a question mark. Luis Valera, as hideous as his photo.

On the floor, next to him lay a large canvas bag with US MAIL stenciled on it in black ink. The drawstring at the top was pulled almost shut, but just inside it I could see a stack of rubber-banded bills. The bag was probably stuffed with cash. If Valera was backward enough to scrape dermorphin off frogs instead of synthesizing the drug, he probably didn't have access to a fancy money-laundering operation, either.

A second glance at the men on the couch revealed two sets of long, greasy hair, pulled back into ponytails. One man's bare arms were inked with tattoos, and on both men, what looked like Santeria charms dangled from leather thongs on their necks. The guy with the tats had a full beard and a big gut. The other man was fit, with jet-black eyes, and a week's worth of dirty, untrimmed bristles on his face. The thought of these men touching Jilly sickened me. I tried to calm my thoughts. I couldn't blast my way into the house; there must be some way to trick these people. It wouldn't be long before they missed their buddies at the hog pen and—

My breath caught in my throat as Shyra walked into the

room. She carried more beer for the men. Her body language with Valera and his thugs seemed relaxed and comfortable. She *must* be related to Valera. She'd said her family practiced the Santeria faith, that they came from Florida. Her call to me had been a setup. *Bitch*.

She left the room, and treading softly, I followed the outline of her progress past curtained windows. She entered the kitchen, where she spooned chili from a pot onto a paper plate, stuck a plastic fork in it, and grabbed a bottle of water. Food for Jilly?

She left the kitchen, walked to the front, and as I hid in the shadows, she came outside, holding the plate of food. I tracked her dim figure, touching the mud plastered on my skin, relieved it was not yet dry enough to cake and crumble off.

Shyra followed a track to the left and stopped at a dilapidated, prefab hut surrounded by vegetation. A dim light from inside threaded through the undergrowth pressing around it. Moving closer and tucking myself behind a leafy plant, I watched as she unlatched a door and swung it open.

I didn't see Jilly, but a man in shackles sat on the floor. Who *was* this guy? Staring, I realized the chain between his wrist irons was attached to a steel cable connected to an overhead wire. He'd be able to slide the cable and hobble back and forth for maybe ten feet. I had to make myself breathe as I stared at his beaten, gaunt face. It held a look of utter defeat.

Damn, where was Jilly? *Please, God, let her be alive, somewhere in Valera's house.* A sudden lurch of nausea hit me. I made myself breathe until the sensation passed

Shyra took a step toward the man. "Get back."

Like a hungry animal, he stared at the plate of food in Shyra's hands before shuffling as far away from her as the overhead line allowed. Shyra set the plate and bottle of water on the floor, then backed away. She latched the door behind her, leaving the man alone in his cage.

I waited until she was gone, then raced to the shed, unlatched the door, and went in.

I put my finger to my lips, and whispered, "I'm here to help." I hoped he wasn't a rival thug who'd just as soon kill me if I set him loose.

He stared at me, wary and unconvinced.

"Who are you?" I asked.

"Steve Craigson."

"The *chemist*?"

His eyes widened. "You know who I am?"

"You're the guy everyone's looking for." I took in his surroundings. Two long tables stretched beneath his overhead tether. The tables were cluttered with beakers, a scale, glass flasks, and jars of what appeared to be chemicals.

"Please," Craigson's voice cracked with desperation. "Get me out of here. They're forcing me to make an illegal drug. It's—"

"Blue juice!" I said, hurrying toward him. "Anything in here I can use to break the chain or pick these locks?"

"Bolt cutters in that cabinet." He pointed at a corner with his bound hands. "But even with those, I doubt you'll be strong enough to break these chains."

The abnormal strength still boiled through my veins. "Watch me."

I darted to the cabinet, grabbed the cutters, and fastened the blades over the chain between his wrists. I gritted my teeth pressed with my elbows, shoulder, and arm muscles. I felt a muffled spasm of pain in my shoulder, but ignored it. The chain broke. I switched the cutter to the chain on his leg irons, and with a loud crack, it snapped.

Panting, I asked him, "Have you seen a girl?"

"No."

"How many men are there?"

"Six, including Valera," he said. "And there's the woman who feeds me."

"How many stay in the house?"

He shook his head. "I don't know."

Thinking out loud, I said, "So there's still four men."

Confused, Craigson said, "No, six."

"I killed one, and another one's out of commission."

He recoiled slightly. "Who *are* you?" he asked.

"Fia. I'm a TRPB agent. You have to go. Follow the path to Flamingo Road. Run like hell, and when that dead-ends, turn right and keep going. Everyone's tied in with Valera. You won't be safe until you get to Okeechobee Road." I picked the machete up from the floor where I'd laid it down with the twelve gauge. "Take this," I said, handing him the machete. "Get help."

"No, come with me. These people are horrible!"

"My niece is in that house. They will kill her." *If she was still alive.* "I'm not waiting for help. *You* need to go!"

We ran from the shed, and when we reached the spot where the path split, I veered away from Craigson and sprinted for the house.

**41**

Once I'd seen a drawing of a Minotaur in a Greek mythology book. The man I saw when I peered into the front room of Valera's house reminded me of that hideous image. He was the fourth man, the one I hadn't seen before now, and he had to be well over six feet. He had a bullish, oversized head. His body was substantial, and as he sat in the middle of the couch, it sagged beneath his weight as if ready to fold in half.

The black-eyed man I'd seen earlier sat on the floor as if loath to share the couch with a bull. Valera was still in his chair next to the bag of money. The man with the big gut and Shyra were absent.

With dismay, I realized I would need a SWAT team to rescue Jilly. What were the chances of shooting five people with six shells? Especially with two people hidden somewhere in the house? A wave of exhaustion began to spread through me. Nausea returned and I retched, only nothing came up. My energy level was crashing fast, pain stabbing at my arms, back, and shoulders. The pounding began torturing my head again. *Damn it.*

My pulse thundered so loud in my ears, I never heard the man who came up behind me. A thick arm snaked around my neck. A powerful hand snatched the Winchester from my grasp. I kicked back, trying to strike his shin, but my strength had dried up and my pitiful effort made him laugh.

It was the Santeria with the large gut. He held a knife to my throat, dragged me and the shotgun through the front door, and into the room with Valera. The air stank of body odor, stale beer, and grease. The man on the floor glanced up, his eyes black holes in his face. He stared, expressionless. The bull man gazed up from the couch and looked away without interest. Valera leaned forward in his recliner, his lips curling into a malevolent smile that matched the brutality in his eyes.

"Ah, the bitch who thinks she can piss on Valera. What have you done with my men? You stupid *puta,* you should never have left Baltimore."

He saw me start, and his eyes gleamed with amusement.

"*Sí,* I know who you are and where you come from. I know where your brother lives and your mother in California."

Fear spiked my blood, replacing the courage that had strengthened me earlier. The first prickle of sweat rolled down my forehead.

Valera rose from the recliner, strode across the room, and pressed cruel fingers on either side of my jaw. "Before you die, you'll learn respect. You will understand who I am." He dropped his hand and looked at the Santeria who still held the knife near my throat. "Put her in the room."

The man with the knife hauled me down the hall. He dragged me past the kitchen where Shyra was cutting a joint of meat. She looked up and quickly dropped her gaze to the floor, as if ashamed. We were almost to the end of the hall when he unlocked a door, and shoved me into a dark room. I fell to my knees, heard the door slam and lock.

Pain stabbed my head so bad, I stayed down, waiting for the

accompanying wave of dizziness to pass, waiting for my eyes to adjust. Cloth blocked what little ambient light might have come through the window. I could hear the receding steps of the Santeria, and then . . . someone breathing.

"*Jilly?*" My whisper was almost a prayer.

I heard a little sob, then, "Aunt Fia?"

"Yes." I crawled toward the sound of her voice.

A shape darker than the space around it rushed to me, and I felt her hands touching my head. She dropped to my level and we wound our arms around each other. I could feel her tears on my neck, and my eyes welled with relief as I breathed in the scent of her skin, the shampoo in her hair, felt the live warmth of her body.

She trembled so hard it shook me. "Jilly, are you okay?"

"Yes." She stifled another sob.

"What happened?"

"That man with the big, ugly head . . . he grabbed me. He, he put his hands on my . . ." Her shaking intensified. "He made me feel horrible . . . like I'm dirty."

"Jilly, you're *not*. He's the horrible one, not you!" I hugged her closer, stroked her hair. "He didn't force you to—"

"No! The other guy, pushed him away—the one with the black eyes. Then Alvera came in the room and got real mad at the man who tried to . . . hurt me. After that, no one but the woman has been near me. She's nice to me."

*Oh, yeah, Shyra's a real peach.* "Good," I said. "Jilly, how did they catch you?"

"Angel brought me here to look for Last Call, and they found us. I'm afraid they hurt him. Did you see him?"

"No. But, Jilly, how did Angel know to come here?" I wondered if the kid had been involved in a setup.

"Something he heard from Mr. Serpentino," she said. "They held a gun on him to keep him back. Then they dragged me into this house. I'm so afraid for Angel."

She should be afraid for herself. "But no one hit you, or hurt you?" I asked.

"No. I guess I'm lucky they didn't beat me up or anything." She was trying to sound strong, but fear rattled her voice.

"We had one bit of luck," I said. "You remember there was a missing chemist?"

"Yeah, but what does—"

"He was here, locked in a shed. I got him out. He's gone for help."

"Oh! How long do you think—"

"I don't know. If I can figure a way to get us out of here before that, I will."

"There are bars underneath the blanket on the window." Her next words were shrill. "We can't get out!"

I felt sick with fear myself. No one but Craigson knew where we were. How long would it take him to walk to Okeechobee Road? For help to come. Would he even make it? A chill touched my spine as a sensation struck me, an absolute certainty a rifle butt was swinging at my head. I ducked, then looked up. There was nothing there. A hallucination. *Damn it.* I shook it off.

Footsteps sounded in the hallway. A key rattled the door lock, and an overhead light switched on, momentarily blinding me. Was I imagining this, too? I blinked and looked up.

The bullish man's massive form blocked the doorway, and I could feel Jilly recoil. In the newly lit room, she stared at me. "God, Aunt Fia! What happened to you?"

My head had to be bruised, and swollen where they'd hit me with the rifle butt. I was still covered with mud, and stripped to a bra above my waist. I felt green with illness and fear. "I'm fine."

Behind the bull-sized man, the black-eyed guy stared at me from the hall. The larger man shambled into the room, leaned over, and pulled me away from Jilly. His dull eyes were devoid of intelligence or humanity.

"You stay there," he said, placing his tree trunk–sized legs between Jilly and me. The black-eyed man moved in and grabbed Jilly's hand.

"No!" she screamed, squirming and fighting like a cat, trying to claw at his face. She was no match for him.

Folding my hands into a club, and rising to my knees, I swung my fists into the bull man's crotch. He grunted, bent over. I sprang to my feet, ready to take on the black-eyed man.

"*Pequeña leona*," he said quietly. "Stop."

Shocked, I stared at him. But had he really said those words? Just one person had called me "little lioness." I knew his voice.

*Calixto.*

He put a warning finger to his lips just before the bull man stood up and came at me.

"Oso," Calixto shouted, "leave her alone! Valera may have plans for her."

Oso laughed. "Her? She look like shit."

"She'll heal, no?" Calixto said. "Leave her alone."

My head spun so fast. Calixto? *Missing at the races, called on to another job.* He was here, undercover. This was real. But his eyes were so black. Of course, he wore contact lenses. I swallowed, took a breath.

I made my voice shrill and angry. "Where are you taking her?"

"She'll be fine. Just a little patience, *leona*."

Oso laughed. "*Sí*, she'll be fine, until the men get to her."

Calixto pulled Jilly through the door into the hall. Oso backed out of the room, making sure I couldn't follow. He killed the lights, closed and locked the door. I could hear Jilly screaming and shrieking as Calixto pulled her down the hall. Her cries broke my heart and the hardest thing I've ever done was not to scream, "He's one of us, Jilly. You'll be all right!"

But would she? I hated not knowing what was going on. Obviously, if Calixto had a plan, my unexpected arrival had interrupted the hell out of it.

Moments later, I heard an engine turn over, then the sound of a vehicle revving up and speeding away from Valera's. Had to be Calixto taking Jilly. But where?

I rose and just for the hell of it, tried the door. Locked. Before Oso had shut off the light, I'd scanned the room hoping to see another door. No such luck. I crossed the room and ripped up a corner of the blanket tacked over the window. Jilly was right. Iron bars secured the window.

Dread turned my insides watery, filled me with weakness. I felt as if I'd burned up my life fighting the two men at the pigpen. Dizziness flooded me, and I sank to the floor. The new wave of terror that gripped me was something I'd never known.

A key scraped at the lock outside the door. Instead of tensing, preparing myself for battle, I cringed, barely keeping from folding into a fetal position. *Damn it, Fia.*

The door creaked open. I dug deep inside, found a scrap of resolve, and prepared to fight.

The light from the hall silhouetted Calixto's body, and I stifled a cry. The night had been like a carnival ride, the kind where you're strapped in, turned upside down, and spun until you don't know which way is up. How many times was I supposed to go from sure death to life?

"Fia," he whispered. "Let's get out of here."

"Where's Jilly?" I asked, stumbling toward him.

"I gave her Valera's truck. She's long gone."

I envisioned her tearing down the road, heard her screaming to release her fear. I suppressed a bubble of wild laughter.

"There's two trucks out front," Calixto said. "Window at the end of the hall. Come on."

I followed him down the corridor to the bedroom I'd seen earlier. The window I'd looked through before had been opened. Calixto boosted me over the ledge and out into the night, before jumping down beside me. As we scurried along the side of the house, a shout sounded from inside.

"*Shit,*" Calixto hissed. "They know you're gone!"

Someone closed in behind me. I whirled. No one was there. "I'm in a bad way, Calixto."

"Get it together, Fia." He grabbed my hand and pulled me forward. His touch was solid, strengthening. We sprinted past the front of the house, trying to reach one of the vehicles.

The front door burst open and Oso ran outside holding the Winchester. Calixto pulled a handgun from his waistband and fired off two shots. One hit Oso, but the man pivoted and stumbled back inside the house.

A loud crack. A shot whizzed past my ear. It struck Calixto. I whirled, saw the man with the big gut running at me with a large handgun. Twisting back, I saw Calixto on the ground. I dove toward him, snatched his gun, and dropped to one knee, firing at the running man. *This* was happening. Two of his bullets zinged past me. I kept firing, hit him. He fell, but started hunching toward me, so I shot him again. He stilled. I cursed at myself for needing so many bullets, for being uncertain what was real and what wasn't.

Shouting erupted from inside the house. Oso staggered back onto the porch and took aim at me with the Winchester. I zigzagged toward him. His gun boomed, but his shot missed me. I could almost smell the heat of the fired shell. I squeezed off more shots, still zigzagging toward him and firing. Miraculously, he went down.

Valera busted out the front door with an assault rifle. I squeezed the handgun's trigger. It clicked—empty and useless. Valera's laugh was hideous. His aim at me was almost lazy, until he started ripping the night air with bullets. But the shots went wide, and he fell forward as a haze of red burst from his forehead. Was I imagining this?

Then Shyra emerged from the house, holding another assault rifle in one hand and dragging the bag of cash with the other. She gazed at Valera's other men on the ground. As if for good measure, she riddled Oso and the other thug with more bullets. I froze, waiting again for my death.

"I ain't shooting you, cop lady." She paused and looked at the motionless bodies of Valera and his men. "Those other two weren't *necessarily* dead yet, so I shot 'em for you. Knowing how you suffer from guilt and all. Anyways, looks like everyone's dead who should be. I were you, I'd get my boyfriend into one of those trucks and haul ass."

Not sure of anything, I was afraid to move. I darted a glance at Calixto. He had rolled to his side and was trying to sit up. There was so much blood.

Shyra nodded at me. "Go on. Help him."

I ran to Calixto and dropped to my knees. "Don't move," I said. "It's over. I'm getting help."

He tried to nod, but his eyes fluttered shut, and he passed out.

Shyra leaned over Alvera, pulled a cell phone from one of his bloody pockets, and tossed it to me.

I caught the phone, called 911, and quickly explained the situation to the dispatcher. When I finished the call, Shyra slung the assault rifle over her shoulder, and dragging the canvas bag of cash, she took long strides to the closest truck. She heaved the cash inside, then turned, giving me a long, assessing stare.

"You ain't gonna see me again, so I'm gonna tell you something you need to know. The man you killed in Baltimore? He's the shithead who killed your father."

My wild carnival ride stopped spinning. Everything halted, and slowly the fragments came together. *These* Santerias had been pushing drugs at Pimlico. *Wendy.* She'd been in on it. My father had found out. They had killed him. Wordlessly, I stared at Shyra, knowing I was right.

"Who ordered the hit?"

She pointed her rifle at Valera's body on the porch. "That piece of shit. He's the one paid the man to do it." As if she'd reached a decision, she nodded to herself. "You and me are even now, cop lady."

She climbed inside the truck and fired it up. Dirt and sand spun from the tires as she revved the engine, tore down the drive, and disappeared down Flamingo Road.

# 42

It wasn't long before a convoy of cops and ambulances barreled down the dirt road and spun into Alvera's place.

Finding dead bodies, so many weapons and shell casings, the senior officer was inclined to hold me there for questioning. But a female EMT with tired eyes that had seen too much death looked me over and insisted I go to the hospital with Calixto.

"This woman's injured, drugged, and suffering from hallucinations," she said.

The officer relented, and I grabbed the EMT's arm.

"What about him," I asked her, staring at Calixto who was on a stretcher and already inside the ambulance.

"He needs blood, but I think he'll be okay."

My body sagged with relief, and after that things got a little fuzzy.

When I finally arrived at home that night, and convinced myself that Jilly was really there and safe, I downed several shots of vodka, and took a hot shower.

As the water and steam enveloped me, I thought about Shyra, realizing Valera must have ordered her to break into my apartment. His thugs had seen my car and license plate the day they attacked Zanin, Jilly, and me. Since Zanin was a known enemy to Valera, and I'd been with him, they'd run my tag and Shyra had broken into my apartment to find out what I knew. Since I kept my laptop with me, they'd learned nothing.

I finally fell into a tortured, restless sleep in the wee hours. In the morning, I crawled out of bed around nine. Though my head still throbbed painfully, the nausea was gone. I called the hospital, but they refused to give me information about Calixto, so I wandered through the house looking for Jilly and Patrick.

Hearing tires on the gravel out front, a sudden fear gripped me, but I made myself go to the front door. When I stepped under the portico, I saw two parked vehicles. One was a FedEx van, the other Zanin's Tahoe.

In his usual uniform of jeans and work boots, Zanin was taking a cardboard box from the FedEx guy, who waved at me before climbing back into his van. It felt odd to walk into such a normal morning. The FedEx van circled the drive and disappeared behind Patrick's jungle of plants and bushes.

I eased out from under the portico and stepped onto the stone terrace, closer to Zanin.

"Jesus Christ, Fia, what happened to you?"

"I had a little run-in with Valera," I said, not wanting to get into a long explanation.

Moving closer, I glanced at the package he held and saw the words FRAGILE, LIVE ANIMALS.

"Oh," I said, "my Bluesters. I should get them inside."

"Fia, wait," he said, staring at my face, putting his hand on my arm. "For God's sake! Tell me what happened. You should have called me, let me help you."

"It all happened too fast," I said.

The front door opened, and Jilly came out to join us. Her

hair shone, her sapphire earrings gleamed, and her eyes were bright. My heart filled with so much emotion, I couldn't speak.

Jilly wasn't having that problem. "I can't believe you guys saved Last Call! It was so cool when I came home last night and there she was . . . in the barn!" Her smile could have lit up half of South Florida. She caught sight of the box I was holding. "Are those the Bluesters?"

"Yeah, you want to put them in their terrarium and give them some food?"

"Sure," she said, "but you two have to come out back and see Last Call."

"In a minute," I said.

She nodded, took the frogs, and went inside. I stepped into the shade of the portico and Zanin followed, his gaze meeting mine.

"So what happened?" he asked.

I told him the gist of the story and he pressed his lips together, shaking his head.

"I wish you could have reached me somehow. I can't believe those two guys took you like that."

"It worked out," I said.

"And this Calixto guy, he saved your life?"

"Yes, he did. And we cleaned out Flamingo Road and the drug problem at Gulfstream, at least for now."

"I'm not sure I like you being a cop. You seem to be in pretty tight with these law enforcement guys, huh?"

Was he jealous? "I *am* law enforcement," I said, suddenly sad to realize that whatever this thing was between Zanin and me, it didn't seem to be working.

"You're going to leave, aren't you?" he asked.

"Eventually. Gunny will assign me somewhere else. But I've got two weeks off, so I'll be here a while. Come on," I said, "let's go see Last Call. Jilly will love you forever for rescuing that filly and bringing her here."

He shrugged. "I guess."

We walked through the house, out the sliding door, and stopped. The sun shone on Jilly who was in the paddock with Last Call, her arms wrapped around the filly's neck. Patrick was nearby scrubbing out the water trough with a long-handled brush.

Seeing the girl with her horse made Zanin smile. "So Jilly will be all right?"

"She'll never get over what happened to Cody, and now she'll have to deal with additional trauma and more night terrors," I said. She wasn't the only one. I'd awakened more than once the night before, envisioning the man I'd killed in Baltimore knifing my father to death. I'd heard the screams of the man I'd thrown into the hog pen, and the ceaseless sound of gunfire had echoed in my head.

"She went through a lot," I said, trying to shake off my own lingering shock.

"What about that kid, Angel?" Zanin asked.

"From what the cops said last night, he hadn't realized what he was getting Jilly and himself into. Didn't understand the connection between Alvera and Serpentino. Alvera's men beat the boy up pretty bad. At least they sent him back to Serpentino alive. After that, he was too terrified to say anything to help Jilly."

"An unpleasant lesson about life," Zanin said.

I nodded, watching the girl in the paddock. She was finger combing Last Call's mane. The horse craned her neck and pressed her nose against Jilly's side.

"You did good when you saved that horse, Zanin."

His face brightened a little. "I guess Last Call will go a long way toward healing her."

"Might save her life," I said.

# 43

That afternoon, Gunny drove me to the Hialeah Hospital, where the ambulance had brought Calixto and me in the night before. My memory of that event was spotty. I'd been suffering from flashbacks, had still been terrified, and apparently had assaulted one of the EMTs when he'd tried to wheel Calixto away from our ambulance and into the hospital.

Once they'd gotten me under control, the doctors had rushed Calixto into emergency surgery, and the staff had tried to keep me overnight for observation. They'd been worried about my behavior, the drug in my system, and a concussion.

I might be a while recovering, but Calixto would take longer. The bullet had burst into the right side of his chest, ripping through a lung before blowing out through his back. But once I'd known he was out of danger, I'd insisted on going home, needing to see for myself that Jilly was okay. A Broward County sheriff had driven me from the hospital to Patrick's.

Now, as Gunny and I entered the hospital's surgical unit and approached the nurses' station, I caught my reflection in the shiny surface of a paper towel dispenser and winced. I really looked like hell. Gingerly, I fingered the purple swelling on one cheekbone. The scratches on my face and neck that had scabbed over and the dark circles under my eyes didn't help, either.

A vigilant nurse eyed Gunny and me suspiciously from behind the counter. She told us Calixto was sleeping, and checked our identification as if hoping to find something wrong with it.

"You can go in," she said resignedly. "Five minutes, but don't tire him out okay? I had to let those FBI folks in earlier. You people should just leave him alone."

We promised not to agitate him and went down the hall to find the room number she'd given us. The night before had been so crazy, and I'd been too out of it to know what to ask. Now I had a million questions.

I stopped walking and put a hand on Gunny's arm. "FBI?"

"Let's see how Calixto is, and then we can talk," he said.

We entered Calixto's room. He looked small and fragile in his hospital bed. Tubes were attached to his arms, and monitors crowded around his body. Thick surgical dressing covered the right side of his chest. Feeling like a voyeur, I pulled my eyes away from the smooth skin and beautifully defined muscles on his left side.

His face was pale. Someone had cleaned the dirt off. His eyes were closed, but he seemed to breathe normally.

There were two chairs in the room and I eased into one, moving slowly since I'd severely strained muscles, ligaments, and tendons during my stint as Wonder Woman the night before. With the concussion and a hangover from the strong opiate injected in my blood, I felt like an old woman and groaned like one as I sat down. I worried about more flashbacks, too.

Gunny stood at the foot of Calixto's bed, his focus on his agent.

"So, what's with the FBI?" I asked him.

"You sure you want to hear this now?"

I spread my palms and nodded toward Calixto. "He won't care, and it's not like we're doing anything else."

Gunny sighed and folded his arms across his chest as if protecting himself. "Luis Valera has been branching out into human trafficking."

I flinched, pretty sure I knew what was coming next.

"The FBI," he continued, "was after a Miami man running a particularly nasty trafficking operation. Valera was one of his suppliers. He was snatching up some of these kids that come into the country illegally. You know, the ones that come in through Mexico with the government dropping them off in towns and cities without paperwork?"

I nodded.

"They're vulnerable," he said, "free for the taking. Valera would give them to the man in Miami for a cut."

I closed my eyes, trying to shut out images of children forced into slavery. "That's what he was going to do with Jilly, wasn't it?"

"Yes."

Our silence seemed to fill the room, the only other sound being the beep of Calixto's monitors. The machines kept time with the pain throbbing in my head.

"Go on," I said.

"Calixto's a damn good agent. He'd worked with the FBI in the past on a joint task force. They wanted him again."

"For Valera and the trafficking?"

Gunny nodded. "So he went in undercover, using the identity of a distant cousin to Valera's family. A guy who died recently in Cuba, a guy that Valera had never met."

I nodded.

"The plan was for Calixto to deliver one of these kids to

Miami, replacing her with an undercover agent. They were going to bust the operation once Calixto received cash for the trade."

"But Jilly showed up," I said.

"That wasn't a problem. Calixto was going to leave with Jilly, stash her with an agent, pick up the replacement, and finish the job."

"Then I showed up."

"You were a problem."

"People tell me that," I said. "So the guy in Miami will get away?"

"We don't think so. With Valera dead, your buddy Morales was talking up a storm early this morning. Knows all about the operation in Miami."

"What about Serpentino?" I asked.

"Morales apparently had plenty to say about him and Copper, too."

"Good."

We were both quiet a moment. I tried to digest what Gunny had told me, but gave up, concentrating instead on how glad I was that Jilly and Calixto were alive.

"You did great work, Fia. Good job getting Craigson out of there by the way."

God, I'd forgotten all about the chemist. "So he's all right?"

"Safe at home with his wife." Gunny paused. Still standing, he stretched his arms, and with a little groan, sank into the other chair. "You and Calixto will make a good undercover team in the future."

"Me and Calixto?"

There was a rustle in the hospital bed. Calixto's eyes were open, and once again a warm brown. He tried to speak, but nothing came out. Gunny and I hurried to him and leaned close.

When he finally spoke, his voice was a grating whisper. "You have a problem with that, McKee?"

"Me and you? No," I said, "no problem at all."

"Good." A smile barely touched his mouth, then his eyes closed, and his breathing eased into the steady rhythm of sleep.

Gunny and I tiptoed from the room, and I closed Calixto's door gently. We rode the elevator to the lobby level and stepped through the automatic doors into the Florida warmth and late-afternoon sunshine.

When we arrived at Patrick's house, Gunny cut the engine on his rental car and we climbed out. As we stood on the gravel near the portico, the sun highlighted the streaks of red in Gunny's faded hair, making them gleam.

"So, Ms. McKee, after this case, do you still want to work for the agency?"

"Yes," I replied, and studied his face a moment. "What about you? Still want me as an agent?"

"Absolutely."

I felt some of the tension in my shoulders let go. "So what's next?"

A glint of amusement lit his eyes. "Take it easy, Fia. You're too much like a race filly. Right now, you need time off. You have to take care of that concussion and I've got someone I want you to see about the mental trauma you're having from that drug."

"Okay."

"But don't worry. There's a lot coming up." He nodded to himself. "You might work the Triple Crown races, the Breeder's Cup, or wherever a problem crops up. Might even send you to Europe."

"Europe?" I imagined sleuthing at France's Longchamp Racecourse with Calixto and smiled.

"Even Australia or Japan," Gunny was saying.

"Wow," I said, but Gunny was right. I needed to heal. Learning how and why my father had died had opened a door for acceptance. I would work my way through that door. Maybe find peace on the other side.

"Okay then, Fia," Gunny said. "I'll call you next week." He moved back to his rental, cranked the engine to life, and rolled down the gravel drive. Moments later, he disappeared into Patrick's jungle.

I let the sun warm my back for a while, then turned to my brother's house. It felt like home, as I went inside.